Also by Scott Geisel

Cinderbox Road & Other Stories

FAIR GAME

A Jackson Flint mystery
Yellow Springs, Ohio

Scott Geisel

Copyright © 2020 by Scott Geisel.

www.ScottGeisel.com

Printed and published in the United States of America

First edition: May 2020

Cover art and book design copyright © 2020 by Pam Geisel.
Cover photo by Alexandra Scott.

ISBN 978-1-7350183-0-0

Thank you to my editors and readers, who helped make this book what it is: Macy Reynolds, Roger Reynolds, Dan Rudolf, and Pam Geisel.

This is a Yellow Springs novel. Many of the places used in this work of fiction are real locations in the village of Yellow Springs, Ohio. All of them are intended to be portrayed in a positive manner.

Some of the events in this work take place in Dayton, Columbus, or other nearby areas in Ohio. As with many small towns, the Yellow Springs community in reality is linked with its neighboring municipal and rural areas. And so it is in this story. But this is a Yellow Springs novel at its heart and core.

1

I KNEW IT WAS A BAD IDEA TO STOP. But it was a long, lonely stretch of road, and it was late and dark and had been raining all day. The girl walking along the berm was soaked.

In another time there wouldn't have been any question. No need to wonder or worry. But the age of the internet and cell phones had made us more wary and cautious. Quicker to anger, to be divided, to point fingers. A man alone in a pickup truck stopping to offer a teenaged girl a ride could be made to look like anything online.

It made me feel more fragile in some way, more scared. But I didn't want it to make me feel less human. I pulled to the side of the road and waited.

I had the motor running and the lights on, and the wipers continued to plod back and forth across the windshield, trying to beat back the incessant water. In the rearview I could see the girl coming slowly through the dark toward the truck. If she needed a ride or wanted help, wouldn't she already have called someone? Texted, phoned, tweeted, chatted, whatever? Wouldn't she be plugged in like the rest of the world, even here in the dark and rain on a back country road?

The shape of the girl hesitated at the rear bumper, then I lost sight of her in the mirror. I dropped the stick into neutral and stepped on the parking brake, and stretched across the passenger seat to roll down the window halfway. Rain began to trickle in.

I switched on the interior light and let her decide.

A head appeared at the passenger window, long, dark hair dripping water from the ends.

"You want a ride?"

A heavy, wet beat passed. Rain scattered the windshield and the wipers beat it away. More rain took its place and the wipers beat at it again.

"Look, I have a daughter about your age. I'm just trying to offer you a ride if you want one. Get you out of the rain. I know I'd want someone to stop for Cali if it was her stuck out somewhere."

The face pressed closer to the open pane of the window, the girl's pale nose almost in far enough to get out of the rain. A long slice of slick wet hair fell forward around her chin. She looped the clump back over an ear, but the weight of the water pulled it back down.

"If you don't want a ride, no worries. But I can call her—my daughter, and she'll tell you." I picked my phone up from the cup holder between the seats and held it out in my palm.

"Tell me what?"

"That I'm an OK guy."

The wipers beat again against the rain. The door opened a crack, then far enough to let both the girl and the rain in. "OK."

I stretched my arm farther toward her, the phone out where she could take it.

Water sluiced from the girl as she climbed into the truck, tracks running across the floorboard. She squished into the seat.

The phone was still out in my hand. "You want to call her?"

She looked me over and shook her head. "No. I'll take the ride."

I don't know what it was. Maybe it was my happy grin, the sincere look on my face, or the gravity of my stretched hand offering the phone. Or maybe it was the dirt on my work pants, the mud on my boots. Maybe she could tell that I was a father, someone who saw the foibles of the human race, the challenges of being young, someone who would stop for a stranger who needed help getting over a tight spot. I'm a big guy, six-two with wide shoulders that I keep that way with hard work and lots of time in the gym. I can look like a threat, and if you knew my training you'd think twice about me before you got to know me.

But something in what this girl saw when she looked me over told her what she needed to know. She rolled up the window to close off the rain and dropped a black backpack onto the floor between her feet. It was heavy with water and whatever she had inside it. The remnants of a plastic garbage bag clung to the shoulder straps. Whatever protection the bag had been against the rain had given out long ago.

There was a clean hand towel hanging from the hand grip directly in front of her. The air conditioning in the truck didn't work, and I used the towel on the windshield when it fogged too heavily, which it would probably do now with two people in the cab breathing on it.

"That's mostly dry," I said.

She picked up the towel and wiped her face and arms, then ran it loosely over her hair. She wore no raincoat. She had on jeans and a black t-shirt that sagged heavily and clung to her as she worked. The windshield wipers kept a slow rhythm with her movements.

"Where you headed?"

She cocked her head to me.

I looked away and put my hands on the steering wheel, tried to look polite and respectful and harmless.

"Yellow Springs."

A grin tugged at my cheeks.

"You know it?"

"Live there," I said. "That's my village."

She must have thought I said it in a funny way because she looked at me like she was reconsidering her decision to get into the truck. Then she turned away and worked the towel over her shirt and her soaked jeans.

"There's another towel behind the seat," I said. "You have to—" I made a strangled attempt to show that she would have to reach down for the lever and tilt the seat forward, then twist behind her to reach for the towel.

"I can do it." She was swift and deft, and she came up with the big blue-and-white striped beach towel I kept there.

I eased the clutch in and pressed the shifter into first. The rear wheels gained purchase on the slick pavement and loose gravel at the side of the road, and we edged out through the rain. "I'm Jackson Flint."

I shifted to second, then third, the sound of the rain picking up as it hit the truck harder. I eased into fourth. "This is where you tell me your name. If you want to."

"Karen."

I looked over. She caught something in it and I looked away.

"Or whatever."

I dialed up the speed on the wipers, pushed the stick up into fifth and let the rpms spin down. It would give us a little more traction. "It's OK. You don't have to tell me your name if you don't want to. I'm not trying to make you uncomfortable."

"I'm not uncomfortable." She said it so quickly and clearly that it took me by surprise.

I pointed to my phone in the cup holder between us. "You want to call someone?"

She shrugged. "No."

I drove. She tried to dry herself. "You don't have a phone?"

"I'm saving it."

That probably meant a minutes phone. She had a prepaid amount and didn't want to use it up. Though this seemed like an occasion when burning a few cents for a call or text would be worth it. I let it go.

Post-Millennials. They did things in their own time and in their own way. "You live in Yellow Springs?"

"No." Talkative.

"Ah. Some place I can drop you off?"

"I'll let you know when we get there."

"Uhn." The headlights swept over wet Ohio farm fields. Dim lights from an old farm house barely glimmered way ahead. She hadn't thanked me for the ride. I would be appalled if someone helped my daughter Cali and she didn't thank them. It's not what her mother and I had taught her to do, what I had tried to keep teaching Cali after her mother was gone. You treat respect with respect. I let that go too. Karen or not-Karen was having a bad day. Probably not at her best.

She shivered, audibly and loud. It was chilly for early June in Ohio, but the truck cab was stuffy from the humidity. I was warm in just a work shirt. I turned the dial up for some heat and clicked the blower up a notch.

Not-Karen turned a blower vent toward her and leaned into the air coming from it. She shook out her hair. "Thanks for the ride."

I gave her a smile that she couldn't see in the darkness. In my head it was a silent nod of respect for her mother, or father, or whoever had been the influence.

"How far?" she said.

"Fifteen minutes. Maybe less. It's slow because of the rain." She looked young. Maybe too young to drive, I couldn't tell. But I took a stab. "Car trouble?"

"Huh?" She got it, then shook her head no.

I waited, glanced over at her and the backpack. "Oh, you're walking."

"Yeah."

"From where?"

She pointed, vaguely.

"Beavercreek?"

"No."

I looked in the general direction she had attempted to point. "Xenia?"

She twisted her head where I was looking. "That direction is Xenia?"

"OK, so not Xenia. Fairborn?"

She looked like she was thinking. "Uh-uh. From the college. Where the bus ends."

That would be the RTA. So she was coming from Dayton or thereabouts. "Long way," I said. "In the rain."

She bent forward again to let more air blow over her head. "You're telling me."

A minute passed, and she pulled at her shirt where it stuck to her arms because it was wet. "If I could just squeeze this out."

"Use the towel. Squeeze that out. Doesn't matter if you get more water on the floorboards."

She tried, but not much water soaked out of her shirt into the towel. The shirt stretched and sagged as she worked. "I can't do it while I'm wearing it."

An alarm bell went off in my head. This was why it had been a bad idea to stop. You try to be a nice guy, then it gets turns around and the next thing you know—

She laughed. "God, you're so uptight. I'm not going to take my shirt off."

OK, she was good. Read my expression in the dark like I was an open Google map.

I concentrated on the road. "We'll be there in a few minutes."

She laughed again, watching me. "Get ready."

"What?"

I heard movement as she squished around in the seat. When I glanced over she had her thumbs hooked under the edge of her belt.

"What are you doing?"

"I'm not going to take my shirt off, but these pants are killing me."

"Don't you—" I reached over to try to stop her, thought better of that and pulled my arm back, then I panicked and reached again and stopped again. The truck swerved and juttered as I jerked it back into the center of the lane.

The girl cackled. She held her hands up to show me she wasn't going to do anything. There was a sharp edge to her laugh. "You are so uptight."

"You said that already. I'm not. It's just in this climate of the internet and…"

"And what? You sound like a teacher."

"I'm just saying…"

"What?"

"Nothing."

"You were going to say *me too?*"

I didn't answer.

"You were."

I shook my head and kept my gaze on the road. "It's just that…"

"I know what it is."

She did, and she knew how to make that work for her. I shut up.

The wipers thumped. The rain had let up a little, and I turned the speed of the wipers down.

"God, it was just a joke."

"Good one."

She was probably smirking. I don't know. I wasn't looking at her.

"The radio work?"

"Sure."

"Can I turn it on?"

I shrugged. "It only gets country stations."

Her finger stopped at the button. "Really?"

"What you get with a truck."

Now I looked over. Her expression was blank. I grinned.

She grinned too. "Good one."

She punched the radio and a Holly Williams song came on. Very country. A little acoustic cross-over.

"Hank Williams' granddaughter."

She gave the blank expression again.

"Hank Williams? Hank Williams Junior—Bocephus?"

Nothing.

She reached for the dial.

"No, leave it. Good song. One won't hurt you."

She snickered. "I was going to turn it up."

She probably wasn't, but the song stayed and we listened. She seemed to be paying attention, like there was something real in the words that spoke of a thing that had touched her life. I guess that's the measure of a good song. That and a good riff in the middle to bridge the sound to its conclusion, which was coming on now. When the verse came back she said, "What are you grinning at?"

"Nothing."

The song wound into a blue-grassy acoustic finish. "I was thinking you'd fit in."

"In what?"

"In Yellow Springs." The rain had slowed again, down to a drizzle. I turned the wipers off and let the drops collect on the windshield.

"I've heard about it."

"About Yellow Springs?"

"Yeah. From my mom. She says it's kind of funky."

"You've never been there?"

"No. That's just what my mom says."

Her mother was right. Small towns have their own flavor and vibe, different from the suburbs and the city. Many of them have a lot of character. Old buildings, mom-and-pop diners, coffee shops, antique stores. People who know each other and say hello.

Yellow Springs went a step beyond that. It had a vibe left over from its hippie days. An artsy town with buskers on the sidewalks, belly dancers, skateboarders, shops, and generally a lot of weirdness. People doing their own thing, and nobody giving them much of a second look about it. LGBTQ flags and book stores. Nature preserves, a bike path, drum circles. Cars went all the way into the other lane and blocked traffic for walkers and people riding bicycles. It was a people town, more than just some place with cool things to do.

We were coming through the last stretch of road before the downslope into town. The girl was looking out her window. "Is there any place to eat when we get there?"

"What, now? Not much." There was one grocery market, two gas stations, three bars, two pizza places, a generous sprinkling of eateries and coffee shops, food carts and trailers, and even one chain sandwich shop. But late on a Sunday in the rain, the couple of blocks of downtown would be mostly quiet under the hazy glow of the street lights.

"Gas station?"

"Not open now."

"Vending machines?"

"In Yellow Springs? No. I think maybe there's one with soda."

"So what's between here and there? I'm hungry."

I hit the brights. They lit up dark fields full of crops just starting to rise. "This."

"Ugh."

"It's not so bad if you like corn or soybeans."

"It all looks kind of brown and uggy to me."

"Uggy?"

"You know what I mean."

"That's one of the things people like about Yellow Springs. It's surrounded by green. Mostly."

She looked out. "Doesn't look very green to me right now."

"You saw it in the daylight, you'd get it."

I turned at the crossroad, and lights from the new medical marijuana plant glimmered ahead of us. It fit right in. People were calling it mellow yellow.

We stopped at the intersection by the high school. "Where do you want me to drop you?"

"Over by the college."

The light changed, and I shifted into gear and drove through the intersection.

She gave a little jump.

I looked at her. "You said over by Antioch?"

She seemed confused.

"We'll go down South College. Just tell me where."

"Antioch?"

"Antioch College. Isn't that where you said you wanted to go?"

"I thought it was called Yellow Springs College." She grabbed her bag up from the floorboard, reached into an outside pocket, and pulled out a wet ball cap that she put on.

I stopped at the sign by Gaunt Park. "No, it's Antioch. Which way?"

"This is the college?"

"No. It's ahead. Where do you want to go on campus?"

She looked out into the darkness of the park and her fingers worked over the straps of her backpack.

"Look, are you all right?"

Her hand was on the door handle before I knew what she was doing, and she jumped out.

"Wait a minute. I—"

But she was gone.

I stomped on the parking brake and jumped out of the truck and ran around to the other side. The passenger door was hanging open, and the drizzling rain was coming in.

I scanned the street, the park, down the road behind where we'd come. "Sonofabitch. What was that?"

No one answered. The rain was mute.

I drove into the park, turned the truck so the lights ran over as much ground as I could get them to cover. I saw nothing. I got out and looked around, drove the nearby streets looking for signs of the girl until what I was doing felt a little creepy and entirely pointless. She was gone.

2

THE NEXT MORNING I WAS DRINKING COFFEE in the Emporium at seven. I would have been drinking coffee there at six, but the Emporium doesn't open until seven.

I have a coffee pot at home and one in my office, but sometimes a cup of joe is better when you don't have to brew it yourself. When you can take your coffee in the middle of a quiet place and watch it wake up and take its shape for the day, yourself included. The Emporium was like that. We liked to call it the village's living room.

The first rivulets of caffeine were working their way into my bloodstream when my phone rang. I checked the number. It wasn't my daughter. I swiped. "Jackson Flint."

"Mr. Flint, I intend to hire your services."

It was a compact voice, controlled and precise but with weight behind it. Someone who knew how to talk and expected others to listen.

I was amused. "Intend to?"

"Yes. We must meet at your earliest availability."

Sometimes, diction is everything. We *must*. At my *availability*, not my convenience. Ah, language, you fickle master. I took a sip of coffee and switched the phone to my other ear. "It's very early."

"The sun has been up for well over an hour. I suspect you've been up for longer than that. I'm told you are an early riser. I have a job for you, and it is urgent. It will pay well."

Huh. I let the line hang empty while I took another sip of coffee, slower this time. "Can you tell me more?"

"I will tell you more when we're in your office. I'm on my way there now."

Huh. Already on his way. "Let me give you directions."

My office was notoriously hard to find. It was in a tiny slot hammered out of a corridor between two spaces above the shops downtown. The only way in was from Kieth's Alley, a narrow passage behind the storefronts that was oddly named after a former editor of the *Yellow Springs News*. The door from the alley was hidden in a corner nook between a couple of buildings. From there you had to go up to the second floor and make several turns and know where to look for the interior door that was hung backward, so it opened out instead of in. If you opened the door without stepping past it first, it would span the narrow passage and cut off access to my office.

The whole thing would be funny in a comedy sketch, but as a practical matter it was more trouble than humor. Such as with many things in life.

"I won't need directions, Mr. Flint. Are you available now?"

I shrugged, but he wouldn't see that. "Let me know when you're there. I'm one minute away."

"Very well," he said, and ended the call.

I didn't even get his name. My mistake. Some days are like that.

I was still distracted from the night before, the girl in the rain. It made me think of my own daughter, who was at home by herself, and still in bed. Cali was maybe a year or two older than the girl I'd given the ride to, both of them coming up on driving age and anticipating their first real taste of independence. But I knew Cali was safe at home, and that she was growing up to be a capable and independent person. It bothered me not knowing what had become of the girl in the rain. If she was safe and comfortable. Dry. If she had something to eat. Who was looking out for her. If anybody.

But we all made our own way through the world, and there are a lot of things out of our control. Maybe that girl was fine. Maybe she was becoming independent and capable in her own way.

I had been getting myself up in the mornings since I was in grade school, when my father handed me a dollar store windup clock and said

Here, figure out how this works. My father didn't choose that because he wanted to, but because my mother wasn't around and he had no choice. He had to be at work, and I had to get myself up, feed myself, and do my laundry, and I damn sure had to get myself to school and get passing grades. The dollar clock was what he gave me to do that. Sometimes you didn't need much.

I wanted Cali to learn the same responsibilities. It was OK if she made a few mistakes, but I didn't want her to miss out on growing up because I hovered. Still, if it wasn't for the mysterious caller on his way to my office, I would have taken my coffee to go and gone home and made a big breakfast for Cali, which she wouldn't eat because she would get up about five minutes before she had to be out the door this morning, and that time would be spent in the bathroom. School had just let out, and she was spending the day with some friends and one of their mothers travelling to look at some college campuses in Ohio.

College was still a few years away for Cali, but some of her friends were older and already thinking about how to get out of the small town they grew up in. I was disappointed when Cali asked me if she could go along with them because that was something I'd wanted to do with her. But they wanted to make it a girls' day, and there was no way I was going to step in front of that.

That didn't stop me from pecking out a text to Cali. *Breakfast sandwich for you in the fridge.* She would already know that. It had lately become our routine. *Lunch money on the counter if you need it.* She didn't know that, and she would take it whether she needed the money for lunch or not. We both knew that.

I tagged on a smiley emoji, knowing I would get one back and that would tell me when she was up and on her way. I wanted more than that from her this morning, but it would have to do.

My stomach growled. I frowned at my phone, checked the time and wondered how long it would take to get a plate of eggs. I could put down a mess of eggs and potatoes and toast in not much more than a few minutes, and it might take about five minutes to get them. Breakfast would help set things right for the morning.

But my phone rang again, the same mystery caller. I swiped.

"Mr. Flint?"

"Yes."

"I'm at your door."

"Are you sure?"

"Quite. It's a bit awkward, don't you think? With the door hung such that you must step around it?"

He sounded like a character from Mary Poppins. "That's it."

"You are, I believe, one minute away."

I sighed. The eggs would have to wait. And I still hadn't gotten his name.

A minute later I was in the corridor outside my office.

The man standing beside my office door was young-looking but probably in his thirties. He was slim and of average height and looked like he worked at keeping himself in shape. He was dressed professionally in a white shirt and gray slacks. Clean-shaven and smelling like soap. Pretty nice for a little after seven on a Monday morning. He would stand out on the street in Yellow Springs, where you were more likely to see sandals and a t-shirt or something loose and colorful.

He extended a hand. "Samuel Thomas."

We shook once. "Jackson Flint."

"Of course you are."

Of course I was. Samuel Thomas looked and talked about as much like a lawyer as a person could without trying to. He held a simple leather briefcase secured by straps, and he carried himself with the casual smile of a man who knew he was on the clock and getting paid well for it.

The handshake over, we went into the office and maneuvered for seats. I took the chair behind my desk. That left the one other chair for Samuel Thomas. Besides my desk and a filing cabinet in the corner, there were some folding chairs closed and stacked against the wall. The coffee pot was on top of the filing cabinet. The best feature of the room was the little window that looked down over Xenia Avenue and the heart of the village.

With me behind the desk that left just about enough room for Samuel Thomas to sit on the chair across from me and get his knees up in front of him to prop the briefcase on. He got up to reach for the door and pulled it closed. "Cozy."

"I'm thinking of expanding."

Usually that gets a laugh. Samuel Thomas didn't even blink. "I'm here at the request of a client."

"Not a surprise. You're a lawyer."

Now he blinked. "Very astute. I believe we'll get along fine."

I pushed my coffee cup to the side, laced my fingers together, and leaned over them across the desk. "You're very straightforward, Mr. Thomas."

"I find it saves time."

"Hmm." I unlaced and relaced my fingers. "Shakespeare said *The first thing we do, let's kill all the lawyers*. But I believe that not all lawyers are evil. I also believe that more often than not it's a safe premise to begin from that if a lawyer comes to see you he wants something, and the bottom line is probably money."

"We all make our own way. There is some very good and important work being done by members of my profession, and often for pro bono consideration."

"Some will rob you with a six-gun—"

"And others with a fountain pen. Mr. Flint, now that we have demonstrated to one another that we can bandy about Woody Guthrie comparing lawyers to Pretty Boy Floyd and Robin Hood, may we get to the business at hand?"

I leaned back into my chair. "We may."

Samuel Thomas flipped his briefcase open. "Do you always greet your clients so warmly?"

"Potential clients."

He looked up.

"I like to reserve judgement."

"Ah. I hope that I may convince you to accept my offer." He removed a large manila envelope from his briefcase and set it on my desk. The briefcase danced on his knees as he worked.

I gestured at the open space on the desk. "There's room for that here."

"No need. This will do."

Protective, maybe. We both looked at the envelope sitting between us. I didn't reach for it. "Where is he?"

"Who?"

"Your client."

"My client, ah, wishes to remain anonymous at this point."

I waited. Took a sip of coffee, studied the lid of the cup, set it down again. If he didn't take the hint soon, I'd have to lace my fingers together and then unlace them again.

Samuel Thomas sat perfectly still during the show and looked perfectly at ease. Finally, he said, "Is that going to be a problem?"

"Yes."

He didn't look surprised. "I believed this might be the case. I assure you that my client is a highly respected member of the community and has more than sufficient resources to cover any fees and expenses you might accrue."

"In Yellow Springs?"

"I beg your pardon."

"Your client is a highly respected member of the community here in Yellow Springs?"

He blinked once, slowly. "I don't think that's what is important here."

"Because if that's what you're telling me, I can think of a handful of families that are well known and might have the kind of money and influence you've hinted about. And a couple of individuals. This is a small town, Sam."

He took a breath. I had a feeling that if he wore glasses this is the place where he would stop and adjust them. But he was handsome and well put-together. If his eyes weren't perfect, he would have gotten Lasik surgery to correct them.

"It's Samuel, please. And I think we're getting off the point. If you're concerned about any improprieties, I can vouch for her—for my client's reputation and the veracity of what you'll be asked to do."

I leaned back in my chair. It squeaked a little. I moved again to make it squeak some more.

Samuel Thomas's eyes cut down. "And now you've narrowed your list of guesses?"

"I have."

"Because I've let slip the gender of my client?"

"Yes."

He straightened himself. "Before I dig myself any deeper into a hole, may we discuss the nature of the business?"

"Couldn't hurt."

He reached into his briefcase and came out with a business card that he laid on the desk. It was for a firm in Springfield. It seemed like every state in the Midwest had a town named Springfield. Ohio was no different.

"You'll be asked to find someone."

I held up a hand. "I don't do divorce, revenge, voyeurism, or anything of the like." Actually, I did. I just didn't like it. But if the money was good, and the case would put someone in a box who needed to be put in a box, and if my cash flow might be a little low, I could find myself doing a little something I wouldn't tell the neighbors or include in my memoirs.

In the dozen years since I'd gotten my private investigation license and quit the Greene County Sheriff's department, since I'd hung the sign out on my door that read *Jackson Flint Detective Agency, Yellow Springs, Ohio*, there had been ups and downs. Clients I liked and clients I didn't. Good money and some leaner times. Cases I was happy I'd taken and cases I wished I hadn't. You lived and learned. Or not. I knew for certain I was still living. I hoped I was still on the learning curve.

One thing I tried never to do was look back at the security of the pension I'd given up when I left the Sheriff's. That was part of the learning. Always move forward, not back.

Samuel Thomas held up a hand. "Mr. Flint, this is not a TV show. My client has a legitimate and ethical interest in locating and communicating with a missing person."

I held up my hands in retreat. "OK. But a missing person is a serious matter. Have you been to the police? Maybe what you need here isn't a private investigator."

"With respect," Samuel Thomas said. "I have checked you out, and both I and my client believe you are suited for the case."

I smiled. "Touché." Then it hit me. "You seem to know a lot about me."

"I have done my homework."

"How'd you know I was an early riser?" I was thinking now that he probably knew I'd be at the Emporium when he called. Huh.

"There aren't many secrets these days. You are known to have resolved some fairly high-profile cases in the Greene County and Ohio area. You are also known to sometimes be difficult to work with. Especially for local authorities. You are most known for the loss of your wife two years ago, and for this village of Yellow Springs rallying support around you and your daughter Calliope when that happened."

He saw me look up at the mention of Cali's name. Nobody called her Calliope. She wouldn't allow it.

"You don't always follow the rules."

"You got all that from a laptop and an internet connection?"

Samuel Thomas held up his phone. "Not even that."

I took another slow sip of coffee. "OK, why me?"

"Why you?"

"For the job. Knowing I can be difficult."

Samuel Thomas considered the question. If he wore a tie, this is where he would straighten it. Maybe press his fingers over an imaginary wrinkle in his shirt. "My client is sympathetic with your situation with your, ah, deceased wife." He paused, raised his gaze, and continued. "And with due respect, she appreciates the way you handled things with your daughter and her—struggles since she lost her mother."

Touché. There were few secrets in a small town. Cali and I had gone through a hard stretch when we lost her mother. We'd tried to keep it private, but that's not easy to do anymore with all of the digital intrusions.

Samuel Thomas pulled a ledger-style checkbook from his briefcase and opened it on the desk. The checks were in the name of the law firm. "I can offer you a retainer."

"I'd like to know who I'm working for and discuss the case personally."

He took a heavy pen from his pocket and twisted it to bring out the point.

"Speaking with your client will help me to avoid unexpected complications. And it will help me decide the merits of the situation and decide if I want to take the case."

"I'm afraid I'm not at liberty to arrange that. I can't share details with you."

"You could call her."

He sighed and retracted the pen and reached into the briefcase. "I can give you cash if you prefer." He laid a fat white envelope on the desk beside the larger manila envelope that was already there. The edges of the smaller envelope were crisp and the corners had been folded carefully like an accordion to give shape to whatever was inside. I could guess what that was.

Then Samuel Thomas said, "I can assure you that finding this missing person would result in a positive resolution for those involved."

I kept my eyes on Samuel Thomas. Neither of us looked down at the fat envelope. "That's not the point."

He folded his hands carefully. "I urge you to reconsider. My client has in mind the best interests of everyone involved."

I shook my head. "I'll need to talk with her."

Without speaking, Samuel Thomas snapped the check ledger shut and stuck it into his briefcase. He closed the briefcase and secured the leather straps. "I'll give you some time to think about it. As will I consider what might next be appropriate." Then he stepped into the hallway, maneuvered the door to get around it, and as he walked away he became only footsteps disappearing down the corridor.

Both the large envelope and the thick, smaller one still lay on my desk. We both knew it. There was no mistake. The lawyer hadn't accidentally forgotten anything.

I stretched my arms and hooked them behind my head, then twisted to look out the window, down on the street below. Traffic was light and walkers were heavy. The bicycle racks were full. It was a good day in the village.

Then I swept up both envelopes and dropped them into the top drawer of the filing cabinet. I stopped, dropped my hand back in for the smaller envelope, and popped the seal to ruffle my thumb through a stack of large-denomination bills. I took one bill out and tucked the rest back inside and locked the filing cabinet drawers.

Interestinger and interestinger. Samuel Thomas had backbone, and he knew how to make a play. For a lawyer, there was something I liked about the guy. Maybe I wasn't ready to do what Shakespeare had suggested and kill him yet.

On my way down the stairs to get that plate of eggs, my phone doodled. *Thanks dad!* There was an emoji of a smiley-face heart.

It was a good morning in the village.

3

I WAS BACK IN MY OFFICE BY EIGHT. I had been distracted during breakfast thinking about what was in the big envelope, but I didn't look before breakfast because I was distracted by my stomach wanting a plate of eggs. Sometimes focus is everything. Sometimes eating is.

I unlocked the filing cabinet and took out both of the envelopes the lawyer had left and set them on my desk. The fat stack of bills spilled out, and I counted the money.

There was a lot. More than made sense for a job I didn't know anything about and hadn't accepted yet. But the whole exchange this morning didn't make much sense.

The larger package held copies of newspaper clippings and a four-by-six photo, which was facing down when I pulled everything out. The news clippings were for a story I recognized. Most people who'd been in town for a generation or so would. A local teen had disappeared twenty years ago, just flat vanished into the ether.

My eyes went to the photos in the stories. There was something familiar about the girl. That something snapped into focus when I looked closer. She looked like the girl in the rain from last night.

My brain wobbled for a moment like the big black-and-white cone in the opening of *The Twilight Zone*. I righted my thinking and scanned through the headlines, then I set the articles aside and flipped the photo over. The color image was clean and clear. The girl from twenty years ago matched the image in my memory of the girl last night in the dark of the truck cab, trying to rub the damp out her clothes with the beach towel.

I read through the articles more closely. The missing girl was Henna Winstrop. I remembered when it happened. The whole town had turned out for days to look for her, with no luck.

Several possible scenarios about why the girl in the rain looked like Henna Winstrop ran through my head on crazy non-parallel tracks, crashing into each other and getting crazier. I let them all waddle around up there for a minute and swiveled my chair to look out the window. And I dialed Samuel Thomas.

"I've been expecting you would call."

I scanned Xenia Avenue below me. I half expected to see Samuel Thomas down there, looking back up at me with his phone to his ear, with that casual look of confidence he pulled out and presented like it was a business card. He was annoying, but eerily impressive. I didn't see him on the street. "Tell me when and where."

"Now. At the Winstrop home."

He didn't need to give me directions. Everyone in town knew the Winstrop house.

Twenty minutes later I was seated in Elizabeth Winstrop's parlor room in a wingback chair, watching her pour tea. The Winstrop matron carried herself like just that—a matron. Her hair had gone halfway to gray and her hands were thin, but she was carefully dressed in pressed white pants and a modestly flowered shirt with lapels. Her hair was stylish and her back was straight. She was slim and the beaded jewelry at her wrist matched the string around her neck. I could detect no makeup, and her skin looked clear and vibrant.

Samuel Thomas was seated across from me in a wingback chair that matched the one I was in. He was the consummate lawyer, wearing a tailored jacket now, his gold watch wristband poking out of the sleeve. His briefcase was at his side, and he held a notepad in one hand with a thick pen clipped to the top, waiting to take the most lawyerly of notes.

The scene would have been complete if there had been a fire burning in the hearth between us, but it was too warm for that on this June day.

"Why the cloak and dagger?" I asked the both of them. "I would have figured out who you were hiring me for as soon as I saw the stories and photo."

"Plausible deniability," Samuel Thomas said. "It could be helpful if—"

"Gentlemen." Elizabeth Winstrop stepped between us. "Introductions have barely been made. The tea is hot and we must get acquainted." She turned to me. "Mr. Flint, do you care for sugar?"

"No, thank you." I didn't even really care for tea. I wanted to start connecting some dots. Thoughts of the girl in the rain were pressing my agenda.

Elizabeth Winstrop picked up a tiny pair of silver tongs from the tray beside her chair. In it was a cube of sugar. "It's lavender sugar. You will regret it if you don't accept."

I tipped my head. "In that case."

She dropped two cubes of sugar into a cup of tea, added a dob of milk, and handed me the cup with a saucer and a spoon. It was all very dainty, but she completed the motions with such deliberation that both Samuel Thomas and I kept our eyes locked on her.

She prepared a similar cup for Samuel Thomas, then one for herself as we sat and waited.

When she had arranged herself in her chair, Elizabeth stirred her tea and took a careful sip and straightened her back. She looked at Samuel Thomas and me, and we both sipped of tea. It had a delicate and slightly soapy flavor that made me feel clean when I drank it. I gave an expression that showed I approved, and Elizabeth Winstrop seemed satisfied. I didn't tell her it tasted a little too much like soap.

The matron set her cup and saucer carefully aside. "Now then. The cloak and dagger. That was Samuel's idea."

He moved as if to protest, but Elizabeth held up a hand. "I wanted no part of that."

I checked the time. Her identity had remained secret for a little more than an hour. "Then why bother?"

"As you will see, Samuel can be very convincing."

The fat stack of money in my office was evidence of that.

Elizabeth smiled primly. "And you will see that I can also be very persuasive." If getting me to drink lavender tea was any indication, she was good.

A clock ticked on the mantel. The tea cooled in my cup. We all looked at one another.

"Samuel tells me that you don't want to work for me."

"I don't know that yet. I needed to know who you are and the nature of the work."

"Yes, Samuel explained that. What is it you would like to know?"

I leaned forward. "Why don't you start at the beginning?"

She tilted her head slightly. "Certainly you recognize the family name?"

"I think just about anyone in Yellow Springs would. I know your husband as the name on the factories in Dayton and Xenia. And I know your family as a generous donor to a number of organizations in the area. You've been here a long time." I waited before I said the last piece. Dipped my head to show some respect. I'd been there. "And I know your husband Robert passed away recently."

Samuel Thomas cleared his throat. "Robert was the founder of Winstrop Industries. He patented several processes for microencapsulation, then later for metal plating and making integrated circuits. He was a genius at chemistry and with anything small. Winstrop Industries owns several manufacturing and research businesses in Greene, Montgomery, and Clark Counties. Those businesses are continuing to operate fully with Robert gone, but the whole of Winstrop Industries has passed to Elizabeth."

Samuel Thomas flipped through some pages on his lap. "There is also the matter of—"

"Wait." I turned to Elizabeth. "Ms. Winstrop, please accept my condolences on the loss of your husband. I know that can be difficult."

Her face softened, but she gave no other noticeable reaction. "Thank you, Mr. Flint. That's why you're here."

A strangled sound came from Samuel Thomas. "He's here because of the stack of money I left on his desk."

Huh. I thought I was there because of the photo. And this was where someone should tell me why there was a girl I picked up on her way to

Yellow Springs last night who looked very much like Henna Winstrop
who had disappeared from this house twenty years before. But I guessed
that was coming. I took a small notebook from my pocket to indicate
my readiness.

I turned my back to the lawyer. "Ms. Winstrop, why don't you tell
the story? What did you mean that's why I'm here?"

"I wanted you. Because you lost your wife. You have a daughter.
And you know how difficult it is in a small town to keep things private.
Everyone talks. And with all this tweetering and twottering about on the
internet, nothing is discrete."

True. Loosing my wife Kat had been hard enough. Watching Cali
struggle along with me to accept the loss was harder. Seeing all of that
ground through the public lens became nearly unbearable.

Elizabeth looked me in the eye. "You're here because I know that
there is something gentle in your soul. I wanted you, but Samuel argued
for prudence."

"It's called plausible deniability," Samuel Thomas clarified for
Elizabeth. "Which could be useful depending on what is to come. If
we find your daughter, there may be legal consequences that will be
best kept out of the public discussion, both for your sake and for your
daughter's."

"Well, that all sounds very prudent," I said. I thought I sounded
clever echoing Samuel Thomas's words, but he didn't laugh.

He looked at Elizabeth instead. "Robert generally followed my sug-
gestions unquestioningly."

"I'm sure he did. And I'm sure that arrangement worked for the two
of you. But I think you are also finding that I am my own woman, especially now that Robert's assets have passed to me and I have retained you
as my legal counsel."

He remained stoic. No reaction. "Yes ma'am."

"I hope also that our relationship will remain, or evolve as necessary,
such that you may think of me as Elizabeth."

"Yes, ma'am."

"We'll keep working on that." I had the feeling that if he were close
enough, Elizabeth would have patted Samuel Thomas's hand.

I reinserted myself. "Elizabeth, as for the gentle soul. That's about half of me. The other part is something very different. I don't like bullies. I don't like blatant disregard for other people or their property. Once I've decided where my sympathies lie, I can be something much less than gentle following them."

"That's no secret. And that's the other reason I wanted you."

I must have frowned.

"Your reputation for getting into scraps precedes you."

Oh, that. "OK, now that the mutual admiration club is over, let's get to it. You want me to look for your daughter."

The strangled sound came from Samuel Thomas again. Elizabeth picked up an old issue of the *Yellow Springs News* from a tray on the table beside her. It was folded open to the story covering the twentieth anniversary of Henna Winstrop's disappearance. There was a photo of Henna when she was sixteen, just before she disappeared. The resemblance to the girl I'd given a ride to was remarkable.

"The story has gotten smaller over the years," Elizabeth said. "But it's still news."

"You think your daughter ran away." It wasn't a question. Elizabeth's opinion on that had been in the news for twenty years.

"Yes."

"She'd be almost thirty-seven now."

"Yes."

"And you've not heard from her in all that time? Nothing since she disappeared?"

"Nothing."

"Have you heard from anyone else who may have had contact with Henna?"

Elizabeth looked to Samuel Thomas. Here it was. The girl in the rain. They knew.

"No one."

I held my pen over the page in my notebook. "Are you sure? Anything you can think of may be useful."

"Nothing direct, but there have been phone calls."

"OK. When did those happen? Over what period of time?"

"Yesterday."

My pen hovered again. "Just yesterday?"

"Yes."

"And nothing before that? Not a hint of your daughter's whereabouts?"

"Nothing. Two calls came yesterday asking for Henna." She picked up her cell phone. "I had our land line transferred to this some time ago. This used to be our home number."

"Caller ID? Did you try calling back?"

"I called back. My phone was unavailable most of the day yesterday and I missed the calls. I called back last night."

"Your phone was unavailable?"

"I own my phone, not the other way around. I turn it off when I don't want to be bothered."

OK. I got that. "Does that happen often?"

Samuel Thomas answered flatly for her. "Yes."

Elizabeth ignored him. "The calls came from a professor's office at Sinclair."

I scratched my pen across the notepad paper. "Why would a Sinclair College professor call about your daughter?" Wait. "On a Sunday?"

"You tell me." Elizabeth played the voicemail message. *Hi. I'm looking for Henna Winstrop. I have this number for her. Is she there?*

That was it. It was a female voice. Muffled and quick. Garbled, but clear enough to make out the words.

Elizabeth ended the voicemail call. "The other was a hang-up, but it was from the same number." She dialed that. A carefully enunciated message came on.

You have reached Professor Jay Canbury at Sinclair College. If you're calling about the logics course, there are no seats available. There are still openings in the ethics course and the Great Female Minds course, where we look past the classical view of philosophical and existential thinking and into the contributions of women to their fields of study.

I wrote the name down. "Why would this guy call you?"

"I don't think he would. And I find it further suspicious that a college professor would be in his office on a weekend."

"Well, at least he sounds progressive." Clever.

"If you're referring to his course on female thinkers, that's long overdue. I'd hardly call that progressive."

OK, not so clever. I shook it off. "I can track this down for you. And I don't know what I'll find. But I have to tell you that it's a little thin. I may not find anything. Just an old number and a mistaken call. It may be nothing."

"I understand."

"And in all kindness, I have to ask about your motivations for finding your daughter right now."

She nodded.

Samuel Thomas's voice floated across the room. "Henna has been written into the will."

We both looked over. Samuel Thomas held a file in his hands that I assumed was the late Robert Winstrop's will. "Probate requires that those designated in the will to receive inheritances be notified, that a search should be done to try to locate designees, and that a further search be done for other family members if such a need is deemed to exist. As the executor of Robert's will, I must satisfy the courts that a diligent search has been made for Henna. The estate will pay for the expenses of that."

That was the envelope fat with bills. "So that's where I come in."

Elizabeth had been sitting very still. One hand went to her cheek, touched it very gently, then returned to her lap. "That's not all of it. I am not motivated only by the legal requirements of my husband's will. We disagreed about how to raise Henna. Robert was more lenient than I was. Mr. Flint, I don't think I have to explain the intricacies of raising a teenaged daughter to you. Henna and I were not on good terms when she disappeared."

I slowed myself down to make sure I chose the words I wanted. "Not on good terms?"

"Henna and I had a fight."

"Before she disappeared?"

"Just before. It has always bothered me."

"It was just the one fight? Was there anything before that?"

Elizabeth's hand fluttered, but it stayed down on her lap. "Henna and I had not been on good terms for some time. It's fair to say that we regularly disagreed. Do you think you know what I'm saying?"

"I do."

"I'm an old woman now. I have regrets, and I don't have a lot of time to right them. Losing Robert has made me see that."

It was a vulnerable moment for her. I could tell she didn't like it. I knew Samuel Thomas could tell. And we both knew Elizabeth could see our reactions.

"Elizabeth," I said.

She looked at me.

"Will you call me Jackson?"

"Yes, Jackson."

"I'll take the case. I'll track down what is happening with these calls, and if it's OK with you I'll ask Samuel Thomas to give me some other information that may help me dig deeper."

She waved a hand at Samuel Thomas. "Whatever Jackson needs."

I looked at the old photo of Henna on the newspaper page. Now the resemblance to Elizabeth came through. The confident expression, the straightforward look into the world in front of her. It was the same thing I'd seen on the mysterious girl in the rain. But we hadn't gotten to her yet. I'd hold onto that card until I had a better idea how to play it. "And if I find something. What do you expect then?"

Elizabeth pushed her chin forward. "Hope."

I wrote that down in my notepad. Elizabeth Winstrop was convincing. But I didn't like coincidences. Who was the girl in the rain? Did they know about her and weren't telling me?

Maybe they knew. Maybe they didn't know that I knew. Maybe they knew that I knew but didn't know if I knew that they knew.

If this were a TV sitcom it might be funny. But this was real. And I had a feeling the ending might not be very funny.

4

HOME WAS AT THE EDGE OF THE VILLAGE. After the house it was farm fields for miles, open spaces with dark rows of trees at the creek lines. Our front porch faced town, one mile away.

During the growing season we saw a lot of tall, tall corn, walling in the roads like a giant patchwork quilt. Soybeans and an occasional sunflower field made lower elevations that cut the landscape like ragged jack-o-lantern teeth. In the winter with the crops cut down there were long, flat, dark vistas and cold winds that bent the trees in the yard over like hunching sentinels.

There were red-tailed hawk, turkey vultures, sometimes coyote yipping in the night, a mink or fox if you could find them, raccoons, possum, and enough deer to host a venison festival.

A lot of people liked to live close to downtown. Only a few minutes' walk to Tom's Market, or the library or coffee shops or places to eat. Near the Little Art Theatre and Glen Helen. Close to the energy of the buskers, the bicycles, the sidewalk benches and the conversations. Young people and older folks mixing together and lots of colorful people and a laid-back vibe.

Cali and I liked having a little distance from all that. It was nothing in the summer to walk or bike into town. We kept bicycles scattered around the house, leaning against the porch railing, outside the kitchen door, waiting to be jumped on for a ride to town. It was different in the winter, when the snow and cold and the prospect of scraping a frozen windshield would slow us down and make us feel more cut off from the village center, only a mile away.

It was different now at home, too, without Kat. She'd been the soul of the house. The decorator and gardener. Master of surprises, orchestrator of dinner parties, weekend adventures, and play dates. Kat had filled the house with exotic and weird music and art, made it the place where Cali and her friends wanted to hang out and fill it with giggles and whispered secrets and the strange and unending energy of youth. Kat dreamed impossible plans and additions for the house. A forest of fruit trees. A tower deck and zipline for Cali and her friends. An Airbnb in the backyard to finance it.

We did a few of those things. New roof and a couple of peach and apple trees in the back. A plum tree that fed more deer than us. An office up in the attic eaves where Kat could work and look out at her gardens and the farm fields.

All of those things were still there, but none of it had been the same these past two years without Kat. I know Cali felt it too. About a year ago I tried rearranging everything. Moved the furniture, bought some new lamps, put a plant in a pot by the kitchen window. Moved out of the bedroom I'd shared with Kat and into the guest room. But that felt wrong, like instead of moving beyond our loss I was trying to wipe Kat away.

We moved it all back. I was still sleeping in our nuptial bed in our nuptial bedroom, and the house looked like it did when Kat lived here. Cali and I have come to a place where we can live with the memories, where the loss is there but tucked into some far corners of our brains where it can't hurt us too much anymore.

But every once in a while I don't like the feeling of being alone in the house. Something strikes me in a way that's unsettling, or a smell or the look of something brings back a memory that's hard to bear, and hard to let go. Today was one of those days.

Just then, Mrs. Jenkins walked through my bedroom door and saved me from my melancholy. Mrs. Jenkins had come to live with me and Cali the summer after we lost Kat. The little long-haired calico cat just waltzed up onto the front porch one afternoon and announced herself, standing on the back of the wicker chair and stretching her neck up to yowl in through the open window screen.

Cali fed her some tuna she begged from a neighbor and rubbed the cat's back as she ate, and that was that. Mrs. Jenkins had decided. She was going to stay with us.

I rubbed my fingers under Mrs. Jenkins' neck the way she liked and started gathering what I needed for the day. Backpack and camera. Baseball cap, sunglasses, change of clothes. Water bottle. My old college history textbook from the shelf in the extra bedroom.

Mrs. Jenkins helped by trailing behind me, in front of me, and under my feet. She poked her nose into anything big enough to get her whiskers through, roamed the back of the closet, jumped onto the bookshelf to examine the open space left where I'd pulled the textbook out, and tried to direct me to the kitchen and her food bowl even though we both knew there was plenty to eat in there.

I gave her some fresh water and went for the last thing I needed for the day, my Smith & Wesson M&P40 and holster.

Smith & Wesson started the line of Military and Police pistols not long before I left the Greene County Sheriff's Office. The M&P was built like a Glock and designed as a service weapon. Some of the guys on the force didn't like it, but I had been an early convert. The weapon was smooth, rounded, and slick. It came with different sized hand grips, and the largest one fit into my palm like a handshake.

It was also easy to hide. Kat hadn't liked several things about my line of work. One of them was seeing the gun. She appreciated the public service I was doing and knew that protection was part of the job, but she'd never gotten comfortable with a weapon in the house. I tried to keep the gun out of sight, slipping it out of my duty belt before I came back to the house after a shift, and we eventually fell into a don't-ask-don't-tell compromise.

When I went private and the duty belt disappeared, I became very good at keeping my weapon out of sight.

Some of the guys with the Sheriff's Office complained about their wives, and their wives' complaints about the guns and the danger and not knowing when or if something would happen to them on a shift.

Kat hadn't been like that. She didn't like the long hours and the late nights. The cold, late dinners when I would get stuck at a scene past the end of my shift. The interruptions into our lives that were part of the commitment. But she never complained about my decision to go into law enforcement.

In the end, it had been me that couldn't take the job. The endless paperwork and hours stuck at a desk or sitting in a car. The sheer number of calls that reminded me just how depressing and depraved peoples' lives could be. It wore a person down.

I left the Sheriff's because I wanted more flexibility, and I got it. I could take a case or not. I could carry the M&P40 or not. And I could use it or not.

I'd have to lock the gun in the truck, inside another locked box, with the bullets locked separately, to follow Ohio law on a state college campus. Lately I'd been thinking more and more about making sure I came home every night for Cali. Some days carrying the gun seemed to make that more likely, and some days it didn't. But new cases always came with unknowns.

I took the gun with me. Mrs. Jenkins followed me out the front door and jumped onto the porch railing where she would be the perfect height for another neck rub, but something moving in the wildflower garden caught her attention and instead she stalked off into the May apples and bloodroot.

The drive to Sinclair College was quiet, all back roads until I hit Route 4, which didn't feel so much like a highway as it did another back road that dropped me right into downtown Dayton.

The college looked much the same as when I'd gone there briefly a long time ago. The campus spread along the river between the highways in downtown Dayton. Concrete buildings radiating out and around from the library in the center were connected by third-floor walkways. It was easy to get around, and hard to get lost unless you tried.

The furniture looked different now than I remembered, and there were flat screen TVs in the lounges. Wifi was everywhere and there was a coffee shop in the library. But the students still looked like students, even in the slower summer semester.

Professor Canbury's office was in one of the old buildings with a large, open atrium in the center. An elbow-height half-wall ran along the perimeter of each level of the atrium, marking off a square around the building. Classrooms and office doors ringed the outside. Anywhere from one of the upper floors offered a view down over the half-wall into the lounge below. And from the first floor you could watch heads and shoulders bob behind the walls above. I'd always liked that before. Now I was hoping to put it to use.

I'd scouted Canbury's webpage the night before. He had everything there. His office, photo, specialties. Degrees, dissertation, dissertation director, publications, conferences attended, courses taught, current course schedule, links to websites he liked. Everything except his favorite foods and daily hygiene schedule. I felt like I already knew the guy.

That level of transparency wasn't my style. My business cards read simply *Jackson Flint Detective Agency, Yellow Springs, Ohio. Professional. Discreet.* There was a phone number. I'd thought once about adding a picture of two crossed six-guns to jazz it up, because I'd read that once in a mystery novel. It was the right decision not to do that.

I found a chair in the lounge where I could see the top of Canbury's door over the half-wall above. I knew where he was. I had his schedule up on my phone. He was ten minutes away from finishing his ethics course, in a classroom on the same floor that I could see if I swiveled my head to the right when I looked up. Easy-peasy.

I pulled my baseball cap down over my head and cracked open my old college history text. Just like a college student, twenty years on.

Huh.

There was a bookmark from where I'd stopped reading a couple of decades ago. Right in the middle of a chapter. Something about the Peloponnesian War and whether Thucydides had been an objective reporter. It seemed vaguely familiar, but I couldn't remember what the point had been. I guess because I'd stopped reading it.

I started in again at the bookmark. History shouldn't have changed that much in twenty years. A few minutes later there was a hum of sound from above, and people started to spill from one of the classrooms that was not Canbury's. I closed the textbook and tucked it into my backpack.

History would have to wait again.

I moved up two floors so I could peer down over the half-wall onto the professor's floor. A minute after I got there the door to Canbury's class opened and a clump of students with heavy backpacks wobbled out. The crowd wafted away in a hurry. Probably excited to try out the ethical thoughts and dilemmas that the professor had put into their heads during the lecture.

Another minute later the professor came out with a young woman talking away at his elbow. She must have been either the most ethically pure, staying to bask with the professor, or the most ethically challenged, needing more of the professor's time than the others.

I realized then that I was too snarky to be a good college student. I probably had been all those years ago too.

Canbury moved like clockwork. He dispatched the clingy student, went directly to his office and opened the door, dropped a book and clipboard he was carrying onto a chair, and walked swiftly down the hallway to the restroom.

I pretended to be intensely interested in something on my phone until he came out again a few minutes later. Canbury walked around the perimeter of the floor below me to the department office. I could see him check his mailbox and chat briefly with a young man who looked like the office manager. Then Canbury returned to his office where the door was still open, picked up a book and folder from this desk, and left. I followed him until he reached his next class, went in, and closed the door behind him. Very efficient. Not his first time at the rodeo.

I noted when the class would let out. It was the Great Female Minds course. I wondered how many men were enrolled. If they were wise, they would know they'd probably find themselves in a class full of women. And if they were really wise, they might worry that they weren't ready for the women they would find there.

I returned to the lounge and tried again to pick up where I'd stopped reading about the Peloponnesian War, but I was distracted by how big the book was. Pretty thick. I hefted it and let the weight settle onto my palm. Probably worth quite a bit for resale at the bookstore, all those pages. The book was twenty years old. I wondered if I could still cash it in?

I managed to waste most of Canbury's class time on my phone looking up the book online and trying to see if it was worth anything. Huh. Pretty much like when I was a student here. The bookmark had stayed on the same page about Thucydides.

Canbury followed the same routine again—open his office door, drop his things, go to the restroom. He cruised through the department office again, but this time with only a glance at his mailbox, and walked swiftly back to his office, sat down, and poured a cup of coffee from a thermos on his desk.

I stepped into the restroom, went into a stall, and slipped off my t-shirt and stuffed it into the backpack. I pulled on a short-sleeved button-down Dickies work shirt and replaced the baseball cap with a John Deere cap. Then I went to see Professor Canbury.

His door was open. "Professor?"

His eyes came up from his coffee. He was a thin man with short silver hair and a crisp shirt and a nice line in his trousers even though it was getting late in his day. He looked grandfatherly in a nineteen-fifties way. But he had a thin new laptop on his desk and a smart phone at his elbow, so the look was incongruent for me.

"Is this your office hours?"

"Yes." He looked surprised, so I waited a moment to let him invite me in. "You don't look like you're here to try to sell me textbooks."

I let out a short laugh. "No." Maybe a twenty-year-old history book. He probably wouldn't think that was funny.

"Then please come in." He gestured to a chair beside his desk, realized it had books and papers on it, and swept them off.

I came in and sat. "Nice office." It was big enough to hold at least a couple of mine, with a coat rack, bookshelves, a large desk, a small table, and more chairs against the side wall.

He looked around the room. "I hadn't thought about it."

"Do you have to share it with anyone?"

The professor's face tightened. "No. Our offices are one of the few things on campus that are still sacrosanct. No one else uses them."

OK. I looked around the room again. "Could use a window."

A big grin spread across his face. "I've been telling them that for years."

We shared the moment, each of us taking something different from it, then the professor said, "What brings you here?"

I extended a hand. "John Hill. A friend of mine suggested I might want to take one of your courses."

His eyes moved over me for a split second. He realized I caught it.

"I know. I don't look much like a typical college student. I'm looking for a change."

"Are you currently enrolled in courses?"

"I'm thinking about the fall."

He turned to his laptop and clicked open a web page. "Have you seen the course descriptions? Everything is online."

"I know. Thanks. My friend Elizabeth Winstrop suggested I might like your ethics course or your Great Female Minds course."

I waited to see what registered. "The ethics course will be available in the fall. The other course will not."

"Oh, too bad. Elizabeth Winstrop says I might especially like that women's thinkers' course."

Canbury pushed away from his desk. "Has your friend taken my course?"

"No. Someone she knows has. But I thought you might recognize her name."

"I do. Mister and Missus Winstrop have been donors to this school. You may know that their names are on one of the mechanical labs."

I nodded like I'd known that.

"And Ms. Winstrop sent you here?"

"Yes." It was true enough.

"I'm very surprised by that."

I did my best to look like I had no idea what he was talking about.

"How do you know the Winstrops?"

"Small town. Everybody kind of knows everybody."

An eyebrow went up, very slightly. "Ah. You live in Yellow Springs."

"Yes." I gave it a moment, then added. "Tragic about their daughter."

His expression flattened. "I'm afraid I don't know about that."

He seemed genuine. I hoped I was right. In the mystery novels, gut instinct counts for a lot. I hoped my gut and I were on good terms today. But if Canbury didn't know the Winstrops, that wouldn't help me understand the phone calls coming from his office.

He reached back to one of the bookshelves and picked up a couple of pages staples together and held that out to me. "This is the syllabus for the Great Female Minds course."

I accepted the syllabus and glanced down at it.

Canbury reached back again and came up with another page that he handed to me. "And this is for the ethics course." Then he launched into a brief but precise explanation of each of the courses. He seemed genuine and sincere. I almost felt guilty that I wasn't likely to be a recruit. Maybe Cali in a few years.

"Thank you, professor." I'd heard enough. I didn't think Canbury had made the calls to Elizabeth's number, but I had some ideas about how to dig deeper.

When I stood up, the professor did too. "Thank you for coming by. I hope you'll think seriously about working on that degree."

Damn. I liked him. I was supposed to stay objective. But my gut was speaking again. I stopped in the hallway outside his door. "Will you be here in a few years, professor?"

He shook his head. "You don't have to call me professor. My name is Jay."

I held my hand out and we shook again.

"I don't know if I'll be here in a few more years. Interest in the courses I teach isn't what it used to be."

I knew that. Things were moving to STEM courses. Job skills. It made sense, but it didn't help a guy like Canbury. "Well, maybe you can get something over in the mechanical lab."

He laughed. "I think I'd rather travel."

"Who wouldn't?"

And I left the professor. I didn't know if my gut was telling me right that the professor hadn't made the calls to Elizabeth, but I did know that it was telling me right that I wanted to take a closer look at the food court. I think I'd seen some blueberry pie there that needed closer inspection.

After I'd spent some quality time with a slice of pie and a cup of coffee, I changed back into my first set of clothes and went back to Canbury's building. From the top floor, I watched him leave his office for his last class of the day.

I spent the hour his class met re-reading the news stories that Samuel Thomas had left with me, and looking for whatever else I could find about Henna Winstrop's disappearance with my phone and the campus wifi.

I felt a pang of guilt when I spied on Jay Canbury again as he made his last trip to his office, to the restroom, and then through the building to the faculty parking area and into his car.

Those pangs got stronger when I followed him home. Canbury drove a Honda Civic that looked as old as my truck and only a little less beat-up. He skillfully navigated the city streets out into the suburbs of Kettering, always moving into the turn lane at the right time and timing most of the lights so he didn't have to stop. I liked him more and more.

I knew where he would go. There are few secrets these days with the internet. His address had been easy to find online. County property search. And there was a lot more when I dug a little. When he parked in the driveway and a woman opened the front door to greet him, I recognized her as his wife Joan. They'd been married forty years and had two grown daughters who lived out of state. Neither Jay nor Joan Canbury kept their Facebook profiles private. They probably didn't know. And it probably wouldn't mean much to them that I'd been trolling them.

But it meant something to me. Joan kissed Jay on the cheek and they went inside. I saw them through the window, a long-married couple still happy to see each other at the end of the work day.

I'd seen what I needed to. More that I needed to. Looking in on them made me feel like a voyeur, which of course I was. I tugged my cap down and started the truck and drove away.

5

I WANTED TO GO HOME, but I didn't expect Cali back for a couple of hours and I felt a little at loose ends.

I pulled over in the Oregon District on Fifth Street in Dayton and fingered a text. *Feeling manly?*

The reply came almost right away. *Always. Come over and we'll move the Buick.*

He wasn't joking.

I headed east. Darnell Brickman's place was hard to find if you didn't know where it was, and hard to get to even if you did. He liked it that way.

I drove to Yellow Springs then went north of town, onto a side road, then another side road, across a low bridge that flooded if there was more than a little rain, and past the drive with the chain across the front and the mailbox beside it. This was a decoy. It was Brick's mailbox, but the real way back to his place was a little farther ahead at the sharp right turn in the road. You had to know to slow enough to see the cut back into the trees that was just tire tracks and weeds.

When I pulled up to the clearing in the woods where the house stood and stepped out of the truck, Brick was positioned in the middle of several large parts from a 1978 Buick Skylark. His muscles bulged beneath a t-shirt that announced *I'd Flex, But I Like This Shirt.*

Brick was the same height as me at six-foot-two, but unlike my light European skin his was darker and hard to place. He looked maybe Asian, Greek, African-American, or Native American all at once. In a certain

light his skin was a heavy shade of mocha but with a twinge of something else harder to identify. In shadow he became darker. His jet-black
hair started to curl if it grew longer than a few inches, and I'd seen him
wear it anywhere from shoulder length that looked like he had a poodle
draped over his head to bald. Today it was long enough to curl and drip
sweat onto his shoulders.

I crossed the clearing and twisted my neck a few times to loosen the
kinks, and I stepped into the arrangement of car parts with him. They
were laid out more or less like they had been when this was an actual car.
I rolled my shoulders. "Been eating your spinach?"

"Ugh ugh ugh ugh." Brick bent to the engine block. "Already had her
once around the yard waiting on you."

I like to work out at the gym, with free weights and nautilus and a
hot tub. A roof over my head when it rained. Air conditioning when it
was hot. Warm in the winter. Brick didn't go much for comfort. He had
the bench and weights in the barn, out of the sun, but he liked to move
the Buick. He had a routine that he said would give you the same results
as the fancy equipment. From the looks of Brick, it would give you better.

We started with the engine block, lifting carefully as Brick directed,
then walking it around the yard to the far side.

We came back and Brick bent to the transmission. "Now that you've
said hello to your big muscles, let's work on some of the neighbors."

From there we moved to the chassis and did several carries he'd de-
vised for the rims, until we had the package of parts reassembled on the
other side of the house and it was shaped more or less like a car again.

I sat on a rim and let out a breath. "You must be getting great mileage
with this thing."

Brick squinted. "What'd I tell you about trying to be funny?"

"Must've had it around the house a hundred times, and I've never
seen you put a drop of gas in."

"Tell you what. I'm gonna think about that for a while, decide if I
think it's funny, and I'll let you know." But his big grin gave him away
and I saw the bounce in his shoulders as he turned and chortled once.
When it was over, he said, "You need more rest, old man, or are you ready
to climb the barn?"

"You just gonna leave old Betty lying here? Show some respect. Maybe you ought to roll up the windows and give her a shine. Betty's been good to you."

Brick looked at the scattering of rusted parts. "Nah. You ever drive a Skylark? She's better for this than she ever was as a car."

The barn climb was a series of long, thin boards Brick had screwed to the outside of the barn. They were separated by gaps and rose up and down in a series of elevation changes. There was just enough room to get your fingers on the top surface of the boards. Like rock climbing, but with splinters. You worked your way around the barn by your fingertips and finished by swinging into the open hay door beneath the peak.

Brick stepped up to the barn and stripped his shirt off. That exposed a black ink tattoo of a tree of life that started on the left side of his chest and radiated up and out toward his shoulder. The top edge of the tree morphed into a large black bird poised for flight, and the top edge of that bird broke into a series of identical smaller birds that lifted away up over Brick's biceps and shoulder. The farthest and littlest of the birds disappeared over the curve of his shoulder onto his back.

Anyone who had a chance to look closely might see that the tree and the large bird and the smaller birds covered a tangle of scars, the largest centered under the bulk of the tree, and a patchwork of smaller scars peppering out under the patterns of the ink.

When Brick flung his shirt away, the tattooed birds rippled against his brown skin as if they might lift off and fly away. He turned and grabbed the first slat on the barn and grunted himself off the ground. "First one to put a foot down is a word you aren't supposed to say anymore."

I knew the word. And I knew I'd probably be the first to put a foot onto the barn for leverage.

We did the circuit three times and I thought we were done, then Brick went back for a fourth. He made the whole trip without setting a foot down. I kept my toes on the boards for most of the last run. Brick saw it, and when I came down I hung my head, but he didn't say anything. I pointed to my biceps. "Didn't eat my spinach today."

"Then that's going to make working the weights hard."

"I thought this was the workout."

He shook his head. "Warm up."

Brick would make you stronger, if he didn't kill you.

We went into the barn and got water and towels for the sweat and worked with the weights for another forty-five minutes, always fast without much time for breaks. The way Brick liked it.

After the last set Brick drank a lot of water and wiped his forehead. "You get what you came here for?"

"I forgot why I came. I'm just trying to remember how to raise my arms."

"Good."

He tried to pull his shirt on, but it clung to the sweat and bunched.

"Careful, you don't want a sartorial disaster." I pointed to the front of his shirt.

He pulled the shirt away and looked at it. *I'd Flex, But I Like This Shirt.* "You think I don't know your big words, but I do. I had more college than you did."

True. I'd known Darnell Brickman since grade school. When we were younger he was a little clumsy and a little pudgy. He didn't have a lot of friends, but he kind of got along with everyone. In junior high he was mostly a stoner and we didn't hang out together much. It was in high school that he found his stride. He played sports. All of them. He lifted weights, ran, worked out. His body became tight and chiseled. He embraced his bi-racial color, the child of a Filipino mother and a father who was a descendent of the African slave trade.

After school he disappeared into the Marine Corps. There were stories at class reunions that he'd moved around into some special units and seen some heavy service. I didn't think much about Brick until he resurfaced in Yellow Springs about a half-dozen years ago. He had PTSD he was trying to hide. We reconnected and took long walks in Glen Helen and John Bryan State Park. Clifton Gorge. Long runs up and down the toughest hills, and the work with the weights. He didn't talk much, but he let me come out to the house to help him work on it. He had a septic system put in and we installed indoor plumbing and rebuilt the kitchen and the bathroom. He unearthed the Buick from the back of the barn and we started carrying it around.

Later, we started sparring a bit, then we worked our way into some martial arts that Brick walked me through. He had skills that he'd learned in the service and overseas that scared me when I first started to see them, but in my line of work I'd been able to benefit from them when things got sticky. Dude knew some dangerous stuff, and he'd taught me plenty.

And somehow he'd put together enough college credits to finish a degree in electrical engineering.

"One more thing," Brick said. He dropped to the dirt floor of the barn and raised himself to his fingertips, then spread his legs farther apart and lifted his left arm behind his back.

I grunted. "It's a trick." This was one thing I could consistently beat Brick at, and I knew he'd been working at it. It killed him that I could do more one-armed push-ups than he could. I tried a fake. "I don't know if I can even do one after that workout."

He gutted out a right-armed push-up, breathed heavily, then barely pushed out one more and popped to his feet. "Where I come from, there are no excuses."

I rubbed my shoulder and twisted the joint around in the socket. "Well, you're a special case. And this old arm is sore and tired. Might be your lucky day today."

Brick shook his head. "It's something different from luck."

I dropped to the dirt and got myself into position. Then I pumped out one push-up that I made look harder than it was. When I figured he'd seen me struggle with that, I pushed off two more sharp lifts and jumped back to my feet. "That's enough for now."

Brick dropped again and managed two push-ups with his left arm.

I sighed and got back down in the dirt. "You know this is my weaker side." I ground out three push-ups. The last one nearly dropped my face into the dirt.

I stood and dusted myself off. "This would be different before a workout." We both knew there would have been a lot more one-armed push-ups, and I would have beaten him by a half-dozen or more. He'd figured out how to narrow the gap to one.

I took my shirt off and went to the big open barn doors and hung it in the sun to let it dry some. When I came back, Brick was in the corner of the barn leaning over his toy, a nineteen sixty-six Shelby GT350 that sat up on blocks. He looked over his shoulder at me like he wanted me to come there, but I stayed back and dropped onto the weight bench.

We'd done this before. Brick would make an incremental step forward in getting the thing roadworthy, and then we'd have a long conversation about the car's pedigree and history.

What I really wanted to know was how Brick had come into possession of such a vehicle. Even with the work it needed, the Shelby would probably bring in a small fortune on the market. If Brick ever finished painstakingly removing, cleaning, repairing, or replacing every part or piece that leaked, didn't work, or had a speck of rust, scratch, smear, streak, or blemish, it might be worth enough to pay off the mortgage on my house and also finance what I hoped would be a college education for Cali.

Brick grunted and switched on a work light that hung from the underside of the car's hood.

I sighed. "You want me to come see?"

"If you want."

"Are you going to tell me that it's an original sixty-six Hertz model that rented for seventeen dollars a day?"

"Yeah."

"And that there were only a thousand of those made?"

"A thousand and one."

"And this is one of the few with the four-speed manual transmission?"

"There were eighty-five."

"And are you going to tell me how you got it?"

"No."

"Then I think I'll just sit here."

Brick unhooked the work light and held it up to shine over the car. The black paint and gold stripes and trim gleamed.

I fell for the bait. "Anything new?"

He held the light to the driver's window. "Everything on the instrument panel works now."

I got up and walked over. The car really was a thing of beauty. If it ever ran, it would also be a thing of speed. I trailed my sweaty hand over the shiny finish. Brick looked at me like I'd farted in church.

I laughed. "Who pays for a job with a car like this?"

"It was a special job."

"Must have been. You ever going to finish this thing?"

"The sooner the better."

"Thinking of selling it?"

"Hell no. I got to get this done so I don't have to drive a jeep no more."

I shook my head. "You could put Betty back together."

"You think a busted-up Buick Skylark is better that a Shelby GT350?"

"No, but it might be better than your jeep."

Brick exhaled and switched the light off and hung it back under the hood.

I grinned. "We done here?"

"Unless you got any more questions."

I walked back to the weight bench and picked up my water bottle and drank.

Brick went to a cabinet screwed to the barn wall and took out an apple, a lime, and a pack of raisins, and tossed them to me one at a time. "You need electrolytes."

I rubbed my biceps. "And a new set of arms."

Brick got fruit for himself and we ate together. I rolled my shoulders. "I need protein after that workout."

"Ugh ugh ugh ugh. You want some peanuts?"

"No. I've got to get home to Cali."

Brick swallowed a bite of apple. "How's she doing? I haven't seen Cali for a while."

"She's thinking about college."

He stopped the apple mid-bite. "Isn't she a little young for that?"

"You'd be surprised. With the college classes they have for high schoolers now."

"Huh." He got up and stretched his back. His muscles bulged and glistened in that usual shade of brown that was hard to classify. "Bring her around sometime. If you think she'd like that."

"I will. She would."

I'd finished my lime and apple and raisins and went out to get my shirt that was drying in the sun. Brick came out and turned toward the house.

I called out to him. "Don't let the push-ups keep you up at night. It's not a competition." My smile gave away the lie. "You have other strengths. Go in and bake yourself a nice frittata or something. Make you feel better."

"You'd be funny if, you know, you were funny."

I slipped my sweaty shirt over my head.

"Hey, Jackson. Don't take this wrong."

"Yeah?"

"Fuck you. And your frittata."

"Is that one of those big words you learned in college?"

He grinned. "What, frittata?"

6

"YOU WANT ANY OF THIS?"

I was standing over the stove, eating from the pan. Black bean and chickpea burgers. Protein to build back muscle.

Cali was at the kitchen table with her laptop. "No. We snacked on the way home." She'd been gone all day with her friends looking at colleges. But not the college I'd spent the day at.

I dolloped some dill mustard on a burger. "Salad?"

"No, thanks."

She got interested when I started chopping vegetables. "Is that cucumber?"

I held up a thin slice, then downed it. "First of the season." It was small, but dark green and shiny.

I caught her eyes moving away from the laptop screen. "You have pepper and onion?"

Aha. I held up the onion and a slice of pepper to demonstrate. "And batard from the Emporium." I pointed the knife at the loaf on the counter.

"I guess I could eat a little." She came over for a slice of bread and dappled it with olive oil butter.

Cali was about ninety-seven percent vegetarian. I was about nine-five. Neither of us could resist a fish taco from Miguel's food truck behind the King's Yard. And a local free-range turkey at Thanksgiving still felt right. Cali was in the plant-based food age group. For Kat and me it had been different. When we stopped eating red meat a long time ago, some of our friends and family looked at us suspiciously with flittering glances. Cali's generation was more open to it. They were helping to save the world's resources one meat-free meal at a time.

I put the cucumber salads together and got down the big jar of nutritional yeast. Cali shook a sprinkle on top of her salad. I drowned mine.

She looked over.

I shook out more yeast. "Amino acids."

Her eyes went over the plate of burgers and the bowl of pistachios I'd set out. "Protein. You've been to Brick's."

"He asked about you."

She poked a finger into the muscle between my chest and shoulder. "Ow."

"You guys are crazy."

"Maybe."

"Is he still climbing the barn?"

"We did that. He's got something new going on back in the woods he wouldn't let me see."

"I'll bet that's gonna be fun."

"If it doesn't kill me."

We took the salads and bread to the table, and I dropped a thick oven glove down and set the hot iron skillet with the bean burgers in it on top. "Careful. That's hot."

"You always say that."

"It's always hot."

Cali rolled her eyes. "You could use a plate instead of eating from the pan."

"Then I'd have to wash it. I'm saving the plates for company."

She dipped her fork into the pan and picked off a tiny bite of burger. "When did we slide down to this level?"

"Happens slowly over time so you don't notice it. Like the frog in the pan of hot water."

"Thanks. That's appetizing."

"No problem. I thought you'd see it that way."

She finished her tiny bite of burger and reached into the pan for another.

"See? It comes naturally after a while."

Not even a grin. I tried another tactic. "Where'd you get to today?" I knew what their agenda had been, but I wanted her to tell me.

"Ohio Wesleyan and Denison. We cruised through Wittenberg on the way home."

Her eyes went to the laptop.

"So?"

"Wesleyan had this big organ in one of the theatre rooms. We played it and the sound was amazing."

"Uh-huh."

"The town was pretty cool."

"Delaware?"

"Yeah. There were bars and restaurants with patios on the sidewalk and things."

"You're too young for bars." That one landed flat.

"The town where Denison is is kind of frou-frou."

I eyed her over my fork.

"What?"

"I didn't know you knew that word."

"You use it all the time."

"Right. That's why I'm surprised to hear you say it."

She made a face. "Frou-frou. Frou-frou. Frou-frou."

"You sound like a chicken." I gobbled up more burger. Cali clicked at things on her laptop.

"Did you like any of them as schools?"

"Sure?"

Hmm. "I know it's a couple of years off. Are you also thinking of schools with science programs?"

Her fork went down and her eyes came up. "Dad, Ohio Wesleyan has very strong programs in biology, chemistry, neuroscience, microbiology." She clicked the mousepad a couple of times quickly. "Botany. Biomedical engineering."

I blinked. "You're looking at that now?"

She turned the screen to show an Ohio Wesleyan webpage.

Damn. A happy warm spot blurbed in my chest. "And are you

interested in any of those areas?"

"Right now, I'm interested in everything."

The blurb in my chest expanded and did a backflip. I wanted to get up and hug her, but she was so confident and proud I didn't want to do anything to soften that. Instead I chewed. "You do anything else today?"

"The food was good. Way better than high school."

She was picking at the crumbles of burger at the edge of the skillet. "Dad, you're a little weird, but your cooking is the best."

Ah. I couldn't compete with modern technology until she was hungry.

"We want to go back out tomorrow."

"What?"

She turned her laptop around. On Google maps she had plotted a route between Ohio State, Miami University, and the University of Cincinnati. State schools. City schools. Not small towns. The opposite of Yellow Springs.

"You should have gone to OSU today. You were right there."

"I know, but we thought it would take too long."

"Gonna take too long tomorrow too."

She deleted OSU from the map. "They're gonna want to see OSU. What else is down around Miami and Cincinnati?"

She seemed so grown up.

"Dad, what?"

"Nothing. You want to go with Jenny and her mom again?"

"They all want to go. Asia and Nadia too."

"Another girls' day out."

I got up and filled our water glasses. When I came back I stepped behind Cali and looked over her shoulder at the laptop screen. "You still have a lot of time to think about this."

"I know, but it's fun going with the others. Can I go again tomorrow?"

"Of course. I have to leave early in the morning but I'll leave you breakfast in the fridge."

"They want to go out for breakfast."

Uh-huh. I reached for my wallet.

"Jenny's mom is treating us."

"All of you?"

"She wants to."

My hand hovered with the wallet. "Lunch money?"

"I've still got some."

I pulled out a bill and laid it on the table. "Back-up funds." At least let me feel like I was contributing something.

She folded the bill and put it in her pocket. OK.

"Would you consider a local college for the first year? See how you like it? You could always transfer somewhere else later." It seemed way too soon to be having this conversation with her, but here it was.

Cali scrunched her face. "Like Clark State?"

"Or Sinclair. I'm going there tomorrow."

"You're what?"

"For a case. Some background information."

Her face scrunched tighter.

"What?"

"You know they make fun of it?"

"Who does? Of what?"

"They like, you know—good schools. Ohio University, OSU. Small schools where their parents went."

"Who does?"

"Some of the others."

"Jenny and Asia and Nadia?"

"Maybe. I don't know. Maybe their parents."

I shrugged. "Eh. There are lots of ways to get through college. Whatever works for you. As long as you're interested and want to try, that's good for me right now."

"But I'd like to see it."

"Huh?"

"Sinclair. Didn't you and mom go there?"

"A long time ago. Your mom transferred out." I transferred out in a different way. I got a job.

"Maybe you can take me sometime."

"You bet." More than you bet. Woo-hoo.

When we had finished eating and while we were cleaning up, Cali said, "I know I've been out all day, but we want to hang out at Asia's tonight."

"You don't have to pack all of summer break into the first week."

"I know, but they have Netflix and there's this series we've been watching."

"Oh, Netflix."

"It's about this mother and daughter who—"

I held up a hand. "Do I want to know?"

She dried the spatula and slipped it into the drawer. "It's set in a small town. That's part of what we like about it."

OK.

"It makes me think a little of Yellow Springs. It's called Stars Hollow."

I knew the show. It had finished its run years ago, and Kat and I had been waiting until Cali was ready to introduce it to her. Kat had dreamed of the two of them watching it together. I clanked down the skillet I was wiping. "Then, yes. Go. Watch that show. Watch all of it." And don't get too sad because you don't have your mother to watch it with you. Because I will.

I picked up the skillet again.

Cali touched my elbow. "What time do I have to be home?"

It was something we'd said we would renegotiate for this summer. We hadn't done that yet. "What do you think?"

Her eyes showed more than a little surprise.

"What time do the other girls have to be home?"

"It's different. Some of them stay up really late."

"What time do you think makes sense for you in the summer? Eleven?" I'd been thinking midnight, but I wanted to see her reaction. "If you're in town and I know where you are."

Her head bobbed yes.

"That's not a hard-and-fast time. I'm not going to count the minutes. Just, you know—eleven-ish. We'll talk about it again later. See how it goes."

"OK."

I finished the cleanup and Cali put her phone on the charger and went to change clothes. I understood charging the phone. Changing clothes to watch TV was a mystery to me.

When she was ready to go, I felt a second wind coming on. "You want me to give you a ride?"

"No, I can walk."

"I can come bring you home then."

"OK." She checked her phone and stuffed it into her pocket. "But I'm OK with me walking home if you are."

I thought about it for about ten seconds. "Text me if you want me to come get you. Always. Any time you need me." If Cali was ready to grow up and be her own independent person, this was the village for her to do that in. That's one of the reasons we lived here.

I followed her out onto the porch, and while she adjusted a lightweight jacket over her arm I fidgeted with the broom, knocking spider webs out of the high corners. I never understood anyone carrying a jacket in June. And Cali could do that for the entire summer.

I felt her eyes on me and stopped with the broom.

"You should go to the gym or something."

I pointed to a biceps. "Brick."

"Maybe a run?"

"Got one in this morning."

She chewed her lip. I knew what she was going to say. And she knew I knew. "You could call Marzi."

"Uh." I plopped the broom into a corner. "It's getting late."

Now I got the old fogey look.

"And dating someone in town might not be a good idea. If it doesn't go well, it'll be awkward."

"You dated Mom."

"We were married."

"You dated. I saw you. You even called them dates. You used to say *What are we going to do with the little one while we're on our date?*"

"In my defense, you were little then."

"I'm not now."

"And being married to your mother was different. I knew the dates were going to work out. There wasn't any question. No risk. They were going to be fun."

Cali shrugged and turned away. "Maybe you're not ready."

"Maybe I'm not." Fifteen going on all-grown-up.

"If it's going to be anybody, it should be her."

Then Cali stepped off the porch and went to be with her friends.

I fooled myself into disbelief that Cali could be so pushy for about two minutes, then I picked up my phone.

Marzi O'Brien was the licensed clinical social worker who'd help me and Cali when we lost Kat. I didn't think we'd needed Marzi, but I was wrong. She'd been good for both of us, especially for Cali.

We saw Marzi often for the first several months, then less often until we stopped altogether after about a year. I'd lost track of Marzi until I saw her in Tom's Market buying bananas a few months ago. She told me she'd moved to Yellow Springs. Probably because Cali and I had told her so many times how great it was here.

Cali and I had seen Marzi around town a few times since then, as you do in a small town. Chatting at the library or waving as we drove past while Marzi was walking down the street.

A couple of weeks ago I bumped into Marzi when we were both reaching for the door into Tom's again. We talked and never made it inside the store, and I walked her home. Since then we'd gone on a couple more evening walks. I learned that she hated almonds, which was funny because her real name was Marzipan.

I didn't want to admit that it felt like things were going somewhere. Cali and I were strong now. Losing Kat had changed us, made us into different people, but we were strong and we had to stay that way. Thinking about Marzi made me feel vulnerable in a way I couldn't quite get comfortable with again. I wanted to stay strong.

I sent a text anyway. *Walk?*

The reply came a moment later. *Drink?*

So it wasn't too late. Maybe I *was* becoming a fogey.

Marzi's place was halfway to town, so we agreed I would walk over there, then we'd walk to town and decide what to do once we got there.

I put some food into Mrs. Jenkins' bowl, poured fresh water in another bowl, and started walking. I hadn't seen the cat for a while, but there was food missing from her bowl. It was either Mrs. Jenkins or some other critter coming in the cat door to eat. I hoped it was Mrs. Jenkins.

It was a good night to walk. Marzi was sitting on the swing on her front porch when I came up. She had on a yellow knee-length dress. I was in shorts and a short-sleeve, button-down work shirt. My eyes went to a thin silver necklace that dipped beneath Marzi's neck. "You dressed up."

"Work clothes. I never got out of them." She stood and flipped a length of auburn hair over one shoulder. The strand had gotten a little frizzy from the humidity, and I wanted to reach up and smooth it for her. Huh.

Marzi and Kat had one thing in common. They both looked great in a summer dress. But Kat had been small and compact, a bundle of tight muscles under chin-length blonde hair and always a giant, mischievous smile.

Marzi was taller and more slender, fit but more petite than muscled. She clutched a tiny purse. "I'm ready." There was not a jacket or thin sweater or anything. Huh.

The walk to town was short. That's why people liked living close to downtown. It would go even quicker because Marzi was walking fast.

I took a guess. "Long day?"

"This was my day at Job and Family Services."

"I didn't know you still did that."

"Not very often. We rotate."

"Sounds like it's not your favorite thing."

"Some people like it. I did a lot of work there when I was starting out." Her pace slowed a little. "It's just a place where you often don't see people at their best."

"I imagine there's a lot of that in your work." It made me think of me and Cali when we'd first met Marzi. Not at our best.

"Sometimes it can be, I don't know—embarrassing." She glanced to me and shook her head. "Not for me so much. I meant for the women who come in. They don't want to be there. Their kids, if they come with them, they don't want to be seen going there. It can be tough for everybody."

We'd come down Short Street, and now we crossed Xenia Avenue and were under the marquee of the Little Art Theatre, with the painting on the underside. "And what about the fathers?"

Marzi steered me left down the sidewalk. "The fathers?"

"You said the mothers come in, and sometimes their kids. Where are the fathers?"

She looked at me like I'd said I was an alien. "We don't see them much. The fathers are why a lot of the women are there in the first place. Some of them send the women in to ask for money."

"For their kids?"

"You'd like to think so."

The Sunrise Café was behind us, and we'd passed Ye Olde Trail Tavern. If we stayed on Xenia Avenue, the only places left would be the Winds Café or Peaches. Marzi took a hard right at the end of the street. "We're here." She steered us in to seats at the bar in the Winds.

Marzi ordered a Manhattan. I had a gimlet with extra lime. I hadn't trained them yet to make a foxpossum, my own drink I'd concocted and was still trying to perfect. Another time.

Marzi sipped her drink and let out a long, slow breath that whispered like wind in the trees. She turned on her stool to face me. "Enough about my day. How was yours?"

"I got a thing with a missing person."

She took another sip, then set her drink carefully on the napkin in front of her. "Tell me more."

Elizabeth Winstrop had asked for discretion, and I mostly stayed faithful to that. I told Marzi it was a cold case and there wasn't any evidence of foul play. It may have been a run-away. And the mother was aging and wanted to find out what had happened to her daughter.

I was keeping it quick and sketchy, but there was enough there to get a good reaction from Marzi.

She nodded as I finished telling it. "Hits pretty close to home?"

"That's part of why I got the job."

"OK, now I'm really interested."

I shook my hands in the air in front of me. "I'm not supposed to tell." Marzi made a pouty face.

"You know how it is. I've said too much already."

"OK. We can talk about something else."

We did. We talked about how she was getting to know people in town and had started taking a yoga class. We talked about Cali and colleges and growing up too fast. I knew Marzi had never married or had children, and it impressed me how much she knew about both of those subjects.

And then the girl in the rain slipped into my thoughts and that got my wheels turning about tomorrow, and I think Marzi picked up that I was distracted.

We both decided that one drink was enough on a Monday night. I paid for both drinks without thinking. Marzi smiled and said, "Thank you."

Huh. So now we both knew things could go somewhere. Or already were going somewhere.

We walked back slowly. I went all the way up to Marzi's porch with her.

She touched my arm and left her hand resting there. "I'd do this again. The walk or the drink. Or both. I'm enjoying them."

I gave her a tiny peck on the side of her cheek. "Me too."

And then I walked home.

At twenty minutes to eleven I was on the front porch with a mystery novel and a reading light. The overhead fan was running low to keep the mosquitoes away, and Mrs. Jenkins was on my lap. Even with the night air and the fan, I didn't need a jacket. Manly.

Cali came up the walk and sat beside me on the wicker sofa. She shrugged her thin little jacket around her shoulders.

I turned my book over. "You're early."

Her head went down on my shoulder. She reminded me of her mother. Long blonde hair that got blonder in the summer and darker in the winter. Small features, but wide shoulders and a strong frame.

"I know, but I was ready to come home."

I turned off the reading light and laid my arm around her shoulder. After a minute that was enough dad time for Cali, and we got up and went inside. Mrs. Jenkins stayed out on the porch, her eyes wide in the dark when I turned the light off.

7

I HAD COFFEE AT HOME THE NEXT MORNING. And breakfast at six.

Cali got up earlier than she would to get ready for school. When Jenny's mother pulled up in front of the house, I handed some bills to Cali. "Leave the tip for everyone."

She smiled and took the money and went out to the car. They were going to the Sunrise Café. If you want the best pancake you've ever had, get one at the Sunrise.

I watched them go with a little tingle of jealousy. If Kat were alive, I wondered if she would be driving the girls.

Nope. Not productive. I shook those thoughts off like a pitcher shaking off a first-pitch curveball, and I packed some things for the trip back to Dayton and Sinclair. I left the history textbook at home this time. That stuff just repeats itself anyway.

There were several different strings to pull on. There was the maintenance and cleaning staff at Sinclair. That sounded like a cliché, but sometimes there was a reason why a thing became a cliché. I could ask around about the cleaning staff's schedule and try to narrow things down, but if that's where the calls were coming from it would probably take a long stake-out to find it. I hated stake-outs. I could hire that out to people who were better suited for it and put that on Elizabeth's expenses, but I hated stake-outs so much I didn't even want to do that.

There was Canbury leaving his office door open while he was away. And there was a gut feeling that Elizabeth Winstrop and Samuel Thomas weren't telling me everything.

I'd keep pulling on the strings until they lead to something. They always did.

I drove to Dayton and parked in the Sinclair College garage, locked the M&P40 in the truck, and found a spot on the first floor lounge in Canbury's building. I hoped my work pants and boots and Dickies shirt said I was just another working-class guy trying to reinvent himself with a college degree. I pulled my ball cap low over my eyes. I must have blended in. Nobody looked at me twice.

Nothing happened all morning. This was the part I hated. My muscles were sore from the workout yesterday with Brick, and sitting made them worse. I was bored almost as soon as I sat down. I would have actually read that history textbook if I'd brought it with me.

Just when I was dreaming of a slice of Flying Pizza with mushrooms and was ready to call in reinforcements, Canbury came back to his office again and followed his regular routine.

As soon as he disappeared into the restroom, a feminine head and shoulders popped into view over the half-wall above and tracked straight for the professor's door. She moved quick and my view was limited, but I was pretty sure it was the girl in the rain.

My mind switched from Flying Pizza to flying Jackson Flint. I bolted up two flights of stairs and came out with a good view one floor down into Canbury's office. The girl was gone. You're fast, Jackson, but not fast enough.

My floor was empty, lined with offices that were mostly closed doors. I pointed my phone's camera at Canbury's door and waited. If I couldn't be fast enough, maybe I could be clever enough.

Canbury came back to his office, picked up some things from his desk, closed the door behind him, and left. Just like clockwork. If the girl had snuck inside, she was still there. But I'd been in the professor's office and couldn't think of any place to hide.

The hallways filled and emptied, and classroom doors closed. A few people settled into comfy seats in the lounge two floors below, and the building got quiet again.

Then the girl came around a corner and went to Canbury's door. She was the girl in the rain. She was wearing the black backpack, and one hand dangled a paper grocery sack by the handles. I got several good photos, then she pulled the professor's door open, stepped inside, and closed the door behind her.

I was pretty sure I knew her trick. If it was what I thought, I hadn't seen that since grade school.

I noted the exact time and waited thirty seconds, then punched up Elizabeth Winstrop's number. It went to voicemail. I noted the exact time again. This felt like a gotcha, but I couldn't tell who it would be sprung for yet. That made my gut tell me I was still a little more suspicious of Elizabeth Winstrop than I had thought. The gut worked better on a full stomach, and mine was empty, but I tried not to ignore the feeling that Elizabeth was holding back.

The door to Canbury's office opened several inches. A hand came out and fingers reached into the jamb where the bolt should have slid and pulled out a wad of paper. Then the door closed with the girl and the hand still inside.

Clever. That trick was just as slick now as it had been when Johnny Gunderson made himself famous for it in the fifth grade.

Some things clicked into place. The calls from Canbury's office to Elizabeth Winstrop happened early on Sunday, the same day I found the girl at night in the rain. If she'd done the trick with the paper in the lock's bolt hole, she would have had to place it there on Friday when the professor was on campus for his classes. Unless the professor came to campus on Sunday and the girl had been there, which seemed less likely.

It was possible the girl had stuck the paper in on Friday and not come back to make the calls until Sunday. I wouldn't pretend to know what motivated a teenaged girl, especially one in this girl's apparent position. She would have had to place the calls from Canbury's office on Sunday, then start soon after that for her trip to Yellow Springs. More strings to pull on.

Then the girl stepped out of Canbury's office and closed the door behind her and walked swiftly away.

I went down a floor and followed the girl. She walked through the library and down to the basement of the Physical Activities Center. I stayed back when she stopped outside the entry to the women's locker room. She looked like she was waiting for someone, and I thought I knew her game again. There was a short hallway into the locker room, with a desk at the end where someone would check your ID and give you a towel. And she would probably make her move as soon as someone else went in.

I was considering ways to confront the girl before that happened, but two women carrying tennis rackets came down the long hallway from the other direction. When they turned into the short hallway to the women's locker room, the girl shadowed them.

I ran down after them. When I flashed past the entry to the locker room, I saw the two women with tennis rackets accepting towels from the desk attendant. There was no one else. This girl was good. She'd slipped by when the attendant turned for the towels. And she'd given me the slip twice now. This time I had guessed her moves, and she didn't even know she was ditching me.

The locker rooms let out into the pool area, and from there another set of doors let out the back. There weren't any other exits. I checked everything.

When I'd circled back to the locker room entrances, two young women came out in street clothes and with wet hair. I approached them. "Pardon me. My daughter is in there." I pointed. "And she has been for a while. I hope there's nothing wrong. Have you seen a fourteen-year-old with a backpack and a grocery bag?"

One of the women smiled brightly. She wore jeans and a summer shirt and looked fit. "She was there."

"That's your daughter?" the other woman said. "Don't take this wrong, but she looked like she was homeless."

I turned my attention to her.

"And someone should teach her a little modesty. I know it's a locker room, but..."

OK, that sounded like the girl in the rain. I said, "That someone would be me."

The woman stiffened.

"It's hard, just the two of us without her mother."

The women exchanged a look, and both of them let their eyes slip down and away.

"She has special needs. We're here for a program that's supposed to help her."

The woman who had snapped at me shook her head. "I'm so sorry. I didn't know. I think she went out the back. If we can help—"

But I was already running down the hall to circle the building.

I pounded up the steps and through the revolving doors and then jammed myself to a stop. The girl was about twenty yards in front of me moving between two campus buildings, and she wasn't in a hurry.

I dropped back and followed her through the parking garage and off campus. She turned away from the Chaminade Julienne High School stadium and headed toward the river.

We cruised past a long stretch of warehouses with high loading docks. I stayed way back, but she never turned around. I could have followed almost right behind and she wouldn't have seen me.

Then she veered abruptly into a narrow opening between two buildings and disappeared.

I moved to where she had gone. The space between the buildings was the width of a broken sidewalk and pitted with mud and trash. A dozen or so yards in, a tall chain-link fence stretched between the buildings. A hole big enough to crawl through wrenched a path through the chain-link. On the far side, the sidewalk between the buildings continued several dozen yards to a slash of sunlight. I didn't see anybody or hear any movement.

I squeezed through the gouged fence. A flat metal door in the side of the building on the right was locked. A door further down in the face of the building on the left was bent and stood open a few inches.

I listened and heard nothing. Cupped a hand behind one ear and listened with that through the opening. Still nothing.

This is where if I had a partner I would call in to that person and explain where I was and what I was doing. Give someone a heads-up where to look if something went wrong. But that was me letting Cali get into my head—making sure I came home to her every night. The Smith and Wesson was locked in the truck, where I hadn't had time to retrieve it. But what trouble could an apparently homeless teenaged girl lead me into?

I opened the door and went in. It was dark like a giant mausoleum. My eyes went to a square of light far ahead and to the right. I gave myself a moment to let my vision adjust. The square of light was an overhead bay door, probably on a loading dock. It was open. There were shapes along the far wall, and now I heard the low hush of voices.

I stepped slowly around the inside perimeter toward the open bay door. The shapes of a mini camp of mattresses came into focus. Mixed in with the mattresses were some bags and duffels and a shopping cart stuffed with belongings. A few of the mattresses were occupied with people sleeping or lounging on them.

Everyone turned to watch me as I walked through the camp toward the bay door. I knew my Dickies shirt and my boots and backpack were too nice. I wasn't wearing enough clothes, and I wasn't carrying enough of my things. I didn't look like I was carrying everything I owned. I didn't look like I belonged here.

Nobody said a word until a man who looked sixty but might have been forty pointed a skinny finger at me. "Who are you? What you want?" His voice was thin and screechy, but it had bite. He had a dirty beard and was gumming a cigarette stub to death between his lips. I tried not to judge.

"I'm looking for someone."

"You from the police?" He stretched it out. *Po-leece.*

"No po-leece."

The gummy cigarette floated fast around his mouth, hanging on for dear life. I made out about a dozen others, all of them up from the mattresses now and inching closer. "You from the owners?"

I shook my head. "No."

The man squinted. His eyes went to a couple of the others, two men who wore clothes too bulky for the warm weather and a young, wiry guy with bright red hair and a torn t-shirt. "Ain't nothin' here worth takin', mister."

"A man's house is his castle."

They didn't look amused. Huh. I guessed homeless jokes were a bad idea.

I held a hand out at about shoulder height. "Young girl, about this tall? Long hair, baseball cap. Backpack and carrying a grocery bag?"

"Mister, she ain't here."

"I just saw her—"

"Some people does that sort of thing." He pointed the bony finger at me again. "We don't. Now get outta here." He windmilled an arm that I supposed meant he was pointing me out the bay door.

"Now wait a minute. I don't know what you think, but I want to help her." I did know what he was thinking. And I didn't like it.

The old man's eyes darted right and left, right and left.

I followed his gaze—right, left, and caught the wiry guy coming at me with a chunk of two-by-four. He screeched out a yell, and his bright red hair made him look like a kids' show character gone mad. He swung the lumber at my head.

I ducked and parried and the lumber went over my head. I came up with an elbow and jammed my arm up and twisted. The weapon skittered away across the concrete floor, and red-hair came down hard on his ass.

Instinct kicked in. I readied for another strike and backed from the crowd so no one could get behind me. They looked haggard and scared, like a frozen zombie apocalypse.

Red stirred.

"Stay down. I don't want to hurt you."

He spat. "You ain't hurt me." But he didn't get up.

I kicked the lumber and it clattered across the floor. "A two-by-four? By god, that's an honest piece of lumber. You could hurt someone with that."

His eyes were slits. "She ain't here. Ain't no one like her been here."

"Get up." I motioned with one hand.

"You tol' me not to."

I took one step back. "Get up if you want to." A little bit of dignity wouldn't hurt the situation.

When he was standing, I said, "I get the feeling you know who I'm talking about."

The tension in his long, thin body was so tight I thought he might start vibrating. He spat again before he spoke. "You and your friends can't have her. She ain't coming back. You won't find her."

"My friends?"

"Git." He took a slow step toward me.

"Don't do that."

He took another step.

"I appreciate your loyalty, but I don't want to hurt you."

He took another step. "Git."

"What friends? What are you talking about?"

The zombies awoke. The crowd lurched unevenly toward me like a slow-motion scene.

"You don't understand," I said. I moved away. This was crazy, like a scene from a bad late-night movie. Next the blob would come out of the shadows and try to suck me up into oblivion.

I took another step back toward the bay door and the block of sunlight. What was I going to do? Go Chuck Norris on a bunch of homeless people in an empty warehouse?

I resigned myself to backing away, and that's when red bolted. His hair bobbed like a candle flame as he jumped off the loading dock and scrambled across the weedy lot behind the building.

He was my best bet. I went after him. He disappeared around a corner of the building.

When I made the corner, he was gone. I looked up, behind me, and scanned the building walls. There were no doors or ladders, no obvious place to go.

I listened. Nothing. How did this keep happening to me today?

I backtracked and from a crouch peered over the edge of the loading dock into the building. The camp had already reassembled around the mattresses.

I had two choices. I could search the building and fight off the zombies, or I could assume the girl had made her escape and look for her before the trail got ice cold.

I chose the exterior search. I jogged to the river and looked up and down the flood banks. I went up to the highway and scanned the long, hot stretch of road. There were cars and noise but no moving shapes along the shoulder.

I went back and circled the building to search for anything that looked like an escape route. Nothing did.

I backtracked to the college and made a half-hearted loop before I went back to the truck. It was late in the afternoon and the energy on campus was shifting, growing quieter.

Canbury's office door was closed and locked, and his teaching schedule said he was done for the day. So was I.

Elizabeth Winstrop wanted an update in the morning, and I'd give her one. The update would include some photos I'd taken and some questions I had for her about who was in them.

The only thing that bothered me about quitting for the day was the girl. I felt a fraternal instinct to find her. But I felt another fraternal instinct to be home for Cali, until I remembered she would be out late again with the girls and Jenny's mom.

I needed to know more about the Winstrop women and why the girl I'd seen today looked like Henna Winstrop who had disappeared twenty years before. Why she'd been in my truck two nights ago. I had a pretty good idea how to connect some of the dots, and no idea how others fit in. I was going to push up tomorrow's meeting with Elizabeth to first thing in the morning.

I twisted my neck and rubbed my sore shoulder and arm muscles. Brick's workout hadn't taken everything out of me. If it had, I might have a new two-inch-by-four-inch shape in the side of my head right now.

Brick meant well, but that guy could kill you without even trying.

8

I TEXTED CALI. *ETA?*

Late.

How's it going?

I got a thumbs-up.

You're good for dinner?

I got another thumbs-up.

I would have replied with a thumbs-up, but they're like jokes. The riff gets stale after two. Three times will kill it.

Cali was having a good time. I needed to get over feeling left out.

My thoughts tumbled around the girl in the rain, circling like a satellite in an unsteady orbit. A nudge and that orbit would degrade. I didn't like thinking about the girl sleeping rough and sneaking into the college showers. Maybe she had someone to take care of her and a home to go to, and maybe she didn't. I didn't like not knowing.

And I didn't like what the tall kid with flaming red hair said about other guys looking for the girl. I didn't like that the girl looked like Elizabeth Winstrop's daughter Henna, but that Elizabeth seemed to have no knowledge of the girl. I didn't like that the girl had ended up in my truck two nights ago. The coincidence looked suspicious. And I didn't like that I hadn't found time to look for Henna, who was almost certainly this girl's mother.

There were too many things that didn't fit together, and that kept things tumbling around in that low orbit in my head, ready to crash.

I could stake out the warehouse and call in backup for an overnight watch. I could set up watch at Sinclair. I could go look for the kid with the red hair and give him motivation to talk.

Pulling on those strings would probably eventually get me somewhere, but there was a different string I liked for pulling right away, and that was Elizabeth Winstrop. I might have to rely on my gut instincts to flush her out if she knew more than she was telling. Good thing I'd fed my gut so it would be at peak performance.

I took out my phone and called.

"Elizabeth."

She responded crisply. "Jackson."

"I want to come over and give you an update."

"Tonight?"

"Yes. Instead of waiting until tomorrow morning."

"I think that's a good idea."

Her answer surprised me. "You got another call. From Canbury's office."

"Yes. Two of them."

"Did they come at exactly—" I checked my notes and told her the time.

"Hang on. I have to—Yes, that's about right."

"You didn't tell me there were more calls."

"We're scheduled to meet in the morning. You're investigating."

"We talked about this. You should have called."

"I recall our conversation. I had planned to tell you in the morning. I don't know the rules with private investigators."

I laughed, in spite of trying not to. "Neither do I. I can be there in thirty minutes."

The pause was brief. "Can you tell me now what you have learned?"

"There's a visual element."

This time the pause was longer. "A what?"

"Some pictures I want to show you."

"Of what?"

"It's a visual."

"Mr. Flint, if you have something to share, please do that. I don't like this coyness."

"Jackson."

"Pardon?"

"You agreed to call me Jackson. And I agreed to call you Elizabeth."

"Regardless of that."

"Regardless of that, I can be there in thirty minutes."

"You're assuming that I'm at home."

"I am." I let her wait.

"Well, I'm home."

"Then how is thirty minutes?"

She sighed heavily. "Let me try to get Samuel Thomas here."

"You won't need the lawyer."

"I'll feel better if he's here. There might be something pertinent."

Let's hope. "Cost you a fortune after hours."

"Samuel is on retainer. Not that that's important for you to know."

"Do what you think. I'm on my way." I almost hung up, but then I pressed the phone back to my ear. "Elizabeth, do you enjoy our banter as much as I do?"

"I don't think so," she said, and ended the call.

I mostly drove the speed limit. Traffic was light. It took me twenty-eight minutes to arrive at the curb in front of Elizabeth Winstrop's house.

I parked behind a dark gray Infiniti coupe that I'd seen the last time I was there. Unless Elizabeth Winstrop was full of more surprises than I'd guessed, the lawyer was here. And he'd beaten me.

The wingback chairs were arranged around the hearth in the parlor. There still was no fire, and this time there was no lavender tea. The beverage cart was out, with brandy and scotch and an ice bucket, and little bottles of seltzer and a shaker of bitters. Three glasses were turned upside down on a tray, and a pair of polished silver tongs rested on top. I glanced into the kitchen but saw no one. If Elizabeth had help with the house, I hadn't seen it. She was probably the hostess.

"Jackson," she said as I sat in a chair across from her. Samuel Thomas was seated to her left. His shirt was crisp and he had a crease in his pants even though it was late in the day. Just like the professor had.

"Elizabeth."

Samuel Thomas tipped a hand with a heavy gold pen toward me as a greeting.

I turned to Elizabeth. "So. Two more calls."

She straightened her back. "Shall we get right to it then?"

I smiled and held up my phone with the time showing. "Exactly thirty minutes." I looked at the lawyer. "Your spaceman here is fast."

Samuel Thomas's eyebrows went up.

"That your car at the curb?"

His eyebrows went back down. Maybe he'd heard this one before.

"An Infiniti?"

"Ah, yes. It's spelled differently from the movie."

Elizabeth looked confused, then a smile crept through. She gathered herself and rolled a finger over her phone screen. "Yes, the times for the calls match up with what you told me."

"Did you answer?"

"No. I was—indisposed."

I looked at Samuel Thomas. Samuel Thomas looked at Elizabeth. Elizabeth looked at me. Like a kids' game. "OK. Was there a message?"

"No. It was a hang-up. And then another a minute later."

"Both from Canbury's office number?"

"Yes."

I leaned in dramatically. "I saw the person who made those calls. It was not Professor Canbury."

Now both Elizabeth and Samuel Thomas leaned in.

"Henna?" Elizabeth's voice came like a waft of warm, flat air.

I shook my head. "It wasn't your daughter."

The tight line of Elizabeth's mouth looked as if it might pull her eyebrows down in a heap. "Well?"

I gave it another few seconds. "Is there something you haven't told me?"

The line of her face got tighter.

"Anyone else involved here that I should know about?"

"Mister Flint."

"Jackson."

"I don't know what you think you're doing here, but—" She pushed a hard look over to Samuel Thomas. His hand was wrapped tight around the gold pen, poised over a pad of legal paper.

Samuel Thomas said nothing.

Elizabeth flicked her eyes to me. "Will you please explain yourself?"

"With due respect, something here doesn't add up. Or it does, and I'd like to know how. Is there someone besides your daughter Henna who may be of interest here? Someone you might recognize if I showed you a picture?"

Elizabeth swiped an angry slash through the air with her hand. "Enough of this. Tell me. Who did you see?"

I let my eyes drift to Samuel Thomas again. He looked like he'd tried to eat something that wouldn't stay down. "Samuel?" I held up my phone. "Do you recognize this young woman?"

On the screen was a zoomed photo of the face of the girl as she entered Canbury's office. I stood and walked the image toward Samuel Thomas. "I took this photo this afternoon at Sinclair College."

Samuel Thomas's grip stayed tight on the gold pen.

Elizabeth craned her neck, then rose from her chair and bent to look at the phone. A choked sound like a backed-up drain gurgled from her, and she went down to her knees on the floor. A hand went to her throat, then continued up and wiped moisture from an eye. "Oh my."

We both looked at Samuel Thomas.

I reached for Elizabeth to help her up, but she refused my hand and remained on the floor. "That's—"

"It's not your daughter, but it sure looks like her."

Elizabeth blinked. "Remarkable." She pulled my hand closer to look at the face in the photo. "Where is she?"

I let Elizabeth have the phone. "There are some other pictures. I don't know where the girl is. Those were taken at Canbury's office just before you got the calls from his number. No one else was in the office. She made those calls."

She swiped to another photo, then another. "You don't know where she is?"

"She got away."

Elizabeth swiped again. Forward. Backward. "Oh my. She looks just like Henna."

"Like Henna twenty years ago. She was sneaking into Canbury's office. This girl must have made the other calls too."

Elizabeth finally broke her eyes away from the phone. "And Henna?"

I shook my head. "I don't know where she is yet."

Elizabeth handed my phone back. "Will you send me copies of those pictures?"

"Of course."

Now she let me help her up. We rearranged ourselves back into the chairs and Elizabeth straightened the seam of a pant leg. "So it seems I have a grandchild."

"Yes, at least one."

Her eyes jumped. "You think I have more than one?"

"No. Wrong thing to say. As far as I know, just the one."

"But why isn't she with her mother? And where is— Why would—"

I'd been watching Samuel Thomas. His eyes were down. He held the pen too tight. He was too quiet. "Samuel?"

His chin hitched up. "I was afraid of this."

Time ticked on the mantel clock while he chose his words. "Robert believed he had a grandchild. He hired someone a few weeks before he passed to look for Henna. He thought if he found your daughter he might find a grandchild also."

Elizabeth's backbone went rigid. "Why would Robert think he had a granddaughter?"

"Grandchild. He never mentioned gender. Your husband—I don't know why he believed that. I asked him, and he simply said it seemed likely. After all these years."

"Of course," Elizabeth said. "And the way Henna behaved when she was younger. It's no wonder he'd think she had a child."

"I never heard Robert say anything disparaging about your daughter."

"No, he wouldn't. I did enough of that for both of us."

Samuel Thomas looked away from Elizabeth. "That was before my time."

Elizabeth watched her lawyer. "We hired investigators. Years ago. They never found anything."

Samuel Thomas flicked his pen in my direction. "Yet here is Jackson Flint. And the photos he has are very convincing."

Elizabeth's eyes flickered. "I see your point."

"Robert seemed to think it was urgent. I believe he knew his health was failing."

"And you never told me about this?"

"Robert asked me not to. He thought it would upset you."

"It has."

Samuel Thomas and I let Elizabeth sit with her thoughts for a moment. Finally, she said, "Robert wouldn't speak to me about Henna because… of how things were between the two of us when she disappeared."

"When whatever happened that took your daughter away from you occurred," Samuel Thomas said.

How did lawyers talk like that? The daughter ran away. We could all see that. I pointed to Samuel Thomas. "And the other investigator didn't find anything? Neither Henna nor any other descendants?"

"Nothing to report."

"How long did he work on the case?"

"Not long. Less than two weeks. Until Robert—"

"Until he died," Elizabeth said. "He didn't find her, but Henna did have a child."

"So it seems," I said.

"Oh for god's sake. Look at her."

I did. "Yeah. So it seems."

"And that means Henna is still alive?"

Both Samuel Thomas and I turned to Elizabeth. "I had assumed so," I said. "It hadn't occurred to me that she wouldn't be."

"But you haven't found her," Elizabeth said.

"No."

"And neither did the other guy, the one my husband hired."

"He didn't appear to." Huh. I swiveled to Samuel Thomas. "What's the guy's name?"

"I don't know if I should divulge that. My agreement with Robert—"

"Robert Winstrop is dead."

Samuel Thomas reached beside his chair into his leather satchel and pulled out a folder that he spent some time sorting through. Elizabeth and I watched him as if it were the most exciting thing in the world.

"William Bennett."

I wrote the name down. "Did he send a report?"

"I don't see one here." Samuel Thomas riffled through some more pages in the folder.

"Could it be somewhere else? Did he send a report to Robert?"

"He could have. I don't recall a conversation about it."

I sighed. "Look, there is some urgency here. A young woman who very well may be Elizabeth and Robert's granddaughter appears to be homeless, and we have no idea where her mother is or even if Henna Winstrop is alive."

"I can look through the items in Robert's estate. And Elizabeth might sort through what she has to look for some kind of report that Bennett may have sent."

"Yes, that might turn up something eventually. But I have another idea that might be faster." I held a hand to my ear as if talking on a phone. "Call him."

Samuel Thomas's eyebrows came up. "Now?"

"Yes."

"It's after hours."

"Pretend he's on retainer."

Samuel Thomas returned a blank look.

"Call. Leave a message if he doesn't answer. Tell him it's urgent. Do your lawyer thing. You have his number?"

Samuel Thomas peered at a page. "Yes."

I mimed making a call on a phone.

"I suppose given the circumstances."

Samuel Thomas made the call. When he got an answer, he started on a lengthy explanation of who he was, his connection to Robert Winstrop, and why he was calling.

When he got through all of that, he listened intensely for a moment, then picked up his legal pad and motioned to us that he was going into the other room. When Samuel Thomas was safely away from us in the kitchen, I looked at Elizabeth. Her eyes were somewhere far away.

"You OK?"

"Yes."

I watched her. "Are you thinking of something that might be useful?"

"No. I'm thinking about a drink."

I got up and went to the beverage cart.

Elizabeth leaned back in her chair. "You'll have one with me?"

"No."

"Do you mind if a lady has a drink without you?"

I turned over a lowball glass. "What's your preference?"

"Brandy and bitters. Lots of ice."

Nice. Almost enough to get me to join her. But a plan was coming together in my head, and I wanted to stay sharp for it.

I poured brandy, added a splash of bitters, and held up the drink for Elizabeth's approval. She nodded once at the bottle of bitters, and I gave the glass another splash and added ice and handed it to her.

She sipped and I saw the approval in her eyes. She took another sip and said, "Why would my granddaughter sneak into a professor's office and call my home?"

"I don't know yet."

"Do you think she knows about me? That she has a grandmother?"

"I don't know that yet."

"And where is my daughter? Why isn't she taking care of the girl?"

"Maybe she is. I don't know that yet."

Elizabeth took another sip of the brandy and bitters. "Do you think she's really my granddaughter?"

I nodded. "Yes. But I don't know that for sure yet."

The drink went up, came down, without a sip. "You keep saying *yet*."

"I do."

She took a tiny sip this time. "I like that." Then she set her glass on a coaster on the beverage tray. "Do you care to speculate?"

I shrugged. "You can guess what's happening as well as I can. I'm not sure that would be helpful right now. I'd like to find this girl and find your daughter. That should clear things up."

Her eyes went to her brandy glass, but she left it sitting on the coaster. The glass was nearly empty. "You sound confident."

"I have some ideas, and Samuel Thomas should get more leads from the other guy. We'll eventually pull on the right string and unravel this thing."

Elizabeth let a very short but unladylike snort slip loose. "Your bedside manner is riddled with poor clichés."

I gestured as if tipping an imaginary hat I wasn't wearing. "I aim to please."

Then Samuel Thomas came back holding his phone like he didn't understand what its purpose was. "That was Bennett."

There was nothing to say, so we didn't.

"He is—cautious. But he recognized my name, and he seems to believe my story. He's aware that Robert has passed, and he remembers that case, as his investigation was very recent. He has a file with some details, his activities, and where he looked and who he talked to."

Samuel Thomas paused long enough to make me impatient.

I rolled my hand in a circle to get him moving. "OK."

"This guy really is reluctant to talk about the case, but since Robert has passed I was able to… persuade him of certain legal obligations it may be in his interest to meet."

"You strong-armed him."

"It was more a matter of finesse."

Samuel Thomas looked capable of either. For a lawyer, there was still something about him I kind of liked. I tapped my head. "Law school wasn't wasted on you."

His parry was deft. "You're welcome."

Touché. "So where's the report?"

Samuel Thomas screwed his face up like he knew he was delivering bad news, but he couldn't quite figure out why the news was bad or he was the one who should deliver it. "Tomorrow."

"Tomorrow?"

"Yes."

"Ask him to send it now."

"I did. He has to make a copy."

"What, you mean like open a file and hit send?"

"He didn't say."

"You think he's going to make a paper copy?"

"As I said, he didn't say."

"You told him this is urgent?"

Samuel Thomas began returning items to his satchel. The legal pad, the folder full of papers. He twisted the gold pen closed and slipped it into his jacket pocket where it would be near his breast. "Look, the guy is a little odd. He's very cautious. We're lucky to have gotten this much from him. He's under no immediate legal obligation."

I studied Samuel Thomas for a moment and rubbed a hand across my chin. "He scares you?"

Samuel Thomas didn't look up. "You'll be dealing with him tomorrow. You can drive to his office in Columbus in the afternoon and get the file."

"Drive to Columbus?"

"You can expense that. Keep track of your time and mileage."

"I don't believe—"

"I gave Bennett your name and phone number. I'll text you his address. You can work out the details with him yourself."

"Give me the address now. And his phone number."

Samuel Thomas picked up his satchel, flung his coat over the top, and turned to Elizabeth. "Is there anything else tonight?"

She had the empty brandy glass in her hand. The ice rattled. "No. Thank you, Samuel."

Then Samuel Thomas left.

I was tempted to have that drink with Elizabeth now. Or go out and stop Samuel Thomas and wring William Bennett's address and phone number from him right now.

Instead, I came back across the room to Elizabeth and gestured to the brandy bottle. "Another?"

"No. I'll have one drink alone in front of you. But the second I'll have in private."

I could sympathize with that.

"You'll let me know?" she asked.

"As soon as I learn anything."

That seemed to satisfy her. "You should go home to your daughter now."

That would leave Elizabeth to her brandy and bitters. "I'd like to. But Cali is out with friends for the day, looking at colleges."

Elizabeth's eyes had taken on a far-away gaze. "It happens so fast."

And before I let her melancholy have a chance to try to reach out and grab hold of me, I slipped away. My gut instinct told me that what I'd heard tonight was true. I liked Elizabeth, and I hoped my gut was right.

9

YELLOW SPRINGS IS BETTER ON FOOT than in a car. And it's good by bicycle. You get the feel of the village better when things are close and they don't zip by through a window. And you feel more of the village vibe when you're really in it and not locked inside a steel and metal box on wheels, with all of its modern distractions.

Tonight I was slipping through that village vibe. Cali wasn't going to be home until late. We were near the summer solstice and the daylight would last until deep into the evening. I hadn't eaten dinner, so I did what a lot of people in the village did. I went to Tom's Market to see what I could find.

During the day, Yellow Springs has a lot of energy mixed in with the mellow—people working at the shops, traffic through town stopping for people at the crosswalks, people chatting with the UPS delivery guy because so many of the locals knew him. Maybe some people eating at the sidewalk tables or hanging out having conversations.

In the evenings the dial swung even farther over into mellow. People like to be outside, including me. This evening I cruised past some casual dog walkers. The dogs sniffed and the walkers waved. I rode past someone tending a front yard that had been planted entirely with a vegetable garden. Beyond that a woman in a sundress was sitting on her porch and tuning a fiddle. At Gaunt Park, there were kids playing tee-ball next to an ultimate frisbee game. Lots of people were out walking or bicycling, one of them pulling a trailer with a dog on it, and another pulling a homemade cart loaded with lumber and tools.

Snippets of the song "The Ancient Egyptians" floated through that mysterious part of my brain that creates music when it's not really there. I tracked the imaginary music in my head and recognized the band as Poi Dog Pondering. They really nailed what it's like to live in Yellow Springs.

I cruised past the grade school with the big schoolyard, then past the Mills Park Hotel where people perched up on the high porch in the big white chairs, looking down over the street. I pedaled past the funky clothing and art shops and the flower shop and the hardware and toy stores, then I swung into Tom's parking lot and looked longingly across the street at Current Cuisine. The deli counter and curried tofu were calling to me, but the sign in the window had been flipped to closed.

So on to Tom's. If the Emporium was the village's living room, Tom's Market was its pantry.

A couple of kids were busking on the steps. A girl on trombone and guy with a saxophone, playing a pretty good cover of "Seven Nation Army." Huh. It worked. I dropped a couple of dollars into the open trombone case and hoped I would remember these two if they ever got famous. It happened. There were some local folks who'd made it pretty big.

I stepped around the buskers to the door, and there was Marzi walking up from the opposite direction. We both stopped at the entrance and Marzi put a hand on her hip. "So. Here we are again."

She was wearing jeans and a Little Art Theatre t-shirt. Her neck glittered with long silver earrings that curved subtly toward the underside of her chin. I held the door open and tried not to let my gaze linger. "Not surprising. I'm a regular here."

She swept past me through the door. "Isn't everyone?"

I went in and drifted back to the produce, and Marzi followed. I lingered over the cucumbers, then held up a shiny pepper. "I think I feel like eating red food tonight."

She laughed. "Meal planning by color is not your typical approach."

I lifted some red lettuce from a bin and dropped it into my hand basket.

"That's mostly green."

"A foolish consistency is the hobgoblin of little minds."

Marzi gave me a curious smile. The silver earrings framed it perfectly. "Is this a test?"

"A test?" I picked up a bunch of radishes and shook the misted water off.

Marzi's gaze followed the radishes. "Red on the outside." She laughed. "And that quote was from Emerson."

"Careful, your education is showing."

She laughed again, and I dropped the radishes into the basket. "I don't think the hobgoblins will complain."

Marzi swiveled her head to survey the other produce bins. "I'd like to see you plan a dinner party by color."

"Oh, I can do wonders with orange and yellow."

"Sounds like a winter palette."

"Indeed."

She held up an eggplant questioningly.

I grinned. "Ah, aubergine, my old friend. What I could do with you and a beet and some purple yams."

"You are a little weird."

"Just a little?"

She replaced the eggplant in the bin. "Another time, Mister Purple."

I looked around. "No more red."

Marzi teased her eyes to the display behind me.

"Tomatoes! Of course." I chose a couple of romas.

"You're like watching a…"

I cocked my head to coax her to finish the thought. She didn't.

"Is everyone in Yellow Springs a little strange?"

"That seems to be the general trend." I hummed a bar of the Poi Dog Pondering song and reached for a bag of baby carrots.

"Those are orange."

"In the color family. They'll play OK with the others. Like second cousins at a family reunion." I moved down the aisle and picked up a baguette, then went for olives. I held the jar up and wagged my eyebrows at Marzi.

It took her a moment to catch on. "Pimentos. Red."

"Very good." I tucked the olives into the basket and turned back down the aisle.

Marzi followed me again. "What else?"

"Protein." I picked up some soy nuts and a bag of nutritional yeast.

She blinked at the yeast. "What *is* that?"

"Amino acids. Tastes like cheese and nuts."

"I'll take your word for it. It looks like something you'd scrape off a rock."

"I think that's pretty much how they make it."

We started back for the front of the store. "I notice you haven't gotten anything," I said. "Just here for the ambiance?"

"That would be worth it, but no." Marzi took my elbow and steered me to the pet supply section. "I'm on a mission." She picked up a can of cat food.

"I didn't know you have a cat."

"I don't." She held up the can for my inspection.

"Yes, a very nice choice. I'm sure the cat will love it."

She waved a hand in front of the can as if she was going to do a magic trick with it.

"What?"

She waggled her eyebrows as I had done with the olives.

"Oh, red label. Very clever."

"Thank you." She bowed as if she'd actually performed a magic trick. "I'm watching a friend's house while she's gone."

"And he has a cat?"

"Well, I'm not going to eat this. She has two cats."

"Ah." The friend was a she. Good.

We made our way to the corner checkout and I swung my backpack off my shoulders to load the red foods. When I'd finished checking out, I refitted the backpack onto my shoulders. "So it looks like this is where we part."

Marzi smiled. "Could be."

I felt the corners of my mouth tug upward. "I'm listening."

"I've already had dinner, but it looks like you're hungry."

"Always."

"I don't doubt that. And you're probably going home to Cali?"

"It's just me. She has a late night."

"Oh, in that case." Marzi took her change from the cat food and slipped the can into her pocket. "I'm on my way home. You could stop there and make your salad with the weird toppings, and I'd give you a little company."

"You'd watch me eat?"

"I'm very good company."

"And what about the cats?"

"The cats can come later."

"You make a very convincing argument." I swept my arm toward the door. "Lead on."

When we came out of Tom's, a group of the usual suspects was carousing on the bench across the street. A few conspirators were lounging in chairs they'd pulled to the curb. They were like the village town criers, announcing that the day was winding down and all was well. Let the tomfoolery begin.

One of the men was wearing a bright red baseball cap and he looked over at me and pointed. He clapped, and a few of the other joined him.

I gave back a snappy salute and a bow that satisfied the bench crowd, and they went back to their official business of chatting and watching.

Marzi went with me to get my bike from the rack. "What was that for?"

"I don't know. They just do that."

"You know them?"

I looked over. "Some of them." I looked closer. "Yeah, I guess I know them all."

"Isn't that a little weird?"

"You get used to it."

I pushed my bike as Marzi walked, and we worked our way back down Xenia Avenue. The kids with the trombone and saxophone were still busking on the steps. They'd moved on to something that sounded like a bluegrass version of Pink Floyd. It was pretty good.

We passed a young couple. She had a toddler strapped to her in a backpack baby carrier, and he wore a fedora with a feather in it. Both of them smelled like patchouli and something else earthy, maybe sweet pota-toes. Marzi and I nodded to them and said hello, and they greeted us back.

We passed two middle-aged men who were holding hands and grin-ning like they'd just won the lottery. We said hello and they wished us a pleasant evening and kept grinning.

We passed a young couple who looked like they didn't care to fit any traditional gender roles, but they looked happy and wished us a nice evening.

"I'm still getting used to that," Marzi said.

"What? Saying hi to everyone?"

"No. I mean that sometimes I feel like the unusual one here. I seem so—traditional."

I looked her over. "You'll get over it. It's hard to place the marker for unusual here. People just seem to be who they want to be."

"You seem to have adjusted."

"I have trouble with the pronouns sometimes. The new ones. And I can't get used to *they* for only one person. I guess the new pronouns don't stick because I didn't grow up with them."

"A lot of people didn't."

"I don't want to seem offensive. It just makes me feel old."

She squeezed my biceps. "You don't look so old."

I flexed my arm. "I like the way you talk."

We turned away from the downtown blocks and headed into the grid of houses. It was a short walk to Marzi's, and when we got there I leaned my bike against the porch railing.

"You can put that in the garage."

"Too fancy for Old Paint. I'll just let her graze out here in the yard."

"Yee-haw. Come on in and let's put on the feed bag."

I followed her. "Just keep the rodeo talk coming."

Marzi's house was light and open and airy with a bit of a beach house feel. The kitchen was small but nicely remodeled. White cabinets, lots of windows and glass, wooden beams below a high, white-washed ceiling. The living room had a fireplace and wooden floor that matched the accents and beams in the kitchen. A side door opened to a veranda and a heavily wooded yard.

Marzi set a colander, cutting board, and knives on the kitchen counter, and we chopped salad into a big bowl and toasted slices of the baguette.

Then Marzi got out two plates and silverware and two glass goblets. "I thought you'd already eaten."

She filled the goblets with water from the fridge. "I did."

"You don't want me to have to eat alone?"

"That doesn't bother me. I'm hungry." She forked salad onto the plates and dressed them. The salads grinned red at us. I dug out a slice of pepper that looked like a toothy grin, then set two olives above like I was making a face.

"That one's yours," Marzi said. "I don't eat anything that smiles back at me."

I dumped soy nuts and a healthy mound of nutritional yeast over my plate and we clicked forks. "Cheers."

After a couple of bites, Marzi reached for the yeast and sprinkled a tiny dab onto a forkful of salad. I pretended to ignore her reaction. She licked her fork in a very unladylike manner and shook out another tiny dollop of yeast onto her salad. "It's good."

"Yeah, if you could taste it."

I refilled our water glasses and Marzi said, "We should have had red wine."

"Maybe better that we didn't. I've got some work things on my mind I want to keep turning over."

"That's what a woman wants to hear when she gets a man into her house."

I set my fork down and looked at her. "Oh, sorry. I'm distracted."

"It's OK."

"Look, I haven't done anything like this for a long time."

"I know."

She did know. She knew the whole story. Everything. Cali and I had told her all of it when Marzi was our counselor and we were mourning Kat. I pushed some salad around on my plate. "This is probably weird for you. Me being a former client."

"It's weird."

"If it helps, it's weird for me too."

"That doesn't help, but weird seems to be the theme here." She un-curled a finger toward my plate. "Eat. And tell me about it."

"About the weirdness."

"No, about what's distracting you."

I gave her the short update. It was a further breach of the discretion I'd promised to Elizabeth Winstrop, but it seemed a reasonably safe breach. Marzi had promised privacy when Cali and I were in grief counseling with her. Anything we told her was privileged information.

But I realized that's not what Marzi and I were doing here. There was no promise of privacy. This was new territory. Marzi wasn't here to ease my mind or rest my worries. This was a different kind of discre-tion. Something implicit between two people who were coming closer together.

Marzi was a good listener, and then she asked a lot of questions. She wanted to know the professor's name, what I knew about the girl in the rain who sneaked into the showers and disappeared from the home-less camp in the warehouse, and about the girl's mother. She took out her phone and looked up the story of Henna Winstrop's disappearance twenty years before. She turned the screen toward me to show an old picture of Henna Winstrop. "That's her?"

"Yeah." I reached in my pocket for my phone and swiped to the pic-tures I'd taken at Canbury's office. "Look at this."

Marzi whistled at the resemblance. "What's going on?"

"That's what's keeping me distracted."

I put my phone back into my pocket and settled into the last bits of my salad and baguette.

Marzi watched me intensely. "You have to find that girl."

"I will."

"Soon."

"Now you're distracted."

"Tell me about what happened in the warehouse again."

I did.

Marzi nodded. "She's looking for her mother."

I crunched a resonant note on an errant soy nut. "What?"

"The girl. She's looking for her mother."

"I've thought of that. It would mean Henna Winstrop is alive, and she's been nearby."

"You think they've been separated." It wasn't a question.

I pushed my plate away. "Yes. And I want to find her. I want to find both of them."

Marzi was looking at her phone again, reading up on Henna Winstrop's disappearance. I took our plates to the sink and rinsed them.

Marzi was still reading on her phone.

I ran some water and added dish soap from the dispenser, then washed the plates and forks and water goblets and set them in the drainer.

Marzi looked up. "Oh." She turned her phone over on the table. "Now it's me who's tuned out."

"This case is like that."

She chewed her lip once, realized she was doing it, and stopped. "You know what would clear our heads?"

"What?"

She stretched out her arm to reach for the can of cat food on the far edge of the counter. "Izzy and Fluffers."

I rolled my eyes. "How could they not?"

We walked over to her friend's house. I pushed my bike. It was after sunset and mostly dark. We talked about how Marzi liked living in Yellow Springs, then out of the blue she asked me if I had a gun.

"Yes."

"Did you have it with you when the guy came at you with the board?"

"It was a two-by-four."

"Of course it was. Did you have the gun?"

"No. It was locked in the truck. You can't take them onto college campuses in Ohio."

A few steps later she slowed. "Do you have it with you now?"

I stopped and lifted my arms over my head. "No ma'am. You can frisk me."

She didn't. "How can you justify…"

We walked several steps. I pushed Marzi to finish. "It's OK. Say it. I've had this conversation before."

"How can you put together living the way you do in this town with this vibe, and carrying a gun."

"I don't put them together. They're two different things. One is business. It's a business that can help other people, but it's also a business that means people sometimes need helping because there are people who do bad things in the world."

Step, step, pause. A moth flitted by. A cricket chirred. I waited for it.

"Have you ever shot someone?"

"Yes."

"Fatally?"

My answer came slowly. "Yes. A long time ago."

Step, step. Stop. Chirr.

"More than once?"

"Yes. It was necessary. Things would have been way worse if I hadn't."

"Does Cali know?"

"She's never asked. I'll tell her if she does."

"But you're so—You fit right in in this town. You don't seem like you'd have a gun. Or that you'd shoot someone."

"If the bad guys didn't carry them, neither would I. But the bad guys do."

We walked some more.

"You seem to have it all figured out."

"I don't. Guns allow people to do much worse things than they could without them. Look at the shooting in Dayton at the Oregon District. That guy had a history. But some of the things happened when he was underage and the records were sealed. We have the second amendment that says we have the right to protect ourselves and our country. A lot of people own guns, and a few of them do very bad things with them."

We walked. Marzi said, "Some other countries have tried limiting gun ownership."

"With mixed results. Some people in this country want to take away all of the guns, and others want everyone to carry one all the time. Like politics, the middle ground seems to be disappearing."

"And that's where you're stuck—in the middle."

"That's where a lot of people are stuck, and if I'm a problem solver

I have to play the game as it's laid out in front of me."

"You're a complicated man."

I thumped my chest. "Yawp. Do I contradict myself? Very well then, I contradict myself. I am large. I contain multitudes."

Marzi stopped and turned her head up toward me under the light from a street lamp. "That was Walt Whitman?"

"W. W. himself."

She turned up the walk to the house we'd stopped in front of. "We're here." And she disappeared into the shadows of the pine trees in the yard.

I left my bike on the sidewalk and caught up to Marzi at the door, where I was introduced to Izzy and Fluffers. They didn't think much of me until Marzi gave me the can of food and I opened it. Then I was their best friend. Cats can be like that.

Marzi pointed at the cats while they ate. "That one's Fluffers, and this one is Izzy."

"I already forgot which is which."

"Easy." She pointed again. "That one is fluffy, and that one isn't, *izzy?*"

I almost let myself laugh. It didn't matter. Marzi laughed for both of us at her joke.

Then while Marzi checked the house, I looked around. The place was modest in size but fixed up really nice. An open floorplan, bookshelves, LED lighting. Wrap-around porch. Hot tub with a solar cover out back.

Marzi took in the mail, went into rooms and turned lights on and back off. I took a tour of the titles on the bookshelf while she worked. There was a lot of science fiction. Some Westerns. A bunch of technical books about electrical circuitry.

I came back to the kitchen. The cats had eaten and were cleaning themselves. I had become invisible to them again.

Marzi finished checking the house and took my hand and led me outside onto the back porch and we looked up at the sky. I pulled her closer and she tucked in under my arm. "Cold?" I asked.

"A little."

I kissed her forehead, and she turned her face up and we had our first real kiss. It was soft and quick, and then it was over and we were looking up at the sky again.

I thought I felt her shiver. "We could go back."

She turned so we pressed together facing each other. "Or we could get in the hot tub to warm up. It'd be a nice interlude."

Her face showed that she'd caught my reaction. She pulled back to look at me. "What?"

"Did you say interlude?"

She nodded.

"I thought you'd said *in the nude.*"

Her mouth turned up at the ends. "We might have to do that."

"Don't you think that's a little fast?"

"Yes."

OK. I did too. But we'd known each other a long time. Something was see-sawing in my mind. I didn't want to let go of Kat, but I also didn't want to let go of Marzi. But Kat wasn't coming back, and Marzi was standing here under the stars with me offering a late-night interlude in a hot tub. It was time to listen to Walt Whitman and be large and embrace my multitudes.

My phone stopped me. I took it out and looked before I could think not to. There was a text from Cali. *Dad it was so cool. I loved Miami. I'm home. Is there anything to eat?*

I texted back. *Veggie dogs in the freezer. I thought you had dinner.*

A long time ago. Then *Found them!*

I smiled and slipped my phone into my pocket and found Marzi waiting. "Oh, shit. I'm sorry."

"Don't be."

"It's Cali."

"I figured."

"She's been out all day and she just got home and…"

Marzi was very patient while I explained. When I'd finished, I said, "I've spoiled the mood."

"Kind of."

"Maybe I should go home."

Marzi shrugged.

"Sorry." I came over and clumsily hugged her and gave her another kiss.

Marzi was not clumsy, and she made the kiss more than I put into it. "Don't worry about it. It heightens the anticipation. Will we or won't we?"

She was holding me tight, and one part of me was trying to answer right now. "Maybe we could re-start?"

Marzi pointed toward the door. "Go home to your daughter."

I did.

Summer night bicycle rides through Yellow Springs are one of the joys of living in a small town, and I felt relaxed when I got home. Cali was excited and wanted to show me pictures of the college campuses she'd been to. She swiped through them so fast it didn't take long, and she yammered about the details all they way. "It's like that old show I've been watching with Jenny and Nadia and Asia. When the daughter goes off to college."

"You have a couple more years before that happens for you."

"I know, but—they were talking about it today. Asia and the others got ahead of me."

"Ahead of you?"

"When I came home the other night. They stayed and watched another episode."

"Oh. When the daughter goes off to college."

"Yeah. One of those."

"And now you're going to look at colleges with them and they're all talking about it. And you're behind on the show."

"Yeah."

I reached into the coffee table drawer for the TV remote. "So you need to catch up with them."

Cali looked unsure. "You'll watch one with me?"

"Absolutely. But don't tell anyone."

She snapped off the floor light. "I won't."

This was the opposite of what I'd planned. It was late, and I was going to get up very early in the morning. I should be in bed. But there was no way I was going to miss this interlude.

10

THE AIR WAS STILL AT FOUR IN THE MORNING. Wednesday. Since Sunday when I'd picked up the girl in the rain. I needed to make progress today.

I lay in the dark and listened to the sounds of the house. The ceiling fan whispered a steady white noise and put a chill on the room that felt good. A lone tree frog croaked a song that wafted through the open window.

I gave a soft two-note whistle, waited a minute, and whistled again. A moment later there was rustling that moved through the jack-in-the-pulpit under the window, then the slap of the cat door flipping open in the kitchen, followed by the almost-invisible sound of Mrs. Jenkins padding through the house.

Mrs. Jenkins stopped beside my bed, then magically transported herself effortlessly up onto the bed with a trick only cats can do. She lowered her head to my hand and rubbed. I obliged her with fingers over her head and under her chin, which she stretched her neck out for and set her purring to a level that drowned out the fan and the frog. Cat, queen of the bedroom.

Before she could settle in for a nap I lifted the covers and said, "breakfast?"

Mrs. Jenkins dropped to the floor and diligently herded me to the kitchen and her food bowl. It was earlier than I needed to get up, but my thoughts were already pushing me to get moving. One of the nice things about a cat is that you can have company at just about any time of the night if you want it. If you can find the cat.

I made a big breakfast of potatoes, eggs, and leftover yellow grits that I sliced like polenta and browned in a skillet. I ate two-thirds of the breakfast and scooped one-third onto a plate for Cali and slid that into the refrigerator. Then I wrote a note for Cali, filled my coffee travel mug, and went to get dressed.

I picked out an old pair of trousers that were worn and too big in the waist. I kept them for working around the yard. Then I pulled on a gray t-shirt and my brown, long-sleeved button-up that was stained with motor oil. I topped it with my gray ball cap that I pulled down low over my ears. Everything would be too heavy and warm for the temperature by mid-morning, but that was part of what I was going for.

Then I packed some extra things into a backpack, turned off the lights, and slipped out the front door into the dark. Mrs. Jenkins was lounging on the wicker porch chair like she owned the world and knew I would be coming out the door to pet her on the head, which I did. All is right in the world when the cat is happy.

The drive to Dayton was quiet and dark and relaxing. The radio kept me company. I made one stop at an all-night convenience store. The exchange was awkward.

The place was small and brightly lit and a radio played Joan Jett's "Bad Reputation." The guy behind the counter was maybe twenty and he was filling in the bubbles on a lottery card with a stubby pencil. I stepped up. "Pack of cigarettes."

He looked blankly at me and waited. Finally he said, "What kind?"

"Doesn't matter."

He cut his eyes over me.

"What kind do people like?"

He reached up to a slotted display over the counter and pulled down a pack that was white with a red stripe in the middle. "You'll probably like these."

I picked them up. "Are these a brand name?"

The guy's eyebrows went up.

"Doesn't matter. I'll take them." I set a couple of dollars on the counter.

He looked at me like I had orange hair.

I pulled out a couple more dollars. He shook his head and rang up the sale.

"You're kidding me." I added some more bills.

The guy gave me my change. "You want a bag for that?"

"Oh, yeah. That might be—"

The look on his face told me how stupid he thought I was for not getting the joke. I pocketed the tobacco and left.

Before I got out of the parking lot I realized I'd forgotten the lighter. When I walked back into the store the guy lifted his head from his lottery bubbles. "Change your mind about the bag?"

I picked up a lighter from the display by the register and handed him a five. He made change again and turned back to his pencil.

I tapped a finger on the counter. "Hey, how about a bag?"

The bored droop went out of his eyes. "You kidding me?"

I pointed at his nose. "Yes."

The rest of the drive was uneventful. I dropped off the highway and into Dayton and parked in a spot down by the river. I locked the M&P40 in the truck cab. If things went sour I'd want it, but if things went really sour I wouldn't want to be caught on private property with it. It was a fifty-fifty proposition. I left the weapon in the truck.

Streaks of color were rising in the sky over the banks of the river. The day was calm and clear. I approached the warehouse carefully. Down the broken narrow walk between the buildings and past the side door I'd gone in the day before. Out into the weedy lot beyond the loading docks and the bay doors.

The carcass of an abandoned semi trailer rested like a fallen creature on the broken tarmac. I waltzed past it like a gawker in a museum. I climbed onto the loading dock outside of the homeless camp and sat under an orange-colored sky that reminded me of the Nat King Cole song. Bands of rusted rebar showed through crumbling bits of concrete that flaked off the dock. I laid back and listened.

No sounds that I could distinguish came from inside. In the distance there was a steady thrum and clack of cars on the highway and crossing the bridge over the Great Miami River.

The sun was warming my feet where they dangled over the edge of the dock, and I felt at peace in a way I hadn't expected. Aloof, detached, free.

I knew it wasn't real. No matter how earnestly Janis Joplin sang in my imagination, freedom wasn't just another word. Being homeless was a hard road. I had a home to go back to. Work and a steady income. A daughter I could provide and care for. Friends. Love. There were no needle tracks on my arms. No urgent need for food or warmth. My decisions weren't driven by the need to sell myself so I could find my next fix. I wasn't a young girl vulnerable to being trafficked in the sex trade by strangers.

All of that rattled in my head. Then I realized I'd been asleep when something made me jerk awake.

I turned my head and saw a girl down the dock from me squatting on her toes with her back over the edge of the concrete. She was so close to the drop I thought she might fall. She wasn't the Winstrop girl I was looking for.

I watched closer and realized she was urinating, and a shaft of guilt sliced through me and I turned away. It was an odd thing. The girl could have found privacy in any number of places around the old building or docks or shipping yard, but she didn't. And the only shame there seemed to be was what I felt for her.

I waited for a few minutes after the girl had gone, then went in to watch the rest of the camp wake up.

I sat at the far end of the ring of sleepers. There were a dozen bodies on makeshift beds in a loose grouping. The girl who'd come out on the dock to pee had crawled back into her bag, and only one of the others was up, a thin man with weathered skin who sat cross-legged on the floor and sang quietly to himself. His voice was too soft for me to make out the words, but it sounded like a children's song.

I took my time looking through the shapes and faces of the squatters. The man with the dirty beard who'd gummed the cigarette and come after me the last time I was here was one of the lumps curled under a blanket. I made a mental note to keep my face turned away from him. Then I remembered the cigarettes and took one out and slipped it behind my ear. Bait.

The flame-haired kid who'd swung the two-by-four wasn't there, and neither was Elizabeth Winstrop's granddaughter. Or Elizabeth's daughter.

The camp woke up slowly, and everyone completely ignored me. Not a word or a grunt or a walk-by, only a few quick glances that turned away when I looked back. After a long time of watching people wake up but not do much of anything except shuffle around and sit, I stood and made a pass through the edge of the group and out to the dock.

A minute later, someone followed me. It was the man who'd been singing to himself. He looked to be somewhere between forty and sixty and was very thin. His clothes were too big and he wore a scratchy salt-and-pepper beard. The man squinted up at the sun, then at me, and he pointed. "That a smoke?"

I touched the cigarette behind my ear.

The man moved closer. "You got another?"

I tugged the cigarette loose and held it out to the man. He closed his hand around the cigarette and made it disappear.

I reached into my pocket and offered the lighter, but the man shook his head. It hadn't occurred to me that the cigarette would be worth saving for later, but there it was.

I kept my face canted away. "Been here long?"

His lips moved for a moment before words formed and began to come out. "I slept here before."

"Cozy."

He looked confused and turned away, but I called out to him to wait. "I'm looking for a friend."

The man's eyes darted over me. "Ruthie can fix you up. She still likes the boys."

"No. Someone else—"

"Mister, I'll give you your smoke back if you want it."

"No, I don't want..."

But he was already shuffling off. He kept the cigarette. This was probably going to be harder than I'd thought.

I went back inside and worked the camp slowly. Most of the others wouldn't look me in the eye, and some of them wouldn't even talk to me. After nearly an hour I hadn't gotten anything useful, and I feared I had worn out my welcome. I walked out of the warehouse and down over the bank to the river to consider my options.

The water and the geese floated by. A cloud lingered overhead. After several minutes, a movement sounded from behind me and someone came down the sloped riverbank and sat to my right. I knew before I looked that it was the girl who'd come out on the dock to pee.

She was young but looked older than Elizabeth Winstrop's granddaughter. The girl wore jeans that were in good shape and a long gray shirt that came down to the tops of her thighs. She had a backpack hanging from her shoulders. I had a feeling that the things she thought were most important were never far away. She didn't hold a cell phone and she wasn't wearing the kinds of clothes that Cali and her friends paid attention to, but other than that she could have been any teenaged girl walking through the city or waiting for the school bus. But she wasn't.

I reached into my jacket for the cigarettes and shook one out of the pack and put in it my mouth. Her eyes followed my movements, and I held the pack out to her.

She took a cigarette and held it in her hand but made no move to put it in her mouth or light it. After a moment she cocked her head. "Are you going to light that?"

I squinted at the sun. "No." I pinched the cigarette out of my mouth and set in on the grass between us. Her eyes followed it.

I offered her the lighter but she shook her head and made the cigarette I'd given her disappear somewhere into a pocket or a fold of her clothing. Then she dropped her hand over the one I'd left in the grass and made that disappear too.

Her gaze went out over the river. "I know who you are."

I let it sit between us for a minute. "Who am I?"

"You're looking for her."

I rubbed a hand across my chin. "Her?"

The girl looked over her shoulder at me as if she were making a decision, then spoke very carefully. "Willow."

I tried the name out, repeating it back. "Willow." Elizabeth Winsrop's granddaughter. The daughter of Henna Winstrop, who Elizabeth had hired me to find.

I let out some line. Waited. Looked casually over at the girl. "Long dark hair. Thin. Black backpack?"

The girl sat on her hands. I interpreted that as a strange kind of yes. "You know her last name?"

She gave a shake of her head that was almost imperceptible. "I saw you earlier."

"I'm sorry about that. I didn't realize what you were doing."

She stared, then her face softened. "Don't worry about that. Nobody does."

My education was expanding.

"I saw you yesterday," the girl said.

Oh. "That didn't go real well."

"Flame is protective of her."

"Of Willow."

"Yeah."

"Flame is the guy who came at me with the lumber? Bright red hair?"

"Who else?"

Right. "You have a name?"

"Kristine. With a K."

"With a K. Getting it right is important."

She turned to look more squarely at me, and I saw there was a spark in her eyes. "They think they know who you are."

"*They* do?" I jerked a thumb over my shoulder toward the building we'd come from.

"They think you're with the others who came looking for Willow."

There it was again. "That was real? Someone was looking for Willow?"

Kristine shrugged. "They were looking for someone. It seemed like it could be Willow."

"You were there?"

Her eyes cried yes, but her voice was calm and flat. "Two men. They slapped Ruth around and hurt her. They tried to scare us."

"Did they? Scare you?"

Her gaze drifted down. "Yes."

"Is it possible that it wasn't Willow they were looking for?"

"They didn't say her name. It could have been something else."

"Like what else?"

She shrugged. "People come through sometimes. They're bad news."

A trickle of sweat formed at the top of my back and began a very slow trip downward. The extra clothes I was wearing to try to fit in were going to be a slog. I took off my ball cap. "But you don't think I'm one of them?"

"No."

"How do you know?"

"You're not like them."

I waited a long time for her to say more. She finally did. "I saw the way you were yesterday. When Ruthie came up to you. You were kind to her. And you didn't hurt Flame." She was searching my face. I wondered what it would reveal to her.

I took off my outer shirt and folded it across my knee. "You recognized me right away today?"

"People look out for new faces."

"I guess they would." I glanced over at Kristine. "You need anything? Hungry?"

Her shoulders moved slightly in what might have been a shrug.

"Cup of coffee? Anything?"

Another quasi-shrug. "I'm all right."

"You can bring anyone you want. Or we can go somewhere you choose, with lots of people around."

Her head came around and her arms shot to the ground beside her. "I'm not afraid of you."

"Whoa." I held up my hands in a time-out sign. "I'm not afraid of you either."

She looked at me for a long time, then stood up. "I know a place."

I picked myself up off the grass.

"The restaurant in the sky."

I raised an eyebrow, but she was already climbing back up the riverbank.

Kristine led me several blocks through town. We didn't talk much. She crossed Main Street by the Wright Brothers Flyover sculpture, and we went across the park by the new Levitt Pavilion. When we passed through the doors of the Crowne Plaza hotel, I quickened my steps and got in front of Kristine before we reached the elevators. "Look, I'm not going to sleep with you."

She pivoted around me and pushed the button for an elevator car. "No, you're not."

The doors opened and we stepped into the elevator. Kristine cut her eyes to me and whispered, "Asshole."

"I heard that."

"I said it so you would hear." Then she rolled her shoulders and let them soften. "It's the restaurant at the top."

The Muzak carried us up. A not-so-bad rendition of a Beatles song.

We stepped out into a lobby that opened to the glass-walled expanse of the View 162 restaurant that took up most of the top floor. I knew the place. I'd come here on dates with Kat years ago before we were married. Kat would order a dessert for us to share, and I would get one bite of it and we'd look out in the dark over the lights of the city.

The place was bright and sunny now, the windows doing exactly what they were supposed to and giving the illusion that we were standing at the top of the city. Just like Kristine had said. The restaurant in the sky.

A young guy appeared from the wings and took us to a table. He was thin and fit and his hair looked like he'd just stepped out of the barber's chair. He could have been an extra in a Hollywood movie. The look was probably good for tips.

There were a few other people at tables eating breakfast. Most of them looked like they were travelling for work, eating slowly and watching the large-screen TVs behind the bar as they ate or tapped at laptops or phones.

The waiter pointed to the lobby. "There's a coat room by the elevator. You can leave your things there." His eyes slid over our backpacks. Kristine had hers in her lap. I'd stuffed mine under the table.

Kristine clutched her backpack tighter. "I'll keep it here."

I shrugged. What are you going to do?

The waiter nodded. "Coffee?"

Kristine and I both flipped our cups over, and the waiter shushed away.

I swiveled my head to take in the views. "Nice choice of places to eat."

Kristine frowned.

"What?"

"Where did you think I'd pick?"

"I don't know. Blimpee's?"

Her frown deepened. "You think that's where I belong? Blimpee's?"

Huh. "No."

"No?"

"No. It's not a reflection on you. Blimpee's is the kind of place I'd choose. It's a reflection on me."

She looked confused. "Blimpee's is closed down."

"Kind of place I'd go to if it were still open."

The confusion gave way to something softer.

I stuck my hand out across the table. "Let's try again. I'm Jackson Flint."

She laughed. "What kind of name is that?"

"My daddy liked Johnny Cash."

I got a blank stare. "Doesn't matter. It might as well be somebody's name."

"Well, Jackson Flint. I'm going to the Ladies'." She picked up her backpack and took everything with her.

The waiter came and poured coffee and filled our water goblets and I looked at the empty chair across from me and shrugged again and he wheeled away to another table.

Kristine came back with a bounce in her step. She'd moussed her short blonde hair and put on a necklace that dangled a silver amulet. Her boney white knees showed under a black skirt. I still had the too-big pants with the cuffs rolled up and the old t-shirt.

She kicked her backpack under the table and sat. "Good. You're still here."

"Tempted to run off with the waiter."

She picked up her menu and didn't even turn to look at him. Not funny, Jackson.

When the waiter came back I asked for oats and yogurt and told Kristine to get whatever she wanted. She ordered biscuits and gravy with an egg on top, hash browns, fruit, and a pancake. Orange juice. Her eyes came up to mine like she was asking if it was too much. I pretended not to notice.

The food was on the table inside of a few minutes, but Kristine had spent that time looking at the kitchen door like it was taking forever. When the plates were all arranged on the table I could tell she was trying to eat slow but she had to work at it. She dug into everything at once, one plate to the next and the next. Biscuits and gravy and potatoes and pancake all in the same bite. Chased with orange juice.

I let her get deep enough into the food that she'd slowed before I picked up the conversation. "You've eaten here before?"

"God, no." She reached for her coffee and took a tiny sip.

"It seemed like you knew the place."

"I do."

OK. I ate a few bites and took some coffee. Waited until she decided to talk.

"I've always wanted to come here, all right?" She ate a bite of pancake, reached for the orange juice again. Picked off a flake of hash browns. "There was a guy at RiverScape. You know the park by the river?"

"Yeah." The other river. Dayton had three. You want water, Dayton's got it. Sometimes too much.

"He used to walk through there. Had a suit and a briefcase. Used to put change and dollar bills into my hand." She swallowed. Looked around the table, considering. What plate to visit next.

"Just you?"

"He gave money to some of the others too, I guess. I liked to think it was just me."

I gave her a prod. "So this place?"

"It's kind of embarrassing."

"OK."

We ate a little more. None of Kristine's plates was empty, but she had slowed way down. Finally she moved some hash browns around and leaned back. "I used to imagine that the guy was kind of like my guardian angel. Like he knew I didn't have a dad and he was, you know, helping me out because of that." Her eyes went up and took in the room, then came back to our table. She seemed satisfied that no one was listening in. "I followed him sometimes. He liked to come here for lunch. I dreamed that he'd take me one day."

I wanted to reach out and touch Kristine's arm, comfort her. But her body language told me I shouldn't. It was her memory, not mine, and I should stay out of it. "You still see him? The guy?"

She shrugged. "Not for a while."

OK, I wasn't learning how to find Willow Winstrop. I tried to steer us out of the weeds and back onto the highway. "What about Willow? Have you seen her?"

"Not since you were there."

I tapped a finger on the table, caught it, and made myself stop. "I'm trying to help her."

"I believe you."

"If you can help me find Willow, I can do that. Help her."

"I said I believe you."

"You don't want to know why I'm looking for her?"

"I can guess. You're not a cop. Somebody's probably trying to find her. Her mother, I guess. Or maybe you're some kind of relative. From what Willow's told me I don't think her mom would have the money to hire anybody."

"That's a very good guess."

The compliment didn't get me anywhere. Kristine stared at the remains of her food and took a tiny sip of coffee.

"Can you help me find Willow? And I can help you—you know. Is there something I can do that would make things a little easier for you?"

"I don't know where Willow is. And I'm not looking for a handout, OK? No one's going to come looking for me. No one's going to take me in and give me a home and meals. Your handout isn't going to change my life. And you're not the guardian angel that's come to take me to lunch at the restaurant in the sky, OK? You're just here because you want to find Willow. I get that. Once you find her, you'll be gone."

I didn't patronize. "You're right."

Her eyes came up.

"But it doesn't mean I don't care. There's just only so much any one person can do." At that moment a Be Good Tanyas song came into my head. "Junkie Song." There are so many people who need something. For a lot of different reasons. You can't help them all. I looked Kristine in the eye. "Have you seen Willow using?"

"She wasn't the type."

"How was she around the others?"

"The others?"

I didn't dance around the truth. "The men. How was Willow around the men?"

"Willow is a virgin."

"What? How do you know that?"

"I don't. But she said so, and I believe her. It's her thing. The others knew. They were protective."

"Protective?"

Kristine wiped her fingers on the white linen napkin. "Look, I've only known Willow for a couple of days. She just started coming around. But she was different. Flame was real protective of her. He wanted to save her. It was like she was his project. He wanted to keep the men from whoring her out."

Ouch. "Pretty harsh way of saying that, isn't it?"

"You got a better way?"

I didn't. My mouth said, "Have you stayed away?" and I knew I'd slipped over the line as soon as it came out.

Kristine didn't shut down. She did the opposite, came straight at it. "I keep away from the junk. It would ruin my chances of a future."

"And a present."

"And I don't whore like the others."

Good. My brain said it, but my mouth wouldn't.

"It's what makes me different from the others. I'm particular about men. Most of the others, they'll do anything. Even the younger ones. Some guy comes along and they'll disappear with him for a while. Get some cash to pump into their veins, or whatever. Then they don't want to do anything. Just lay around and wait for nothing to come along and make things better. You don't want to know what those guys would do with someone like Willow if they could get to her."

"We both know what they would do."

Kristine sighed like I'd ruined the spell of the restaurant in the sky. I guessed I had. "There are options," she said.

"Shelters?"

"Boys I like."

I tried to hide my surprise. I didn't do that very well.

"I find them. I don't go with men who are looking for it. They don't treat you good."

I nodded like this was something I understood.

"I pick them up outside the bars. Or in the places I can get in because they don't check IDs. Or the places that let you in anyway. I pick the guys who are alone. They're just lonely. I tell them I'm hungry, or I need some money. They take me some place and give me what I need. It's like the opposite of what the other women do. I pick the guys up. Who I want. I make them a little less lonely."

Nod. Just listen. Don't try to say anything.

"They don't all want what you're thinking. And it's my choice. A man alone in a bar is safer than a man with his friends."

At that moment I wanted to take Kristine home. Have her come live with me and Cali and figure out what she wanted to do with her life, and how to do it. Like she was a stray cat I could take in. But she wasn't, and I didn't know how to help her.

Kristine looked at me like it was my turn to say something. I did. "You got a longer-term plan than that?"

She blinked.

"You're living at that warehouse?"

"Not really. Temporarily, sometimes."

"How'd you end up there?"

Her eyes dropped. "My mom."

I waited.

"She's in jail."

OK. "Your father?"

"Never met him. If you see him, tell him I said hi."

Just then the waiter came by and looked over the remains of our meal. "Anything else?"

I pointed to Kristine's plates. "Can you put what's left in a box to go? And if it's not too early for the kitchen to handle it, add a sandwich to go."

"I think we can do that."

Kristine shook her head. "You don't have to do that."

"You never got your lunch here. Club sandwich?"

"Turkey."

The waiter wrote that down and picked up the plates and whooshed them away.

Kristine folded her napkin onto the table. "I'm getting out."

"Out?"

"The Air Force. As soon as I turn eighteen they'll let me in. Like my brother. He ran away, and he got in the Air Force and he has everything he needs now."

Great. "You finished high school?"

"Last year."

"You don't look that old."

"I'm seventeen. I skipped first grade."

"So you're pretty smart?"

"I took the ASVAB. That government test?"

"I know it."

"I had a really high score. I can do whatever I want after I get in."

"You could do other things."

She blinked.

"Besides the Air Force."

"Like what?"

And I understood very deeply in that moment that where you are in life sometimes has very little to do with what you deserve or have earned. It often has more to do with what the world around you reveals may be possible. Kristine could go to college and she would probably fly through. She could get a career, go to grad school. But nobody was showing her how to get there. And she probably wasn't going to see a lot of options from the view she had of the world. Military service was it.

"How long?" I said.

"Two months. My birthday is in August."

"You need anything until then?"

"I need a lot of things."

"Money?"

"You don't owe me anything."

"I know I don't."

She hesitated. "The cigarettes."

"I figured you didn't smoke?"

"And it's obvious you don't. But you wouldn't believe what you can trade them for."

I took the pack out and set it on the table. She made them disappear somewhere.

"I'm like the guys," I said.

She tilted her head.

"You pick them up. They give you a meal, or whatever you need. You chose me. Like you choose the others. You came out on the dock this morning because you chose me. And you followed me down to the riverbank."

She stayed mum.

"Can I ask you a couple of questions?"

"I can't promise I'll answer, but you've been real nice to me."

"Fair enough. Do you think there were men looking for Willow? That someone was trying to find her?"

She gave a little shrug. "I don't know. Some guys came and asked for a girl who could have been Willow. She wasn't there. They didn't like it."

"They weren't nice guys?"

"Scary. Especially one of them."

"How many?"

"Two."

"Why do you think they were looking for someone who could have been Willow?"

"No idea. I stayed out of the way. They slapped Ruthie around and she ran away."

I tried to keep mental notes so I could write them down later. "Does Willow have any connection to Sinclair that you know of?"

"The college? Why should she?"

I sighed.

The waiter came back with the box of leftovers and the turkey sandwich. He set those by Kristine and he set the bill by me and pointed to the register. "Whenever you're ready."

Kristine opened the carryout box and looked inside to make sure it was all there. She opened her backpack and rearranged some things to fit the take-out in on top. "If you want to find Willow, you should try looking for her mother. Willow wanted to find her."

I knew that. She'd told me in the truck when I gave her a ride in the rain.

"I think her mother's from Yellow Springs. Willow kept talking about it. Maybe you ought to try out there?"

"On my list. But I need to find Willow's mother. I need to find both of them, and I think her mother is still in Dayton." I thought Willow was still in Dayton too. I'd seen her yesterday at Sinclair.

Kristine stood and tugged the backpack onto her shoulders. "You want to find them, I'd look at RiverScape. I know Willow's been there."

"Thanks. Want me to walk you down?"

But she was already moving away for the elevators. I didn't let myself go after her. I hoped her story of the Air Force and her birthday in a couple of months was true. If it wasn't, the forty dollars I'd secretly tucked into her backpack might help for a little while.

I took the bill to the register and handed over my bank card. A feeling of guilt tugged at me, and I didn't know how to let it go.

11

I WALKED BACK TO THE TRUCK and pulled a change of clothes out from behind the seat. Lightweight pants and a thin, button-down shirt with short sleeves. It was a relief to get out of the heavy clothes, and that reminded me again of Kristine and her backpack and the burden of having to carry or stash away hidden somewhere nearly everything you owned.

Then I traded the boots I'd been wearing for running shoes. I was dressed respectably enough but fairly casual. It would have to be good enough for my next stop.

The guy Robert Winstrop had hired without his wife's knowledge wasn't making things easy. He would only talk to me about the case if I met with him personally in his office in Columbus. And he had only a narrow window of time when he would be available.

That didn't leave time for me to snoop out RiverScape park for signs or sightings of either Elizabeth Winstrop's daughter or granddaughter. And it didn't leave any time to sniff around Yellow Springs to see if Willow might have tried to get back there again. I didn't like it.

So I was already irked when I hit traffic on I-70. Like other Midwestern states, Ohio after the spring thaw became open season for orange barrels and road work. And for some people that also meant open season for road rage.

When three lanes of highway dropped down to one, traffic slowed. But a few idiots zoomed around the merge to the head of the closure where they poked the noses of their vehicles into the line of cars and demanded to be let in.

It was nothing new, and I tried to ignore it. I focused instead on the iced coffee I'd gotten from the Emporium. It sat in my cup holder and dripped sweat while I listened to weird new music on WYSO and watched the aggressors do their thing. And I imagined that I was back home in Yellow Springs walking instead of sitting in a box with wheels in the sun on a long, hot, crowded strip of concrete and asphalt.

Just before the last open lane dropped and I would have cleared the merge and entered the single line of vehicles squeezed between a concrete barrier and a row or orange barrels, the whole pack stopped completely. Then a bright red Mustang screamed down the open lane and thumped to a stop beside me. I eased the front bumper of my truck up to a few inches from the car ahead, and the driver of the Mustang looked over and shouted something I couldn't hear over my radio. He was a small man who I assumed had an equally small penis. But you never know about these things. He flipped me off and punched his way in front of the woman driving the car whose bumper I was parked on.

If Kat were alive and there with me she would have told me I was making things worse. I should have just let the guy in. And she would be right. But there's something in me that makes me want to push back against assholes. The trouble is that you can't tell these days who's packing a gun, or who might be willing to go the distance to play out their rage or sense of empowerment or entitlement, who will be enough of a bully to be real trouble. That's why I had the M&P40 and why it was tucked in the glove compartment now. And why I wanted it to stay there.

Maybe if I wasn't so willing to push I wouldn't need the gun. Maybe if our brains were wired differently and the genetic drive for competition and survival wasn't as strong, there wouldn't be so many bullies and bad guys. Or women, the way things were going. But the world wasn't that better place yet. We were all still swimming in the same soup.

The line started moving again and I saw the woman in the car in front of me glance back in her mirror. I smiled and waved and we moved into the narrow constriction of cones and barriers. And I glanced behind

me and saw the same scene I'd just been a part of repeating itself. A car
nosed in at the head of the line, demanding that sense of entitlement
that was built into our brains. All of us cooking in the same soup.

A funky bass riff from the song playing on WYSO took me away. I
reached for the sweaty cup of iced coffee and soldiered on. All things are
better with iced coffee on a hot day.

By the time I reached Bennett's office I was feeling pretty worn
down. This would eat up a good part of my day when I could have been
doing other things.

His office was in a nice stretch of neighborhood between the Short
North and Victorian Village neighborhoods of Columbus. I drove along
the edge of Goodale Park looking for the address, past the big stone
houses with their tall chimneys and turrets and porches. That irked me
too, though I had no reason to be jealous and no desire to live or work
anywhere other than Yellow Springs. Humans are an odd sort.

When I made it to the right place, Bennett opened his door with
one hand holding a phone that was clamped to an ear. He let me in and
waved me to a chair.

I gave him a minute. When he took three, yammering with someone
about the cost of repairs to his car, I stood up.

Bennett immediately pulled the phone from his ear and looked at
me. He ended the call without speaking and circled behind his desk and
sat. I sat down across from him and we eyeballed each other over the
shiny walnut surface.

Bennett's eye twitched. "You're here about the Winstrop girl?" He
had a medium build and looked fit but not overly. His white shirt was
crisp and his dark hair was short and looked like it had just been cut. I
knew a restaurant at the top of Dayton where he could probably get a job
if he was twenty years younger. And a lot more charming.

"Yes."

He eyed me like I'd wounded him.

"The Winstrop woman," I said. "Henna Winstrop would be a full-
grown woman now. Not a girl anymore."

"Of course." His mouth was almost too tight to let the words out.

I had a good view of Bennett, and Bennett had a good view out the window behind me. I turned in my chair to look. The window opened onto an urban park across the street. "Nice view."

The scowl on his face turned to a smirk.

I had planned to be nice, but the day was getting away from me. "Any particular reason you wanted to do this in person?"

He waited too long to answer. When he did, I didn't like what he said. "Mr. Flint, are you carrying a weapon?"

I shrugged. Usually I ask people to call me Jackson. "Probably not." It was a weird way to start the conversation.

Bennett leaned forward and put his elbows on the desk. "I could pat you down."

I gave it a moment to settle. I could tell him the gun was locked in the truck. I could stand up and turn around and show him there was no place on me to hide a gun. I could tell him carrying a weapon onto private property was asking for trouble.

Instead I leaned in and put my forearms on his desk so my face was close to his. "You could try."

He didn't blink. I'd wanted him to. I laced my fingers together. "Look, this is supposed to be a friendly transaction. Simple. Elizabeth Winstrop's lawyer contacted you to get a file her husband paid for. Easy. You could have sent it yesterday. Email or fax or take some pictures with your phone and finish the whole thing without even getting out of your chair. I know that Elizabeth has paid you for your time and a copy of the file."

I took a breath like I was laboring hard to keep calm and finish this long and taxing story.

"But you make me drive all the way out here in traffic and waste my time, and now I'm sitting here wondering what your problem is. Do you have a problem here?"

Bennett leaned back. I took my arms off his desk and did the same.

"I have several problems here."

"You have my full attention."

"First, I don't like being told what to do by a lawyer."

I lifted my shoulders into a shrug.

"The guy Robert Winstrop used. His wife is using him too. I don't like him."

"Samuel Thomas?"

"That's the one. I don't like him."

I looked around the room. "He's not here."

Bennett's eyes said *smartass*. His mouth said, "Second, I don't like you either."

Huh. Swimming in the same soup. I held up my hands. "Fair enough. You're not the first one today. You can make me go away if you just hand over the file. Easy-peasy."

I could almost hear the wheels turning in his head. "And I do not like to be second-guessed."

"Second-guessed?"

"I reported what I found to Robert. He doesn't need someone else sticking their nose into it."

"Robert's dead."

Bennett's stare was long and careful. "I'm aware of that. It's a way of saying things."

"Here's another way of saying things. The report you made is a part of Robert Winstrop's estate. That estate has passed to Elizabeth Winstrop. And now she wants a copy of that report. And you've already promised to deliver it if I drove out here. Now my patience is growing thin, Mr. Bennett. What is the holdup here?"

It was an age-old problem. Territory. I was stepping on his. Like pissing on the neighbor's lawn. Nobody likes that. And now that I'd done it, here I was waggling my dick to shake the drops off, right there over his rose garden. Shame on me.

I ran a hand over my chin, then up to rub my temples. "Look, I'm sorry if my diplomacy is not at its best here. It's been a long day, and a long and hot drive. I don't see the point of me coming all the way to Columbus so you can..."

His frown had faded, and the look that replaced it seemed almost congenial. He juked his head a fraction of an inch. "One question."

I bugged my eyes at him. Odd guy.

"You're sure no one found the original report I sent to Robert?"

"No."

"It wasn't in his things?"

"Hasn't turned up."

Bennett tapped some fingers on his desk. "So the easiest thing for Elizabeth to do is just get another copy."

"You'd think."

"She could have asked me herself, instead of having her lawyer do it."

I pulled my phone from my pocket. "You want me to call her? Have her make nice and ask sweetly for the file?" I had a feeling Elizabeth wouldn't do it.

Bennett's smirk came back. "No. Watching you is good enough."

I fought the urge to make things worse. He made me want to break one of his fingers. And I liked to think of myself as a fairly nice guy.

Bennett's hand went to a desk drawer and drew out a large, thin manila envelope that was fastened with red twine around a clasp at the end. He pushed the envelope across the desk.

I unwound the twine and flipped through the contents. There was a one-page typed summary. I glanced at a few lines. It read like a police report. There were some photocopied hand-written notes and a few printed photos. The photos were of Henna Winstrop at the age when she disappeared, and some shots of a run-down house that could have been anywhere. I'd have to look closer, but nothing seemed to indicate Elizabeth's granddaughter, Willow. "You didn't find Henna?"

Bennett grinned like a cat watching a bird from the bushes. "I found her."

I looked again at the case summary.

Bennett gloated. "You're not familiar with the case?"

"I know that Robert Winstrop hired you to look for his daughter."

"And he didn't tell his wife."

"He didn't."

"But he told his lawyer."

"He did."

"It's a sad world when a man will talk to his lawyer but not his wife."

I sensed the angst of personal experience.

Bennett scrunched up his face like he was a smoker letting out a long stream of smoke he didn't want in his face, but he had no cigarette. "You don't find that odd?"

"What?"

"That Robert Winstrop didn't tell his wife he was looking for their daughter."

"I guess not."

"Seen a lot of things, huh?"

"I guess I have."

"Winstrop didn't tell his wife because I told him not to."

I looked up.

"I found Henna but I didn't initiate contact with her. I didn't have to."

Bennett knew he had my attention. I didn't try to hide it.

"There was no need to talk with Henna. I could see what she was. Henna Winstrop is a druggie and a tramp, and I told Robert he didn't want to have anything to do with her."

I scanned the bottom of the case summary. There it was. "Pretty harsh."

"It is what it is."

I tucked the pages and the photos back into the envelope and re-wound the twine around the clasp. "So when Henna disappeared..."

"She ran off. With one of her druggie friends."

"Why would she leave all that family money behind? Why wouldn't she come back at some point and try to get some of it?"

"Robert hadn't made his fortune yet when Henna ran off. He was still just a working schmuck. Hadn't invented that micro-thingy yet."

I patted the envelope to flatten it. Henna was gone before her father got the patent and the investors and built his factories.

"His daughter never knew. I told Robert to protect the family money. Keep Henna away from it."

"But she was family."

"Not for a long time. He was an old man who was trying to re-connect while there was still time. But reconnecting with his daughter wouldn't have made him happy."

I shrugged. You never knew.

"Better to do something good with the money. He would have willed it to her and she would have wasted it."

"There's Elizabeth."

Bennett waved a hand. "He would have left a fortune to his daughter. It would have been a mistake."

"So Robert never met Henna again?"

"No."

Bennett must have seen the judgement in my eyes.

"He would have. If he hadn't had the heart attack and died. Robert would have found someone else to take him to his daughter."

"But it wasn't going to be you?"

He shook his head. "And now that's what his wife is doing. She's using you to get to Henna."

"And you think that's a mistake?"

"You should do Elizabeth Winstrop a favor. Tell her to forget it too. That her daughter is dead. She doesn't want to see her."

"I think I'll let her decide."

Bennett sighed. "Of course you'd say that. But you and I aren't so different as you might think."

"If you say so." I stood and reached the hand with the envelope behind me and tucked that into my belt. "There's just one more thing."

"Oh yeah, Columbo? What's that?"

"You tell me."

He didn't. No mention of Henna Winstrop having a daughter. Not a whisper of Willow Winstrop. Instead, he offered a personal assessment. "What's that supposed to mean, asshole?"

It was the second time that day someone had called me an asshole. I was starting to think they might be right. I didn't answer him. I turned my back and left.

12

THE STAB OF GUILT I'd felt in the morning when Kristine walked away back into her homeless world revisited me on the drive home. But then the image in my head of Kristine morphed into Willow Winstrop running away in the rain, and the feeling changed from guilt about Kristine to a dull, thrumming desire to find Willow.

Kristine had a vision of her future, a way out that she guarded carefully and that kept her moving forward. I didn't know what Willow had going for her, whether she was happy-go-lucky or on the brink of disaster. Why would she run away into the rain like that? And the slow progress keeping my promise to find Elizabeth Winstrop's daughter bothered me, and wasting more time on the road in traffic.

It didn't help that I was driving into the sun. The big, brutal ball of fusion pounded into the cab of the truck. I didn't know how the settlers had managed it when they traveled the old U.S. National Road that ran just north of I-70. Did they stop early in the day and give up against the sun that bore down on them from their westward destinations? Or did they tip the brims of their big hats down, or the rims of their bonnets, and wipe their brows and bear the heat and grit, eking out the extra miles that the longer solstice days afforded?

I turned up the fan blower, but it just pumped out hot air. The air conditioning in the truck had been out for years, and like my father did when I was young and the air went out on his pick-up, I let mine go too. I had what my father had called two-sixty air conditioning: roll down two windows and drive sixty. It was the best you were going to get.

I punched the radio on and turned up the volume against the sound of the wind. Johnny Cash was singing "Ring of Fire."

Oh, hell no.

I scanned what else was playing and gave up and came back to Johnny. He was just finishing up telling me it burns. Thanks, Johnny.

I had a lot of questions. Somebody, or a lot of people, knew more than what they were saying. Finding Henna and Willow would answer questions. And I wanted those answers. But even with the sun near the solstice, there wouldn't be enough light left in the day to search everywhere that held promise. RiverScape Park? Or the warehouse by the water? Back to Sinclair College? Or even back in Yellow Springs?

But the timeline said Willow Winstrop had been in Yellow Springs only for that one night, then she'd gone back to Dayton. I listened to my gut. It said RiverScape Park. That's where I went.

Once the gut spoke I was committed. When traffic cleared the highway construction and the lanes opened up, I dropped my foot on the accelerator. Now I had two-eighty-five air conditioning. Much better.

I bounced around the radio stations until I got within range of a good signal for WYSO. I could barely carry the sound over the wind from the open windows. *All Things Considered* was playing. Those people will talk about anything.

Then I was cruising down Route 4. Trees and fields and horses. Then Huffman Dam, marking the lower end of what used to be a giant wetland prairie where the Wright Brothers made their magic among grasses and flowers and rattlesnakes. Progress. Well, the flying machine. Losing the prairie didn't feel like progress.

Then a few glimpses of the Mad River and into Dayton and down a very quiet Monument Avenue. No one was blocking off lots and charging to park. No action at the baseball stadium. The Dayton Dragons baseball team was on the road.

I saddled the truck to the curb near RiverScape Park and went into the summer evening. The spring had been mild and wet, and the flowers and shrubs and trees in the park had exploded with green, yellow, pink, and red. I walked the entire length.

A few people were out along the high bank of the river, protection for the city since the big flood had come over a century ago. A happy couple lingered on a swing and looked down at the water and a flock of Canada Geese.

I jogged down the slope to the bike path at the river's edge and looked under the Main Street bridge. Nobody there.

I was already working up a sweat, but I jogged down the bike path to the Riverside Drive bridge and made it a really good sweat. Nobody there either.

I jogged up the slope and slowed to cool off and wander the pathways. There were some people and some chatter, but nothing that got my attention. I didn't know a lot about the homeless, but I had observed some things about people in general that I thought were fairly universal. They liked to gather in clumps. Like ants, people tended to follow breadcrumbs. Some were lonely and looked for others to be with. Some were hungry and followed the gravy train. Some were looking for trouble or someone to bully. Others just felt safer in numbers, or simply felt the pull to not be left out.

I didn't have the patience to sit or wander the park all night hoping for a trail of breadcrumbs. I could get someone to do that, better than me. Brick knew people from his days on the other side. People who'd served and learned to track. To be patient and watch and wait. It was a professional flaw for me. Surveillance wasn't my best suit.

I was already thinking of making the call for back-up when I heard the hooting.

"Hey, baby. Chicka-chicka. Over here."

A kayaker slipped the rapids down on the river. His paddle glinted with sunlight. I rotated away from the river and listened.

"Hey. Hey, you. With the ponytail. Over here. I got something for you."

I went toward the sound. Three men sat on the low concrete wall of a flower bed near the road. In front of them a teenaged girl was waiting at a bus stop.

You're kidding me, right?

I tried to let it go. The girl didn't seem that bothered. You can't save the whole world, and people don't like a buttinsky. I waited.

The girl was maybe fourteen and pretty, with dark, clear skin that looked Black or Asian or both. She had a long black ponytail hanging down her back.

"Hey, I'm *talking* to you."

The girl had earbuds in, but she heard. A twitch in the way she craned her neck looking for the bus to arrive gave her away.

The heckler let out a high-pitched whistle like you'd use to call a dog.

I never liked bullies, but you have to choose your battles. I hoped for the bus to arrive so I could let this one go.

But then the guy stood up and made a lewd gesture. It was pathetic, but it was clear what he meant. "I got something you need, honey." When he danced toward her she backed away.

Well, damn.

I closed the gap between us and stepped between the man and the girl. It was close quarters. The other men stayed sitting on the wall. They looked away. All three men were thin and reedy and overdressed for the warm weather. I guessed that they could be about my age, but they looked much older, worn down by whatever it was that ate away at people who ended up living their lives like this.

The man with the big mouth looked back at his companions for support. They didn't give it to him, and I figured the game was over. But there was something in him that needed to be acknowledged. Something he needed from the exchange that he hadn't gotten yet.

He tried to wave me aside. "I was talking to the girl."

"No you weren't."

He mugged for his companions. Their eyes stayed down. He mugged for me. "Hey, man, get out the way."

I took one long, slow breath in and let it out.

The bus came and stopped at the curb and the girl got on. Then the bus rumbled away and I pulled my baseball cap off my head and wiped the sweat that had gathered there. I replaced the cap and walked away.

When I was about a dozen steps away I heard it.

"Chickenshit motherfucker."

I kept walking. This exchange hadn't won any battle. It was just men pissing on the ground around them because they still had a primal urge to fight for something, but they'd lost most of their ancient outlets to express that. I put myself in that category too.

I wondered if this is what happened when a man didn't know how to or wasn't able to gain respect in more honorable ways. He reached for what felt like respect in any way he could. What was anyone going to do to change that? How do you hand out dignity?

The park had mostly emptied and I was ready to take the hunt back to the empty warehouse I'd followed Willow Winstrop to when I heard a new voice. It was loud, deep, and happy.

"Change, change, change. Does anybody have any change?"

A large, chocolate-skinned man sat on a bench shaking a can of coins. His voice went up a little but stayed well within the bass range, and he repeated the line with a hint of tremolo. "Does anybody have any change?" Then dropped again to the bass growl. "Does anybody have any change?"

I walked up. He tipped his hat. "Sorry to trouble you, sir." His speaking voice was as melodious as his singing and resonated in a range lower than I could ever reach.

"It's no trouble," I said, and took out my wallet. Then I remembered that I'd tucked the last of my cash into Kristine's backpack.

I reached into my pocket and pulled out what was there. "Change is all I have."

"Much obliged," the man said as I dropped the coins into his jar. "May this kindness be returned to you." Then he shook the can and jangled the coins and went back to singing.

The kindness had already been returned. His basso profondo put a swagger in my step as I walked away. A hitch in my giddy. A shimmy in my gimme. It felt good.

When I got back to Monument Avenue, a lone figure sat on a bench between me and the truck. He was tall and thin, and his shoulders were hunched and his head hung down. His attention seemed be on one of his feet, which was bouncing and made his knee bob like the kids' horsey ride at a department store. I was planning a route across the street to avoid walking past him when something felt familiar.

The man looked up and I saw his hair. Short, bright red, and tousled. I'd last seen him coming at me with a piece of two-by-four. Flame. The one Kristine had said was protective of Willow Winstrop.

His knee stopped bobbing and his head jerked up. And he ran.

Flame had a good lead on me and took a jagged zig-zag pattern through the park, over shrubbery and across the walking paths. We were near the Riverside Drive bridge and I thought for a moment he'd be foolish enough to take that and head across the river to McPherson Town. He'd be easy to reel in on the bridge, with nowhere to go. I'd have him before he reached the middle of the crossing.

Then Flame zagged away and broke through traffic to cross over toward the baseball stadium.

A car squealed its tires and skidded to a stop, and another swerved and bounced up to the curb and stopped. The vehicles were still askew when I reached the intersection. I dashed around them. Flame was a juttery bob of red hair under arms and legs akimbo racing up Monument Avenue. Now I'd catch him easy.

Then Flame surprised me and flung himself into the tall iron fence surrounding Day Air Ballpark and catapulted himself over.

I pumped my legs into a higher gear and raced alongside the brick facade of the stadium until I reached the fencing. And I flung myself over too.

Flame was clearing the infield seats when I landed. Mistake. I'd catch him in the open field.

But then I made a mistake. As I vaulted out of section one-sixteen, over the home team bullpen onto the field, I looked in at the plate, and I imagined a hitter connecting on a long fly ball. Two on, home team up by one. Two out. Ninth inning.

Jackson Flint tracks the ball under the lights, puts his head down and sprints for the fence. Looks back, times the ball, makes his leap. He's on the wall at the three-eighty-one marker. He stretches the glove, spreads the web. There's a moment of mystery as Jackson hangs in mid-air, then the ball drops into his glove.

He's on the ground, holding up the glove with the ball to show the ump. The ump looks in from the grass beyond second base and pumps a fist in the air. Heeeee's out. Jackson Flint flips the ball to the center fielder and jogs in. The catch re-plays on the jumbotron. Home team wins. The giant dragon heads on the scoreboard belch smoke, their eyes glow red, and the foghorns ring out across the stadium and the river and downtown. It's a web gem night for Jackson Flint.

Then the sound of the crowd died away and I was alone on the grass. And Flame was racing away toward the opposite field bleachers.

I dropped my head and sprinted. Flame hopped out of the field and tumbled ass-over-elbows up through the seats. He was all angles and bright red hair tumble-weeding toward the First Street fence.

I was at the bottom of the fence when he went over, and I caught him when he came down hard on the sidewalk outside the stadium. The tackle was rougher than I intended. He went down and stayed there.

A couple of cars went by, and one of the drivers looked over at us. I reached a hand out to Flame. "You hurt?"

Another driver slowed and rubber-necked. The car behind honked and the driver sped up and drove off.

Flame lifted himself up and curled into a ball, arms hooked around his knees. "Don't hurt me, man."

"I'm not going to—"

"Oh lawd, don't kill me."

"I'm not—"

"You ain't gonna find her. No matter what you do to me."

"I'm—"

"And I ain't never even hit you with the wood. I ain't hurt you none."

I waited. Flame's eyes darted. Up, down, at me, down. Up at me again. The confidence he'd had when he was on his home ground, swinging lumber, with the others behind him, was gone. He looked pitiful. It made me feel something for him.

I squatted and tried to look Flame in the eyes. "I think we may be on the same side here."

"I can't tell you nothin'. You may's well just let me go."

"I'd like to do that. But this is important. If you run, I'll catch you again."

His eyes said he heard me.

"I don't want to hurt Willow."

Something flickered across his face. Her name?

I tried it again. "Willow Winstrop?"

His eyes darted again.

"Look, I'm not with Childern's Services. I'm not going to—"

"Children's Services? Man, those guys are with nobody like that."

"What guys?"

He shut up.

I shifted my hips and sat on the concrete next to Flame. The sun was dropping and the shadows were getting long. This could be a really nice evening. We were at a baseball park on a warm June evening. But there was nobody on the field, and I wasn't here to see a game. No cold beer and seventh-inning stretch. This wasn't fun.

I laid my forearms over my knees. Flame looked young. Thin and nervous. I spoke without looking at him. "So look, you can do what you want. You're a man. We're just talking here man to man."

I waited. He was listening.

"So just hear me out for a minute."

He stared ahead.

Good enough. I went on. "I don't want to hurt Willow. I was hired by someone to find Willow's mother."

Flame looked at me like I had antennae growing out of my ears. His favorite martian. "Why you want to find her?"

I squinted into the shadows. "It's a long story. A family thing."

I leaned back and turned my head and spat on the sidewalk. We were just two old friends here, talking on the street, catching up. See? I wasn't one of the bad guys.

Flame let an eye wander over to me. "So you're not one of them?"

"One of who?"

He made a shivering motion with his shoulders. "Man, those are some bad dudes."

"The men looking for Willow?"

He shut up again.

"You've seen them?"

"Those dudes like hurting people. Just because they can."

That explained a little more why he'd come at me with a two-by-four when I showed up at the warehouse. "Why are they looking for Willow?"

He shrugged.

"They like young girls?"

Flame made a face like he'd eaten something rotten. "What d'you know about it?"

"I'm trying to help her."

"You know what people like that do to people like Willow? They mess them up so bad they can't never get straight again."

I looked more closely at the twitch in Flame's hands, the tick in his eye. "How old are you?"

"What does that matter?"

"It matters. How old?"

He shook his head. "I'm nineteen. A man."

That was my opening. A man. Like I'd told him. Old enough to know what he was doing. Young enough to be saved, maybe. But he wanted to be a man. I tipped my head like I was agreeing to something. "Listen, guy like you probably sees things. Knows what's going on. You can see the score. I need help from someone like you. I need you to help me find Willow and her mother."

His eyes were hooded, and his mood looked the same.

I held out my hand. "Man to man. At least hear me out."

He didn't reach for my hand, but he looked at it.

I pulled my hand back and stood up. "I'm going to find Willow, and I'm going to find her mother. If there are other people looking for Willow, for whatever reason, I need to find her before they do. I think you want that too."

Flame stayed down on the concrete.

"I can find her without you, but you can help me. You can help Willow."

I could almost see the wheels turning in his head. Why trust me? Maybe I was baiting him.

I rolled my shoulders. "I could use something to eat. I'm going to walk down here to the corner and get a sandwich. Why don't you come with me and think about it?"

He rolled an eye up.

"I'm buying."

That did it. Why hadn't I learned this trick before? It would have worked on me.

13

WE WENT TO A PLACE ON THE CORNER I hadn't been to before. The baseball game crowds weren't there because the Dragons were on the road, but enough people sat inside and out on the patio to keep the place busy.

Flame hustled to a back corner and sat at the most remote table with his back against the wall. His eyes darted from the bar to the tables, the front door, and the entry to the patio, like he was keeping track of the exits. He probably was. He looked like a teenager shopping for clothes with his mother.

I hung back and let Flame sit while I texted Cali. She thought fifteen was old enough to be left on her own. For Cali that was mostly true, but that didn't make me feel less guilty about my absentee parenting the last couple of days. Or the last couple of years.

I erased the text I was writing and tapped out a new one.

Pick up.

Then I called Cali's number. I was smart enough to know that teenagers could ignore a phone ringing, but a text would get through their radar.

"Dad."

"Hi, sweetie. Are you at home?"

"Asia's."

"OK. Listen, I'm going to be stuck with work for a while."

"Uh-huh."

"I hate to do this to you again, but can you get your own dinner?

There's leftovers in the fridge, or there's money if you want to order a pizza or something."

"It's OK. I already ate."

"Oh." I checked my watch. Of course. "What did you have?"

"The leftover bean burgers. I finished them."

"All right. What are you doing now?"

"Binge watching."

Ah. That TV show they were consumed with.

"We *were* watching it."

"What's that mean?"

"They had to pause because you called."

"Oh." I thought about it. "And what if I'd texted?"

"They wouldn't pause for a text."

"Sorry, I didn't know the rules."

There was a brief silence.

"So Asia still has it paused now."

"Ah. And what are the others doing while they're waiting for you?"

"Watching me talk to you."

"So that's probably not much fun for you."

"Dad…"

"Listen, I'm sorry to do this to you again."

"Yeah, I'm fine."

"I don't know when I'll be home."

There was a murmured exchange of dialogue in the background.

"Why don't I just stay at Asia's tonight?"

"Is that OK with Asia?"

Asia yelled yes from somewhere in the room.

"And what about her mother? What's Asia's mother's name?"

"Bonnie." Cali yelled for Asia's mother.

A moment later Bonnie Douglas's voice came over the phone. "It's OK. Cali can stay here tonight."

"I'm sorry to leave this with you."

"If you saw the girls having fun together you wouldn't be sorry even a little."

"All right."

"And Jackson?"

"Yeah?"

"I know it's been hard. But having Cali over here with Asia so much these last couple of—you know, the last couple of years. That's been terrific for us. The girls are so good together. And Cali can be a real sweetheart."

"Yeah, sometimes. You're sure it's no trouble?"

"Like I said. I'm putting Cali back on."

The phone switched again and Cali's voice came over. "What time do I have to be home tomorrow?"

"How about I leave that to you and Asia and her mother to decide? But don't make yourself a burden."

"Thanks dad."

And she hung up.

I packed my guilt away with my phone and went to the table with Flame and sat down with him.

Flame's knee jerked up and down. "You buyin'?"

"Said I was."

He picked up a menu and buried himself behind it.

Brixx Ice Company had bar food and beer, and a view of the ballpark. The food and beer looked good. We didn't have a view of the ballpark from our back corner. A woman came over and stood at our table. "Drinks tonight?"

I glanced behind the bar. "You have a coffee pot going?"

"I can put one on for you."

"Don't mean to trouble you. A lot for just one coffee drinker."

"It's OK. Pete usually drinks a couple of cups when he comes in anyway. And it'll remind me how to do it."

I had second thoughts. I'd seen what can happen when someone who doesn't usually make coffee brews the joe. But the woman was grinning like she'd made a great joke, so I joined in and grinned with her. You can't expect a barista at a sports bar.

The waitress looked at Flame. He was still hunched behind his menu.

I said, "You want coffee?"

The menu came down and his eyes came up. "Last thing I need."

I looked at the tic in his hand and the jitter in his leg.

The menu went back up. "Coke."

The waitress smiled at us and left.

The menu came down again. "It's not what you think."

"What do I think?"

"I get anxious. Excited."

"OK, I guess that's not what I was thinking."

His face brightened to a shade that was several steps down from his red hair. "I'm not using."

"I didn't ask."

A leg bobbed. "I don't usually tell people that."

I shrugged like it was nothing. It wasn't.

"A lot of the others. They…" The menu went up, down. "That stuff will kill you."

I let a weird silence sit between us. "Heroin?"

He shuddered. "I've seen what it's done to some of them."

I waited again. "Willow?"

He shook his head.

"You're sure?"

"It's so easy. It's all around. They try to get you started."

OK, so he trusted me. A little. But I could tell he didn't like it. "Is that what the men wanted? The ones you think were looking for Willow?"

"God no." His knee jumped. A hand went down to his leg and the leg settled to a slow trot. "I mean, I don't know. They were just—the whole thing was wrecked, you know?"

"So they weren't looking for Willow because she was involved with drugs somehow?"

Flame's head darted like he thought the cops were at the door to cuff him. He put his hands out in the universal shush sign. "Willow is staying away from the stuff. And other things. I'm trying to help her."

"She's clean?"

"As Snow White before she got mixed up with Doc."

A memory from my childhood flickered through my brain. Flame had ruined it a little. But then a gear in my head turned and ratcheted my worries down a notch. Like a wooden wheel with pegs and a cog, slipping down one joint. Thunk. OK, not that. Maybe Willow was clean. Good.

"Them motherfuckers get a two-by-four up their ass they try to whore her out."

I raised an eyebrow. "Where'd that come from?"

"I'm just sayin'. They gonna have to get through me to get to her."

The wheel in my head slipped. The cog slid across the peg but didn't climb back up a notch. This worried me.

Then the woman came with coffee and a coke. She placed the coke on the table, then set down a mug and filled it with fresh coffee.

I tasted the coffee. I looked at the woman. "You've been holding out on me. This is terrific. You made this?"

She gave a tiny mock curtsy and put her hand to her heart. "Cream or sugar?"

I waved her off. "Doesn't need it."

Flame leaned forward. "I'll have some."

The woman gave him a quick, odd look.

"Cream and sugar," Flame clarified.

A hand went into her apron and she laid cups of creamer and packets of sugar on the table.

Flame scooped the booty from the edge of the table into a neat pile in front of him. He sniffed at the coke. "No straw?"

"We're trying to save the fishes and the turtles."

Flame's lip curled up. "So you can eat them?"

The waitress sighed and extracted a compostable paper straw from her apron.

I rolled my eyes to her as an apology.

She gave me a knowing look back. "You've decided?"

Flame pointed to me. "He's buying."

"I am."

He swished the menu through the air in front of him. "Onion straws." He laid heavily on the word *straws*. The waitress didn't bite on that. "Giant pretzel. Peanut butter pie."

She wrote it down. "Anything else for you?"

"Can I get extra whipped cream on the peanut butter pie?"

She wrote that down and turned to me.

"Fish tacos. Hold the cheese."

She tilted her head for a split second as if thinking about it, then her pencil moved. "No cheese. Excellent choice."

I'd been eating out a lot lately. It wasn't always the healthiest food, and I preferred plant-based protein when I could get it, but I wasn't going to pass up a good fish taco in land-locked Ohio. And I could put all of this on expenses.

The waitress left and Flame stacked the coffee creamer cups in a precarious tower and made tents of the sugar packets. When he'd rearranged things a couple a times, he looked out over his construction. "You have to help Willow."

"I intend to."

"I try to, but..." His hand tick-tocked behind the creamer wall.

"One person can only do so much."

"Right. I can't do everything."

I tried to see Flame for more than what I knew of him, but what his life must be like eluded me. I took him in over the sugar-packet tent city he'd built. "Where are you staying?"

He shrugged.

"You've got a place?"

"My dad's sometimes. Let it go."

OK, he was right. I said we'd talk man to man. This wasn't. I shut up and drank coffee.

The woman came back in a few minutes with a tray of food. She refilled my coffee cup and set the plates in an array on the table, working her way around the creation Flame had built.

I scooted my coffee cup over to make room. "Fast."

"And good," she said. "We aim to please."

Flame picked up an onion straw and dragged it across the whipped cream on his peanut butter pie.

The waitress smiled as she watched him. The smile looked practiced. "Anything else?"

Flame thankfully said nothing.

I breathed in the fishy aroma of my plate. "Nope, this looks good."

We tucked into the food. The fish tacos were good, but it wasn't easy sitting across from Flame while he dipped onion straws into his whipped cream and peanut butter pie and ate them like they were guppies in a fraternity fish-swallowing contest.

More guppies went down. I waited, but I wanted to get down to business. I cleared my throat. "When was the last time you saw Willow?"

Flame's throat worked as he swallowed. "You was there."

"When you tried to whack me?"

"I wasn't tryin' to whack you. I was scaring you. I thought you were one of them."

"One of the guys who came looking for Willow?"

"Yeah. I think they was looking for her. It sounded like her."

He reached for another onion straw, worked it in the pie and dug out a chunk of peanut butter cream.

"Wait a minute. You don't know for sure if it was Willow they were looking for?"

"They were looking for someone. It sounded like they meant her."

This again. "What about the others? Kristine said some men were looking for Willow."

His eyes came up. "You know Kristine?"

"We've met."

He picked out another onion straw. "What did you and Kristine talk about?"

"Lots of things. We talked about Willow. She wants to help me find her."

The persuasion was not lost on him. "Anything else?"

"Your name didn't come up, if that's what you mean."

"Ouch."

"Sorry."

"Nah, I kinda knew it anyway. She's not into guys like me."

She wasn't. I let it go. "Kristine thought the men were looking for Willow."

"They were all guessing. That's just the way it looked."

"So you don't know if they were looking for Willow specifically?"

"I wouldn't swear to it in a court of law."

I laughed.

"What?"

"That doesn't sound like something you'd say."

"It's not. My daddy used to say it a lot."

I tried to fit that in with the little I knew about Flame. "He doesn't say it much anymore?"

"I wouldn't know. I ain't seen him much."

That shouldn't have come as a surprise.

"He ain't been doing so well."

Heavy.

Flame dropped the sliver of onion he'd been holding and knuckled a finger in my direction. "I don't need your pity."

"Good, because you're not going to get it. Wouldn't do you much good anyway."

"Can't put it in the bank."

I laughed. "Your father again?"

"Nah. Old Rosie. Seems like she's always sayin' that. Cain't put that in the bank, sweetie." He did it as an impression. I didn't know if it was accurate, but Flame seemed to enjoy doing it.

It didn't make me laugh. I took out my phone, swiped, and set it on the table in front of Flame.

He leaned in. I pushed the phone closer. He enlarged the image, and said, "That's not Willow."

"Her mother. A long time ago."

"Looks a lot like Willow."

"You've seen her mother?"

He shrank the image, looked at what else was in the frame. "She don't look exactly like that anymore."

"Where did you see Willow's mother?"

He shook his head.

"I thought we were on the same side here? If I can find Willow's mother, it'll help me find Willow. Then I can help them. Both of them."

"How you gonna help her?"

"Willow has family. They'll take her in. Willow and her mother." I was stretching what I knew here, but I could make some guesses about the elder Winstrop. I hoped the guesses were right.

"Willow has family she don't know about?"

"Yes."

Flame swiped to some other images. He found a newspaper story from when Willow's mother disappeared two decades before and lingered on that. "How do they know about her?"

"They didn't. They hired me to look for Willow's mother, and I found Willow. And I need to find both of them now."

Flame's eyes skimmed over more of the old news story. "Their family wants them back?"

"They do."

He pushed the phone away. "I don't know where she is."

"Willow? Or her mother?"

"Neither."

"You know where I should look? Where they've been? Where they'd go?"

He was quiet. I didn't know if he was thinking or deciding or holding back or something else. Then his eyes focused on me and he said, "I might know a place."

"That would be a help."

"I still don't know if you're what you say."

I spread my hands. "Tough call. You want me to call someone? Have them speak for me?"

"Who you gonna call?"

"Willow's grandmother." I was taking a chance here, but I felt close to something and I didn't want to lose it.

"Willow got a granmum you gonna let me talk to?"

"Yes." I hoped Elizabeth would answer. And that she would agree to talk. I was pretty much all in on the bluff here.

Flame wagged his head. "I can't talk to no one's granmum."

"Your call."

His head dipped down.

Then the waitress came and asked if everything was all right.

Flame waved a hand at his food. "I'm done eating. Can you bring me a box for this?" He hadn't touched the giant pretzel. The onion straws were almost gone, and the pie was eviscerated. Most of the coke was still there.

"Sure." She looked at me.

I pointed to my coffee cup and pinched my fingers a few inches apart to show her I'd drink a little more. "And I'm going to stay and finish eating. But I think he has to go." I nodded across the table.

The waitress made a waitress move. A little look that said she'd seen it all before and she didn't need to know anything more. "Bring you the bill then?"

"When you have time."

Flame fiddled with the tented sugar packets while we waited for his box. I ate more fish taco. Still good.

Then Flame got his carryout box and he broke up the giant pretzel and stuffed it inside. Then he scooped the pulpy remains of the peanut butter pie in. I realized now he'd probably planned it. The pretzel would last in the warm weather. I would have gone for protein, but that wouldn't last as long without spoiling. The sugary pie was probably the worst choice. That stuff will kill you. But for Flame, sugar and carbs would be the lesser of evils he was surrounded by.

He got up and tucked the leftovers under his jacket, which he hadn't taken off even though it was warm. He stuck a hand out. "Gimme your phone."

I raised my eyebrows.

"I gotta write something for you."

"I'll get a pen." I twisted to look for the waitress.

"OK boomer."

"I'm not—" I wasn't anywhere near that old. But I shut up and gave him my phone.

Flame swiped and typed with the little keypad. Then he set the phone face-down on the table and walked away.

I waited until he was gone to look at what he'd done. He'd opened the memo app and put in an address. Beneath it he'd typed *she's been there with her mother sometimes.*

I knew the neighborhood, but I looked up the address on Google maps. It was close by. There would be just enough time to get there before dark.

14

THE HOUSE LOOKED LIKE ANY in a neighborhood of old homes. It sat tight on the lot, the windows of the neighbors close enough they could look in on you if you weren't vigilant about the blinds. A long porch stretched across the front, overlooking a thin strip of garden surrounded by a low wrought-iron fence painted black and showing rust. A few feet of tired grass sloped down to an ancient sidewalk and the curb.

White, two stories, old windows, a steep roof. It needed some paint and new windows, but the house was in as good of shape as most on the street. It would be a nice place to raise family. It would have been a great place to raise a family a hundred years ago. Now of lot of the homes were probably rentals, on the way down the slippery slope of deferred maintenance.

I got a good look at the house and the neighborhood before the sun tilted away. Just a guy driving by. Phone in the dash holder. Nobody taking pictures. Nothing here to look at, folks.

I parked a couple of blocks away and took a walk down the alley behind the house. Hat pulled down, eyes forward but canted to the side for a better view. Phone in my hand, texting. Nobody taking pictures. Nothing to look at here.

I looped around a couple of blocks, then made my way back to the truck. The evening had moved well into dusk, but there still had been good light when I snapped the photos. The images were sharp. An old wooden garage with carriage doors bordered the back of the lot. A rusty gate opened to a concrete walkway that ran up to the back door.

Windows were open up and down. There was a light on in the kitchen at the side of the house. Box fan in an upstairs window. Blue glow that was probably from a TV in the front parlor. No images of people in the shots, but somebody was home.

There was a church across the street a block and a half down. The church was dark and the little parking lot beside it was empty. I snugged the truck into the far corner of the lot where a weak light on the side of the building gave a little illumination. Then I turned the automatic dome light off and scooted over to the passenger seat. Just waiting on my wife who's in talking to the pastor. Nothing unusual going on here, folks.

I squinted to re-read all of the files, photos, news stories, and notes I had taken, intermittently looking up at the house for lights, movement, somebody coming or going, anything. I couldn't see the back of the house or the garage or alley. My attention was divided. And I didn't like sitting. It felt like shooting in the dark. It kind of was that exactly.

The case files from Bennett weren't as much help as I'd hoped. Instead of pointing me toward Henna, they opened up questions about exactly why Robert Winstrop had hired an investigator without telling his wife, and not long before he suffered a fatal heart attack. Why not search for Henna more seriously years before? Did Robert know that his health was failing? Was he thinking about the family business and his legacy?

And what about the mysterious men who were looking for Willow? Why could no one, neither Flame nor any of the others who were squatting at the warehouse, say for sure it was Willow the men had been looking for? I was well aware that eyewitness testimony was often unreliable, especially when the witness was under pressure or stressed. Flame coming at me with the two-by-four and the reactions of the others were evidence enough of stress. Could there be something more going on there? Maybe they were covering something up? What had Samuel Thomas said about Robert Winstrop's will?

Bennett's notes listed an address in Columbus as Henna's last known home, with a note that she no longer lived there and had probably become homeless. There were notes with speculations about drug use and trafficking, but nothing that looked like solid evidence of any of that.

One of these strings lead to a connection that I was missing. If I had left the Sheriff's office on a little better terms, I might still have a friend there who could run a couple of database checks, look at some records I didn't have access to. But the other deputies had mostly seen me as abandoning them. I escaped and they were still grinding it out and doing the paperwork that would eventually lead them to a pension, if the system held up to give them one. I hadn't meant it that way, but I could see why we hadn't stayed friends after I gave up my badge.

So I used the resources and friends I had. I called Brick. He picked up on the first ring. "Yeah?"

"I need someone to sit on a house."

"Where?"

"Dayton."

"The case you told me about?"

"The missing daughter. Yeah."

There was the sound of shuffling, footsteps maybe. Brick moving around. "You there now?" he asked.

"Yeah."

"What do you need?"

"Light work. Someone to watch. See if the woman or her daughter comes or goes."

"And if they do?"

"Tail them. Alert me. Don't be seen."

"OK, what's happening there right now?"

"Nothing."

Brick laughed. "That's why you want someone else to do it."

"Of course."

"Well, not me."

"Not you. One of your guys."

"Uh-huh."

We'd done this before. Brick knew people who knew surveillance and intelligence-gathering, among other skills. People who'd been in the military and special forces. He'd helped some of them make the same transition he had, back to the secular world where their past lives kept them hard and edgy and made them look dangerous.

"Can you try to get Danny?"

"Danny's gone."

"Gone?"

"Somewhere in the desert. Said he needed to see the sky."

"The sky?"

"Yeah."

"You can't see it from here?"

"More of it."

"OK. When was that?"

"Month ago, maybe."

"So not Danny."

"Not Danny."

I called up another name. "What about Nerbert?"

Brick grunted. "You know that's not his name."

"You know who I mean."

"Bertie got a girl. He's holed up with her and her momma somewhere down in West Virginia. He won't want any work."

"Her and her mother?"

"That's what I heard."

You do what you can, I figured. "You got anybody?"

"Not me."

"Anybody that's not you?"

"There's somebody."

He didn't offer any details. "Not you?"

"This person is a special case. Just got out."

"OK."

"She needs some work. Something to give her focus."

"Uh-huh."

"J'Leah is intense. Head's still in the game."

"I just need someone who can sit. You tell me she can be trusted, I'll put her on it if she wants. If she can sit."

"She'll want it. You giving the usual rate?"

"Compliments of my client and my expense account."

"Give me some time to see if I can set it up. You got something to keep you busy?"

"Is that a joke?"

"You think it's funny?"

"No."

"Then it's not a joke."

He hung up. I was already bored again.

I had my fingers over my phone ready to text Cali, then I stopped. The girls would probably still be up watching their show, or doing whatever they'd moved on to by now. Dad sticking his nose back in would probably make me feel better, but it probably wouldn't do much for Cali.

I texted Marzi instead. She was in bed reading. We exchanged some fairly benign emojis and ended the exchange.

Then I was bored again.

I read through the files and notes two more times. I didn't have a breakthrough. Brick called back about an hour later.

"She's in."

"Good. Give me her number. I'll send the address here and some photos."

"She's already on her way. Already located the news stories and is reading up. I'll text her your number and you can give her the address en route."

"How is she already on her way?"

"She knows you're in Dayton. Speed up the op if she deploys sooner. She'll correct her course to rendezvous with you."

"You're slipping."

There was a long pause. "What?"

"You're talking like you're back in the game."

"I'm not. I'm out. But keep your eyes open. J'Leah is fresh. She's itchy."

"Just what I need."

"You'd rather sit there yourself?"

I didn't have to answer.

Brick grunted. "You're not worried about working with a woman?"

"No. Should I be?"

He grunted again, a sign of approval. "Text me when she gets there." And he ended the call.

J'Leah started a text exchange with me, and ten minutes later we had the details worked out. I told her it wasn't safe to text and drive. She told me she was using bluetooth and an audio app and she was trained for this and to fuck off if I didn't like it. Fair enough. I let that go.

Then I watched the house. I zoomed in on the pictures I had taken and tried to find some useful detail, a hint of a figure or a face in the background, but there was nothing.

I yawned and stretched my legs in the cab of the truck. Then the driver's door opened and a shadow slipped in and sat down. "Jackson?"

"J'Leah?"

She held out a hand and we shook. Her grip was strong. J'Leah was slim, black, and attractive. She looked like the kind of young woman you'd want to be your doctor or dentist, or to run for public office. But Brick didn't send those kind of people to do this kind of work.

J'Leah changed some settings on her phone. "You wanna take off, I got this."

"You need anything?"

She held up a slim backpack. "No. Stocked up."

I peered out the windshield. "You got a car?"

"Nearby."

Of course. "Gonna be a long night."

"No sweat. I'm used to getting jacked for sixteens."

I looked at her. J'Leah was compact, coiled, alert. The gears in my head clicked. Hours? She was used to sixteen-hour shifts? I turned to ask, but J'Leah had her door open and she dropped back out into the night. She skirted the fence around the church parking lot and in the time it took me to realize what she was doing she had evaporated into the alley and was gone.

Military folk. They made it look routine, but there was some drama at play here. A buzz they got off the excitement of the chase.

Not me. I wanted to go home.

I fired up the truck and eased out of the church lot. It was after one in the morning and the street was dark and dead quiet. I probably could have waited until dawn to get someone in to watch the house. But I had a feeling J'Leah would like the night watch better. Wherever she was.

15

SOMETHING BUZZED IN MY HEAD, like a mosquito trying to hammer its way out. I rolled over.

The buzzing grew louder, like a drone circling the bed.

Phone.

My eyes clicked open. The room was dark, but a faint hint of weak gray light framed the windows. Where was Cali? She wasn't here. Where was she?

I sat up. Asia's. Cali was staying the night at Asia's. Why would she call so early?

I rolled over to reach for the phone. The sound was a text, not a call. Maybe J'Leah. Something was happening at the stakeout. But at five-thirty in the morning?

I swiped. It was a text from Brick.

Hill climbs.

I set the phone down and rolled away. It buzzed again.

30 min.

I fingered a message back.

Late night. He knew that.

Another text arrived before I could set the phone down.

You know you want to.

I don't.

Today is the day.

It's not.

The phone was almost back on the nightstand before another text came.

Be good daylight by the time you get there.

Then another.

I know you're already up getting ready.

Dammit. I was.

There is a stretch of road near John Bryan State Park known affectionately, or disaffectionately, as the devil's backbone. It is notable for its steep and tightly wound turns. Driving it was nerve-wracking, walking up it was a challenge, and running up was one of Brick's favorite things.

But he rarely beat me at it.

When I arrived at the base of the hill and stepped out of the truck, the sun had risen and the temperature was cool but it was already humid. I downed a bottle of water and walked over to Brick. He was already sweating. "You've warmed up."

"A little." He grinned.

"Looks like more than a little."

"Today I'm gonna win them all."

I stretched out my hamstrings. "I might be kind and let you take one."

I did a couple of slow starts up the first steep stretch of road to wake up my muscles while Brick kept loose. Then two women appeared from around the first high curve above and walked down to the bottom of the hill to where Brick and I were readying. One of the women was older, and she greeted us. "It's a good morning for the hill. My daughter and I try to walk up once a week."

Brick gave them a quick two-finger salute. "Looks like it keeps you in shape."

The woman gave him a big smile and she and her daughter turned and started their walk back up the hill.

Brick pointed out an imaginary starting line on the pavement in front of us and stepped up to it. I stepped beside him and we started the jog.

We passed the mother and daughter at the first turn up the devil's backbone. Brick stepped up the pace. My muscles hadn't loosened yet and I felt like I was running with a suit of armor on.

At the second turn Brick stepped up the pace again and opened a gap between us. He looked back over his shoulder as he ran. "Today is the day."

"First one is a warm-up."

"You already warmed up." He opened the gap wider. "Little old lady and her daughter gonna pass you."

I kept up a steady pace but let him go. I could still try to reel him in at the last steep run at the top.

I didn't catch Brick. He was bending over, casually stretching, when I finished my kick at the top. Trying to pretend he wasn't breathing heavy. He looked over. "The bad guys are gonna get away while you're warming up."

"Bad guys don't warm up."

We walked back down the hill, waved to the mother and daughter as we passed them, and turned around and ran up again. My legs loosened and we went after it this time.

Brick and I rarely ran more than eight climbs. But we were tied three-three at six races and four-four at eight. When we reached the bottom again I held up a hand. "Last one. Or we might be here all day."

"You won't last all day."

"Last longer than you."

He grinned. "I only have to win one more."

I bent and leaned forward. "Today is not the day."

Brick held up his arm and dropped it, and we ran.

One hard hill climb was enough to push me to the brink of oxygen depletion. I tried to time my reserves on each run so I could run faster at the top and kick to the finish with just enough left to keep from falling down. But this time I bolted off the line.

I opened a gap, but I paid a price. By the second turn my legs were hot and heavy. I could hear Brick's footsteps behind me, but I didn't turn to look.

I deepened my breaths and lifted my knees higher. Just keep going. He caught me at the last turn and we struggled up the final slope. I willed my legs to go higher and faster, but it was like stepping on the gas pedal and the car wouldn't go. Then Brick stumbled over the finish line two steps ahead of me.

I dropped to the pavement and gasped and waited for the world to go from a funny shade of gray back to full color as my oxygen came back. Brick tried to grin at me but he was heaving too hard to make his face take the shape.

I stood up. "One more."

Brick heaved. "Asshole."

"So I've been told." I concentrated on settling my breath as quickly as I could. Then I got down on the macadam and spread my legs behind me and eked out a shaky one-armed pushup. "But you can't do that."

Brick dropped and pumped halfway up in a one-armed pushup, then his elbow jerked and he fell on his face.

I looked down the hill. "The little old lady might still be here. She can come and help you up."

Brick spat out road debris. "I could carry Betty up the hill faster than you can run it."

I pictured the two of us trying to carry the engine block from a '78 Buick Skylark up the hill. "We could race up the hill with the rims. How much did they make you hump in the military?"

"Sixty pounds was for sissies. I could carry two rims easy."

"Two is for sissies." Yee-haw, this was fun.

We drank water, then cooled down with an easy jog through the Glen Helen nature preserve. The land was private property that had been preserved for generations. It made Yellow Springs more than a funky small town. It gave the village a wild border, and that wild area backed up to John Bryan State Park, and beyond that to Clifton Gorge.

We jogged down the fire road past the old pine forest. I filled in Brick a little on the Winstrop case, but we spent a good stretch of the run just gliding along quietly in the dappled sunlight. Ebony and ivory. Or mocha and ivory. Or some unidentifiable shade of brown and pasty white. It didn't matter. We were just two guys running through the woods.

This place was like a cathedral for Brick. He'd spent a lot of time in these woods and along these creek beds after his return from the desert wars, trying to quell what he'd brought back in his head. I slowed my breath and let him set the pace. This was his ride.

We jogged down to Yellow Springs Creek where it met the Birch Creek crossing, then back up the trail until we reached the loop around the Raptor Center and over the Cascades waterfall. I wanted to take the short route out of Glen Helen because I was hungry, but Brick took us on the longer tour of the yellow spring and the long wooden footbridge over the ruins of the old dam. He knew I wanted to finish the run and eat. The longer route was payback for beating him again at one-armed push-ups. It was worth it.

We raced up the ninety-six steep, twisting stone steps out of Glen Helen. Brick's jeep was parked there in the gravel lot and we climbed in so he could give me a ride back down the hill to get my truck.

Mud spun off the jeep's tires and clunked against the underside of the wheel wells as we motored down Corry Street. I leaned forward to look through the windshield at a clean swath rubbed into the hood. "So this thing is supposed to be green?"

"I guess so."

Air hissed into the cabin from a leak in the soft top. I held my hand up to feel the stream. "How old is this thing?"

"Drinking age."

I patted the dashboard. "Looks like the old lady's had one too many."

"Har har."

But the old jeep got us there, and I jumped out and got in the truck and followed Brick back up to town. That landed us on Xenia Avenue just in time for the doors to open at the Sunrise Cafe. There was coffee on the table as soon as we sat down. Brick waved a menu away. "Veggie scramble. Wheat toast."

I didn't look at my menu either. "Eggs and potatoes."

The woman waiting our table nodded. "How would you like your eggs?"

"Surprise me."

"And what kind of bread?"

She didn't need to ask. We'd done this before. "Whatever is your favorite today."

She went to put the order in.

Brick dabbed cream into his coffee. "They ought to name that after you, you order it enough."

"The Sunrise surprise?"

"One of these days you're going to get something really weird."

"Like what?"

"Raw egg in a beer mug, like in *Rocky*."

"I'd eat that."

"Nah. You don't eat a raw egg so much as you slurp it."

"Yeah, but Rocky ate like ten raw eggs. Probably only take a shot glass for two eggs."

Brick sipped coffee. "Lowball glass would be better."

"Wouldn't raw eggs kind of make the point about that line on the menu about consuming undercooked eggs?"

"I guess it would, anybody silly enough to order a raw egg."

The waitress looked over at us from behind the counter. "He's not going to give you a raw egg." She looked back into the kitchen galley. "I don't think."

Then she came out to refill our coffees, but our cups were still full.

I took a sip. "Too soon."

"I know, but didn't you forget something?"

I looked at Brick, looked at the woman. Oh. "Pancake!"

She trickled coffee into my cup until it was back up to the rim. "You'd think after all these times you'd remember your order."

"Good thing I have you."

"Good thing." And she swished away. Man, I loved this place.

Brick took his phone out. "You should ask your daughter to join us."

I cocked an eyebrow. "Cali won't come out this early. It's summer break."

"You have to ask her right." He worked his fingers on his phone's screen.

I heard something sizzle on the grill. That was a good sign. No raw eggs. Then Brick's phone buzzed and he looked at the message. "She's coming."

"What did you tell her?"

"I told her her daddy wants to buy her breakfast."

True. But I had doubts. "I think the attraction may be you. She wouldn't get up this early for me."

"She's a smart girl."

She was.

Our breakfast came and we picked up the flatware and tucked in.

Brick stabbed a spear of broccoli and looked at it. "Maybe we should wait for Cali."

I ignored him and kept eating. When our plates were nearly clean I looked at the pancake in the middle of the table. The pancake was the size of the dinner plate.

Brick set down his fork and looked at the pancake too. "Lot of food for a growing boy."

"You want half?"

"At least."

I cut a jagged path across the pancake and Brick's phone buzzed. "Let me guess. She's going to be late?"

Brick thumbed to the message. "No. There's been an event."

"An event?"

"J'Leah."

"Is that Army talk? An event?"

"I don't know how they talk in the Army. J'Leah and I served in the Marines."

"She needs some relief?"

Brick shook his head. "Ain't even been half a shift yet."

"Why is she texting you and not me?"

"We've bonded."

I guess they had. I wasn't even really sure what J'Leah looked like yet. Just a dark shape with dark skin in the truck last light, then slipping out into the night. "What's she say?"

"You're gonna get a text."

I checked my phone. "When?" Then the phone buzzed. The message went to both me and Brick. I scrolled through. "She says a guy just chased someone out of the house with a baseball bat. Says she thought he might kill him."

"I see it."

"A woman came to the door."

Brick swiped his screen. "Keep reading."

J'Leah said she was going to send a photo. Both of our phones chimed and we were looking at a woman in a long t-shirt and slippers holding the front door of the house open and shouting at a man who stood in the yard with a baseball bat.

Another message came in, with a photo from one of the news stories I'd sent to J'Leah. The picture was Henna Winstrop from the time when she had disappeared twenty years before.

I flicked back to the photo of the woman in the door frame yelling at the man with the bat. "That's not Henna."

Another message. *On her right. The other woman.*

The old news photo had a couple of people in the background that you'd see if you looked closely enough. I hadn't.

The one on her right. So left side of the photo. I zoomed in. The woman with Henna Winstrop in the old photo had an uncanny resemblance to the woman who was just a few minutes ago standing in the door of the house that J'Leah was watching. I looked at both photos again. I was sure it was the same woman.

I glanced up at Brick. "J'Leah's very good."

"Affirmative."

Another text. *Guy with the bat is gone. The woman is still there. I am holding position.*

I replied. *On my way. Stay on her if she moves. Give me an update if you need to.*

Roger.

I forked off a big chunk of pancake, shoved it in my mouth, and got up as I chewed. "You staying?"

Brick pulled the pancake toward him. "Call if you need me." He dabbed more syrup on what was left of the pancake. "How you gonna pay for Cali's breakfast if you're not here?"

"She has a credit card. She's allowed to use it if it's important."

"I think this qualifies."

"You'll explain it to her?"

"Yeah."

I bent to grab another bite of pancake and a swig of coffee.

The waitress came over. "Leaving so soon?"

"Can you put this on the bill with my daughter's when she gets here? She'll pay you for both."

She saluted with a wave of the coffee carafe. "One Jackson Flint breakfast special and coffee. Got it."

16

J'LEAH HAD VIDEO. She and I watched it on her phone, sitting in the truck in the church parking lot.

In the video a skinny guy in a black t-shirt was standing at the door of the house. J'Leah provided commentary. "He'd just knocked."

The door opened and a beefy guy with a dirty blond beard and matted hair appeared. The two men held a brief conversation. There was sound, but it was background noises, cars or a bus in the distance. None of the conversation was audible.

About a minute and a half in, the conversation became more animated. J'Leah paused the playback and zoomed in. "This is where it gets interesting."

She tapped and the video resumed. The skinny guy who'd knocked had his back to us. The guy in the door frame was waving an arm. It looked like he was shouting. Then he reached back into the house with one hand and came up with a baseball bat.

The skinny guy ran, and as J'Leah had described, the wanna-be ball player gave chase and looked like he might kill the other guy. The runner stumbled at the curb and went down on his knees. His hands came up to cover his head.

Dirty-beard held the bat up in a dangerous exclamation point. The video picked up muffled shouting.

J'Leah turned the volume down. "I'm gonna mute. You can't make out what they're saying. But the gist of it was *get the fuck out of here until you have my money."*

Then the guy in the video held the bat with one hand and pointed down the street with the other. The posture was grotesquely similar to Babe Ruth calling his famous home run shot.

I groaned. "That's just wrong."

"Yeah, that guy's way bigger than him."

"I mean the Babe Ruth stance."

I got a blank look.

"Never mind."

The video continued. The guy went back up onto the porch and leaned the bat against the side of the house, and he went inside. After a few more seconds the video ended and J'Leah backed up to a frame that had a good angle on the guy with the bat and zoomed in again.

I glanced up through the windshield and squinted at the house. "Drug deal."

"Good guess. Guy came jonesing but didn't have the money."

"Probably already behind. Might have been moving product and skimmed some."

"That could be it. You never know. Could be something else."

"I can think of a few things, but none of them fit as well as a drug deal." I reached beneath the seat for a pair of mini binoculars I kept there and took a very quick, discrete look. "The bat's still by the door."

J'Leah's eyes cut to the house and back.

I lowered the binoculars. "Maybe he's trying to leave a message."

"Maybe he just didn't want to carry the bat in."

"Leave the bat out. Like pissing on the lawn to show who's boss."

She shook her head. "It's nothing like that."

"Why not?"

"Because one you have to smell, like a dog, and the other—god, I can't believe I'm having this conversation."

"I'm just saying."

"Do you think where the bat is placed is important?"

"No, I just like baseball. And that looks like a good bat."

J'Leah rolled her eyes. "Baseball and canine references aside, there is an opportunity right now."

I tucked the binoculars back under the seat. "You have my attention."

"The guy is still gone. Left in this vehicle before I contacted you." She showed me photos of a Toyota sedan, black, scratched, a dent over the left rear tire well. One shot zoomed in on the license plate. "Can you run it?" J'Leah asked.

"No."

"You don't know anyone?"

"No."

She looked at the image for a moment. "I'd already have this if we were deployed."

"Welcome to the outside."

I got another blank stare.

"How long has it been?"

"Not long enough."

OK. I shut up about it.

J'Leah reached into her slim, black backpack and pulled out a very thin, very compact laptop. "I can get property data."

We both looked up as a woman came into view walking her dog down the sidewalk toward us. J'Leah hesitated. "We need cover. We shouldn't be sitting here in the open."

I picked up a white pastry bag from the seat beside me and reached for a napkin from the wad I'd tucked into the cup holder. Then I stuck my hand in the bag and pulled out a soft pretzel. I held it out for J'Leah.

"What's that?"

"A pretzel."

"I can see that. Your cover is pretzels?"

"Not just pretzels. Smales."

"What's a smales?"

I waved the pretzel. It was soft and still just a little warm. "You don't know what you've been missing."

She rolled her eyes but held a hand out for the pretzel. "I can't believe you wasted time on this."

"It's real close. Took a minute. Little family place that's been there like a hundred years."

She sighed. "If I told my platoon sergeant my cover was a bag of pretzels…"

I handed her a packet of mustard and a water bottle. "This isn't a battlefield. Just people going about their everyday lives. Pretty soon that woman's dog is gonna look for a place to squat, and she'll put all of her attention on scooping it up into that plastic bag she's carrying. She won't even notice us."

"That's gross."

"That's what people do. It's life."

"Someone here could be the neighborhood watch. Or just like looking out their window. Or have some reason to."

"Hence, the pretzels. Just two people sitting here enjoying a snack before the morning shift at the potato chip factory."

The woman with the dog moved by. Neither of them looked up.

J'Leah sighed and sampled the pretzel. "I will never get used to you people." She dabbed mustard and took another bite. "You going to have one?"

I pulled a chunk off of a pretzel. "Just for cover."

J'Leah opened her laptop. She'd already looked up the address on the Montgomery County property search website. "The last name for the owner is the same as one of Henna Winstrop's friends who was interviewed for the news story when Henna disappeared."

I looked at J'Leah's screen. "Ms. Sarah Halstead." I was swiping through my phone for archival news stories but J'Leah already had it up on her laptop. She highlighted a passage with a quote. Kathy Halstead, Henna Winstrop's friend, said when Henna disappeared that she just wanted her friend back and would anyone who knew where she was please help bring her home.

We compared photos again, the image of Kathy Halstead from the old news story and the image of the woman on the front porch this morning. Some features were different, a thinner more aged face and shorter hair, but the resemblance was clear.

J'Leah played a second video she'd taken. The woman came down from the porch in a long t-shirt and slippers and stooped over the man who was still crouched at the curb. She touched his shoulder and said something, and he got up and walked away, and the video ended.

I took out my little notepad and put down a few details. J'Leah watched me. "So what do you think?"

I scribbled more notes. "I think this is Kathy Halstead, Henna's friend from high school, and she's living in a home owned by one of her relatives."

J'Leak looked at the property data again. "Sarah Halstead might be her mother."

"Aunt. Something like that. And I think Henna Winstrop has been here. Recently. For a visit, or maybe more."

"The intel from the kid?"

"Yeah." I didn't think Flame would like being called a kid. And what he'd given me didn't seem like what I would call intel. But it had gotten us here. Maybe not so different from J'Leah's world.

J'Leah folded her laptop and slid it back into her pack.

I closed up the bag of pretzels. "What we don't know is who the guy with the bat is, or when he's coming back."

"And we've been wasting time eating pretzels."

"Smales are not a waste of time."

J'Leah held back a grin. I wondered if she was having me on. You people.

"OK," I said. "I'll go talk to her. Can you keep watch? Give me a signal if he comes back?"

She didn't answer.

"What?"

"I could go."

"You want to talk to her?"

"I've been trained to approach locals in urban situations. Specifically the women. We were to gain confidence as a means of gathering information."

"I've heard of that."

J'Leah cut her eyes over. "It never worked as well with the men."

I believed that.

"We were also trained to de-escalate."

I thought about it. "That woman is older than you."

"You ever talk to a man older or younger than you?"

"Yeah." Flame, last night.

"It's still man to man?"

"It is."

"And this is still woman to woman."

I was already convinced, but one more thing came out. "You're sure it's a good idea for an African-American woman to knock on a door in this neighborhood?"

J'Leah twisted her neck like she was loosening something. "I'm as safe here as you are, or anybody. Probably safer. And I don't care to be limited by my skin tone."

I liked that a lot. "I don't either. I was trying to be protective. I'll stop. You go."

She texted me the photos she'd taken of the Toyota. "He left from the garage in the alley. You can get a position to watch, and if he comes back that way you can text me—just the letter p—and get out in front of him and try to slow him down. Look inept, like you're trying to text and drive or something."

She was giving me back the texting and driving thing. OK. "Why the letter p?"

"For ping. It's quick."

"And what if he parks out front?"

"We don't have time to assemble a team. We have an opportunity now. What do you want to do?"

"What's your cover?"

"My cover?"

"What are you going to say to her?"

"I'm going to knock on her door and tell her I saw a man chase someone away from her house with a baseball bat. I'm going to tell her I've been thinking about it and I can't just do nothing. I have to ask her if she needs help or if there's anything I can do."

"You think that will work?"

"If she'll answer the door."

"OK. And how does that get us to finding out more about Henna and Willow Winstrop?"

J'Leah turned to me slowly. "This isn't some street shakedown. It'll require some finesse."

"That's why I'm asking."

She blinked. Then smiled. "The first step is we think about the person—the woman—and what she needs. Something for her first. Then after that we see what we can get, if she's willing to help. It's got to be up to her."

"It's the guy with the bat I'm worried about."

"I am trained in firearm use, combat situations, and containment. I have a licensed gun and CCW permit."

"You're packing?"

"No one gets to know that unless they have a reason to find out."

I had a reason, and she knew it. It was a matter of trust.

I gave her a thumbs-up. "Go."

The M&P40 was locked in the glove box. She didn't ask, and I didn't tell. That was also a matter of trust. J'Leah pulled her backpack onto her shoulder and got out of the truck.

I stayed where I was in the church lot. J'Leah exited through the alley and a few minutes later appeared walking down the street. I watched her step up on the porch and knock on the door. The baseball bat was still there. It looked like a good bat. I wanted to try the balance, swing it and get a feel for the weight of the lumber. Distraction. I swept that thought away.

It didn't take J'Leah long to get in. A minute or so talking on the porch and the woman opened the door and J'Leah walked in.

I waited for about ten minutes, with nothing to do. Then my phone jumped.

I'm going to get my car and pull up in front and Kathy will get in. Follow us. 2 minutes.

OK. I didn't get any more details.

Two minutes later a dusty maroon Honda maneuvered to the curb and the woman from the house came out carrying a small bag over her shoulder and got into the car. J'Leah must have gone out the back door. I never saw her leave the house.

The Honda pulled away, and I followed it.

17

J'LEAH DROVE TO A COFFEE SHOP at the edge of the South Park District. I waited for her and the woman to get inside before I followed them. They were seated at a table in the back.

The woman kept her eyes down as I walked up. J'Leah said, "Kathy, this is Jackson Flint."

I held out a hand. "Kathy Halstead?"

She took my hand in a weak grip and we shook once, awkwardly. Then she said, "You seem to know a lot about me."

I looked at J'Leah for a cue.

J'Leah picked up my meaning. "I've explained most of it to Kathy. Why don't you get us some coffee and the three of us will talk?"

"I can do that."

Kathy Halstead perked up a little. "Tea for me if you don't mind. Cream and honey. Thanks."

"Happy to. Anything else?"

J'Leah pointed toward the counter. "Pastry. The lumberjack pie seems like it would suit you."

"Lumberjack pie?"

Her eyes sparkled. "You've never been to the Ghostlight?"

"Never."

"Seems like your kind of vibe here."

I looked around. She was right. Ghostlight Coffee would be a good fit for Yellow Springs, if we didn't already have three coffee shops in a village with only two blocks downtown.

But I wondered why J'Leah would think this was my kind of place. She'd probably googled me as she sat there in the dark last night watching the quiet house. Jackson Flint Detective Agency, Yellow Springs, Ohio. I wondered what else she had found out about me.

I got coffees and the tea and scones and asked for a slice of the lumberjack pie.

"Uh, that's seasonal. I don't think we have that right now."

"Oh. February and March?"

The woman working the counter cocked her head. "We usually have it starting at the end of the year."

"OK. What else is good?"

"Uhm, everything? The bagels are house-made. Home grown herbs."

"So everything is good."

"It is. We have a paw paw biscuit that's a specialty."

I raised an eyebrow.

"Does that mean yes?"

"You bet it does," I said.

I'd already eaten the Jackson Flint breakfast special at the Sunrise Cafe and a soft pretzel from Smales. I couldn't afford to keep stuffing myself. I could lose my edge. Little old ladies running up the hill past me as Brick cruised by carrying pieces of a '78 Buick Skylark. But a paw paw biscuit? Oh, hell yeah.

When I brought everything back to the table, Kathy and J'Leah seemed to be talking fairly comfortably. Kathy had never been to the Ghostlight either. She was reserved and mostly followed J'Leah in the conversation. I sipped coffee and ate paw paw biscuit and listened. The biscuit was excellent.

When Kathy didn't respond to J'Leah's oblique attempts to insert me into the conversation, J'Leah took a more direct approach. "Jackson wants to ask you a couple of things."

Kathy turned to me. "I'm only here to help Henna."

I smiled. "Me too."

Kathy moved a piece of scone around on her plate.

I started. "It would help if I knew where Henna is."

She pushed the pasty around some more.

"Henna was staying with you?"

The pastry stopped traveling and Kathy looked up, a decision in her eyes. "I've known Henna a long time."

"That's you in the photo from when she disappeared?"

"Yes. J'Leah showed me."

"You know what happened?"

Kathy pushed a wisp of dark hair back over an ear. It was the first good look I'd had of her. She was thin, with small shoulders and a narrow face that looked much the same as in the old photo, mysterious and a little exotic. She carried her nearly forty years well.

"Henna ran away."

I tried to give an encouraging look.

Kathy focused on J'Leah instead of me. I guess the look hadn't been very encouraging.

"I was over at Henna's all the time when we were younger. We were attached at the hip in grade school."

I took out my little notebook and a pen. J'Leah kept her attention on Kathy.

"But Henna's mother was real strict. Henna started coming to my house instead, and her mother took it, you know, kind of personally or something."

I tried to make that fit with what I knew of Elizabeth Winstrop. It did.

"Then in high school we started hanging out at...other places."

Something from the newspaper stories I'd been reading about Henna's disappearance clicked into place. "Henna didn't go to Yellow Springs High School."

"No."

"And neither did you."

"We both went to a private school. Starting really young."

"But you lived in Yellow Springs?"

"When I was little. My dad used to drive Henna and me to school on his way to work, and we'd wait around after for him to pick us up."

"The school was in Dayton?"

She nodded. "And then we moved to Dayton around the time I started high school."

"But you and Henna stayed friends because you were still at the same school."

"Uh-huh."

"Catholic school?" As if I wished.

She grinned. "It was independent."

"So the Miami Valley School."

Kathy gave a little shake of her head. "We were supposed to be the achievers. Good education, all the opportunity we wanted. And look what happened to us."

I shrugged. I'd seen worse. I tried to find something nice to say, but the words weren't coming. Then something else clicked into place. "That's why I didn't really remember Henna from when I was younger." I nodded to Kathy. "Or you."

"Everybody knew Henna after she disappeared."

I supposed so. I wrote some notes in my little book and then looked back and Kathy. "And what about Henna's father?"

She wagged her head. "I hardly ever saw him. A couple of times when we were really young. He was at work a lot."

"OK. This is really helpful. And then Henna disappeared?"

"Because of a guy."

I scribbled some notes. "You knew the guy?"

"We all knew him. He was popular with…a certain crowd."

I took it slow. Set my notebook down and ran a hand through my hair. "Would you like me to guess?"

Kathy's head ticked up.

"He was trouble?"

"He was what a girl from a good family would want if she was trying to make her mother mad."

"Is that what Henna was doing? Trying to get at her mother?"

Kathy's shoulders moved up and down. "I don't know. It's who Henna was. But I guess her mother would have taken it that way."

"Why would Henna want to rebel?"

"Why would any teenager want to rebel against her parents?"

That hit a little too close to something. I kept my daughter Cali in that safe place in my imagination where she was always protected. Happy, self-aware, confident. Destined for great things. It's what every parent should want. But I'd had to leave Cali on her own a lot these past two years. I couldn't always be there for her. She might discover an urge to rebel, and I wouldn't even be there to know it.

Kathy wanted to fill in some more blanks. I was grateful that it pulled me from my thoughts.

"Henna was a party girl. I mean, a lot of people were doing it, but she made it kind of an art form."

"And that's where the boyfriend fit in?"

"If you mean was he part of the party crowd—yes. He was the plumber."

"The plumber?"

"The guy who came with the necessities to make a party."

Oh. "You called him the plumber?"

"I don't know why they did that. He wasn't big time. Just for friends."

"And do you think Henna's mother knew about that?"

"She knew enough. She hated him."

I clicked my pen a couple of times. "I think it's time we give this guy a name."

"OK, but you won't find him. He's dead. Michael Wellsburg."

"Dead?"

"Iraq. Years ago."

"He served?"

"How else would he get dead in Iraq? The last time I saw him he was headed for rehab. And when Michael came out he enlisted."

"And Henna ran away with him? Before the rehab and he enlisted?"

"Before all that. She ran away because her mother forbid her to see Michael. Henna and her mom got in a big fight."

That also fit with what I knew from Elizabeth Winstrop. "Why would Henna run away? Why not just sneak around?"

"They did that. But then Michael's brother was going to Seattle and he wanted Michael to go with him. Michael said he wanted to get away from the small-town mindset. Henna wanted to go with him."

I worked on the timeline in my head. "So Henna is dating Michael, and her mother won't let her see him, and they run away together with Michael's brother to Seattle?"

"That's what Henna said she was going to do. I guess she did."

"And then Michael goes into rehab and joins the military and gets killed in Iraq."

She nodded.

"And where was Henna in this?"

A shrug. "Henna was gone."

"She didn't stay with Michael?"

"No. When I heard about Michael, nobody knew where Henna was."

"So she disappeared somewhere out in the Great Northwest."

"Somewhere."

"And you didn't keep up with her?"

"Not for years. Then she turned up on Facebook. She'd kind of drop in and out."

"You know what she was doing all that time?"

"What everybody does. She had jobs. She had boyfriends. Or men she stayed with."

And she had Willow.

"Then Henna turned up in Columbus about a year ago. I drove there and we had lunch. I met her daughter."

"Willow?"

Kathy nodded. "Henna was trying to be a good parent. The opposite of her mother. She told me she gave Willow a lot of room. She wanted her to find her own way." Kathy paused, then gave testimony. "Henna was clean. She'd stopped using. She was trying to get things together. I think she came to Columbus because she was trying to get back closer to her family."

I nodded. Her father would have been still alive then. "Do you know if Henna was in contact with either of her parents?"

"I don't know, but she talked about them. She thought her mother would never speak to her again."

"Why would she think that?"

"I believe it's what her mother said."

I let a sigh escape. "Well, her mother wants to find her now. But I'm afraid her father has recently passed away."

"I know."

"OK. Based on the timeline, I'm guessing Michael Wellsburg wasn't Willow's father?"

Kathy wrinkled a brow. "I guess not."

"Do you know who Willow's father is?"

"No idea."

I ran some more questions through my head. "Just a few more things. Has Henna been staying with you?"

A nod.

"Is she still there?"

"No."

Kathy's eyes dropped straight down. I look to J'Leah. She reached out and patted Kathy's hand and said, "It's OK. Jackson wants to help."

Kathy's chin ratcheted up a notch. "Henna came to me about a month ago. She needed a place to stay, just for little while. Her and Willow. But Roy…"

"The guy with the bat?"

Another bob of Kathy's head. "Roy's not my husband. He's just— you know, sometimes you need someone there to help you get through a tight stretch. Just somebody. Roy was that. He's…"

"But the house is in your family name?"

"My aunt's. She left it to me. The title is getting switched over to my name, but the house is mine."

"OK. So it's your place. But Roy didn't like having Henna and Willow there?"

The skin on Kathy's forehead tightened. "No. He liked it too much."

I sat back.

Kathy spilled it. "He was interested in Willow."

"You don't have to tell me."

"Roy is such a shit. He'd fuck his own daughter if he thought he could get away with it."

"I think I—"

"Henna knew it. Roy was going after her too. She was looking for another place to stay when Willow ran off. Then Roy got really mad and Henna got out of there too."

I looked to J'Leah. Her eyes were on Kathy. Kathy's head was down, but I didn't see any marks. No bruises or cuts. Nothing on her arms that looked like Roy had knocked her around recently. Thank god for small favors.

Kathy's shoulders went up and down once. "Willow was smart to get out. God, I wanted to help them, but now it's all such a mess."

History repeating itself. With a twist. Henna ran off to be with a guy, and her daughter ran off to escape from one. My gender wasn't making a very good showing here. "Maybe it's time for you to get Roy out of there," I said.

Kathy choked back a grunt. "It's not that easy. He won't go."

I felt heat at the back of my neck. "Maybe with the proper leverage." I was thinking of Roy's baseball bat leaning against the front of the house.

Kathy wilted. "You don't know what…"

J'Leah pushed her chair back and swung herself around to me. "I don't think Kathy needs a man coming in right now trying to solve her problems for her."

"I was just trying—"

"I know you were, but give it a rest for now. She needs some time." J'Leah patted Kathy's hand again. "And she's not entirely on her own here."

OK. I pushed my chair back to open a space between me and the two women. "Kathy, I'm sorry. I didn't mean to press."

She waved me off with a weak flick of her hand.

"But I have to ask you a few more things."

Her head bobbed in something that could have been yes, or no, or I give up. It didn't matter. I was going to ask anyway.

"Does Henna have a phone? Some way you can get in contact with her? Or Willow?"

"Henna had a minutes phone. One of those things you add money to it and then you can send texts or make calls or use data or whatever, and when it runs out you have to add more money?"

"I'm familiar."

"She used to run out. Willow would use it and Henna would get upset with her for using up the credit and the phone wouldn't work."

"So she didn't have an automatic function? To add more time?"

Kathy shook her head no.

"Does Willow have a phone?"

"I don't think so. If she did, I never saw her use it."

Or maybe it was out of credit. I remembered Willow in the rain when I picked her up, how she'd said she had a phone but hadn't called anyone for help or a ride. "So you don't have a number for Willow?"

"No."

"But you do for Henna? You could call her right now?"

Kathy held her phone up to show me call logs. "That's Henna's number. I've called..." She checked the screen. "Twelve times in the last five days."

I counted backward in my head. "What day did Henna leave your place?"

"Saturday."

"And when did Willow—"

"The day before."

"OK, it's Thursday, and I picked up Willow in the rain Sunday night. So it's almost a week since all of this started."

Kathy frowned. "You did what in the rain?"

"I'll have to explain that. I didn't know it was Willow when I picked her up. And I hadn't been hired yet to find Henna. And..."

J'Leah was shaking her head no.

"Or maybe J'Leah can tell you the details later."

Kathy looked at J'Leah and J'Leah nodded.

"Have you tried texting Henna?" I asked.

Kathy swiped her phone and showed me half a dozen unanswered texts.

"What happens when you call?"

She dialed and put the phone on speaker. A mechanical voice said the number was out of service. "It does that every time."

Well, damn. I really was hoping it would be that easy. Just call and say hey, your mother would like to see you after twenty years, and by the way, does your daughter happen to be there with you too?

I tapped Henna's number into my phone. "Do you think Henna knew where Willow was? Or is?"

Kathy shrugged. "Henna said it wasn't unusual for Willow to disappear. She'd done it before."

"Did Henna seem worried?"

"Of course she did. She knew Willow took off because of…"

I didn't make her say it—because of Roy. "OK. So Willow was gone and Henna was looking for her, and then Henna left too because of Roy. Where do you think they might have gone?"

"It was… kind of fast. Henna left in a hurry."

"Any idea where I could look for either of them?"

"They had some places. I know Willow was going downtown and over by RiverScape. Henna mentioned the library."

"Good. Did either of them ever mention Sinclair?"

Kathy blinked. "The college? No."

"What about an empty warehouse? Maybe down by the river?"

"A what? No."

"OK." I made a few more notes in my little book. "Does Henna have a car?"

"No."

"So she's not sleeping there."

"But that doesn't mean she's not sleeping in someone else's car."

"You think that's a possibility?"

"No idea." Kathy flipped her hands in a gesture of frustration. "I just said that because…"

"I know. You want to help."

"Yeah."

"Me too. Look, do you know any other way to try to find Henna? Someone else she knows or who may be able to help? Have you been in contact with Henna's mother?"

"Henna's mom didn't like me."

I dipped my head to look Kathy in the eye. "That was a long time ago. I think Elizabeth Winstrop may have a different opinion of you now."

Kathy didn't comment.

I tried one more time. "Can you guess where Henna might have gone? Where I should look?"

"Shelter, probably. That's where I'd go."

The quickness of her answer told me she'd thought about it. That if Roy ever crossed some line she would leave her own home to get away from him. And I knew if that happened, and I found out about it, like it or not, I'd look up Roy and give him some persuading. Maybe with a baseball bat, he liked them so much.

I twisted my neck until it cracked. "Which shelter do you think might be a good place to start?"

Kathy's eyes grew big and soft. "I don't know. I can't name even one women's shelter. I guess I'm not a very good friend. I didn't even try to find her."

"I wouldn't say you weren't a good friend."

"What was I gonna do if I found them? Roy wasn't going to…"

It tugged at my sensibilities as a human being. Such feelings of the inescapable. That nothing can be done. "Kathy, you've been a big help. I'm going to find them. But is there anything else I can do for you right now? I can—"

J'Leah held a hand up in a stop sign. "I got this."

I sat back. Then I tipped my head and stood and backed away. "I believe you do."

18

LITTLE DOTS lit up the map on my phone as I sat in the truck. Homeless shelters. A handful were close to downtown Dayton and Kathy Halstead's house and looked like good places to start.

The YWCA.

Daybreak.

St. Vincent de Paul.

Which one first? I had no good cover story ready and no one to run interference. No poseur to front for me. No credentials in my pocket to help me get past the door or loosen up some tongues. Given some time I could put together a plan and make a good run at bluffing my way to information, if information was there to be had. But I'd never been good at waiting. It was time to push this thing. Henna and Willow had been gone for almost a week now. I had to know if they were okay.

But first I swiped to my contacts and tapped the number to call Cali. She answered on the first ring. "Dad."

"You picked up."

She laughed.

"What?"

"That sounds funny."

"It does?"

"My phone was already in my hand. I didn't have to pick it up."

"It's what people say. You used to have to pick up the phone to answer it."

"Dad—I know."

"So what do you say now?"

"We don't. We text."

"Ah, so this is a stretch for you? Using the actual calling capabilities of your phone."

"Har har."

OK, I liked this. "Are you at home?"

"Yeah."

"I'm not there."

"I've seen that."

"And it might be a while before I can get back."

"I knew you were going to say that."

"You probably did. Do you need anything?"

"Like what?"

"Food. Companionship. Medical care? Parental oversight? I don't like leaving you alone again. I've been away a lot with work."

"I'm not alone. Mrs. Jenkins is here with me."

It was a private reference for the two of us. When we lost Kat I didn't work much for the first several months. When we eventually started trying to move toward what would become our new normal and I took on more work, Cali spent a lot of afternoons and sometimes evenings with neighbors and friends.

There wasn't family nearby to rely on. Kat's parents were dug in across the country in northern California where they had a huge network of friends and had more recently begun dabbling in commercial real estate development. My father had passed away years ago, and after that my mother went back to Maine and moved in with her older sister in the ancestral family home.

Even with the Yellow Springs community there to help us, there were lots of bits of time when Cali was left at home alone at only thirteen or fourteen. We were sensitive to that, and we'd fallen into saying that Cali wasn't home alone. Mrs. Jenkins was there with her.

"How is the old lady?" I said. "Will you give her a scratch behind the ears for me?"

"She's frisky. I will."

"Are you all right by yourself for a while? I could be a long time."

"I'll probably go out with Asia and Jenny later."

"Out?"

"Walk to town. Get some popcorn or something. We'll probably watch more Netflix."

Yellow Springs was a good town for that. I felt as good about Cali walking to town with her friends as I did about her being home alone. Or with Mrs. Jenkins.

"Sure. Make yourself happy."

"I will." We ended the call.

Then I studied the little dots on my phone again. They weren't talking to me.

I texted Marzi. She was at work and probably with clients.

Call me if you can.

Then I got out of the truck and stretched. Walked the two short blocks to Park Drive and the strip of park that was the street's namesake and made it a boulevard. I strolled in the shade under the trees and waited for Marzi to call.

It was a quiet afternoon. Someone was painting a house a dark shade of burnt orange. At the end of the boulevard I made the turn and came back up the stretch of park. The house being painted had a second story wall that was accessible by a low roof over the porch. Someone had climbed up there and painted a giant orange jack-o-lantern with the new color. The toothy grin looked out over the neighborhood like a sentinel. I grinned back.

J'Leah's car was still outside of Ghostlight Coffee when I got back. I left the women inside to their own devices and checked my phone, but I already knew there was nothing from Marzi.

I chose the dot on the map that was the Y. It made as much sense as any place to start.

I went in confident, but the women there handed me my proverbial hat. They told me it was a safe place for women and they weren't going to tell me anything about any adult who may or may not have been there unless I had some authority and a really good reason. I didn't have either. And they were right. Fools rush in, that was me. But I was better at pushing than waiting, so I soldiered on.

At the Daybreak shelter I learned that the organization was for youth, and while it made sense that Willow may have gone there, it wasn't meant for families or parents and children. They politely declined to share any information if I couldn't show that I was a legal guardian, but if I would like to make a donation to help their cause they could accept a credit card.

I gave them fifty dollars and moved along. I probably couldn't justify the donation on my expense account for Elizabeth, but I was sympathetic to a good pitch, and they'd given one.

Marzi still hadn't called or texted. My lack of progress was lowering my mood, but that didn't stop me from eying the little dot on the map that was the St. Vincent de Paul shelter. I could go for the trifecta. Three dead ends and blown leads.

My phone rang and Marzi saved me from the failed hat trick. "It's me. Sorry I couldn't call sooner."

"That's OK. You have a minute?"

"Yes."

"What do you know about homeless shelters for women in Dayton?"

It took her about two seconds to catch up. "This is the case you told me about."

"Yes."

"The woman and her daughter. From a long time ago."

"Twenty years."

"You found her at Sinclair. There was that warehouse."

"That's the one. The youngest was there."

"You think they're at a women's shelter?"

"Maybe."

"Both of them? The mother and daughter?"

"I don't know. Listen, if you have a few minutes, I could catch you up."

She did, and I did.

When I was finished with the short version, Marzi said, "So where have you been?"

I told her about the Y and Daybreak, and what had happened.

"I could have helped you. My agency has worked with people at both of those places. I probably could have found someone there I've talked with before. Or someone in my office who has."

"That would have been helpful."

"You should have waited for me."

"I know."

"Now you'd have to wait for another shift. If I went with you, or for you, we'd have to wait for whoever was there when you were to leave for the day. It'd be too suspicious for two people to ask about the same person in one day."

"I've thought of that. But I'm surprised to hear you thinking that way."

A beat passed. "Surprised in a good way? Or in a not-so-good way?"

"In a surprised way. I wouldn't have thought you'd work like that."

"Sometimes you do what you have to do for the best interests of a client. Especially someone who really needs it."

"Agreed."

I heard Marzi take a breath. "I probably won't be able to get free from here for a couple more hours. Can you wait until then?"

I took too long to answer.

"Jackson?"

"I want to press."

"What does that mean?"

"I don't want to wait."

"It sounds like you haven't had much luck on your own."

"I was hoping you'd give me some pointers."

"About what?"

"About how to get someone to talk to me."

There was another long breath. "I think it would be better if you could wait and I could go with you."

"We can do that, but give me something to help me at least feel like I'm making progress while I'm waiting."

A few seconds. Another breath. "Have you been to Homefull?"

"No, just the places I told you about." I checked my phone. "But I see it on the map. I know someone who worked there a long time ago."

"Well that could help you, but I'm not suggesting you go there on your own."

"Then what do you think I should do?"

"They have mobile food markets. The women in the programs work them. I think there's a location at the Second Street Market."

"That's close to where I am." I looked up the market on my phone. It would be closing soon.

"Jackson? Just listen. Look around. Don't press too hard. These aren't women like who you met at the desks at the other places. These women might talk to you, or they might not. They might be friendly, or they might just get suspicious."

"OK." I rubbed a palm over my eye sockets. "You aren't just trying to keep me out of the way until you can jump in and help me?"

"Moi?"

Uh-huh. "OK, I gotta go."

It was a quick trip to the Second Street Market. The place was in a long, narrow brick building that used to be part of the Baltimore and Ohio Railroad. Like the monopoly game, except I was driving a truck instead of pushing a boot or a wheelbarrow. Monopoly would be better if there was an old pickup truck for a game piece. Maybe with a chainsaw and a load of lumber in the truck bed.

I drove a couple of slow zig-zagging loops around the side streets near the market. Nothing got my attention, so I took a spot in front of one of the old bay doors that lined the building.

I went into the market and cruised past the coffee stall, the crepes, and organic produce. The soups, jams, handcrafts, and cheese. The Mexican and Greek food. The plethora of food stalls and wafting aromatics. The people and energy.

I lingered at Rahn's Artisan Breads. The ciabatta and baguettes and salted rye called to me. It would be foolish not to listen. I scored a rosemary baguette.

I'd heard rumors that Rahn might be thinking about packing it in. That he'd had enough nights spent baking instead of sleeping. That he was going to pass the baguette to whoever would take up the ovens for the next generation. I felt for the guy, but say it ain't so, Rahn. I grabbed a couple of pain de raisin and told myself it was in case the rumors were true. But I would have bought them anyway.

I almost missed the Homefull location. At the far end of the market two women stood behind a counter loaded with bunches and baskets of leaf lettuce, mesclun, early peas, and strawberries. A sign above the display announced who they were, and some brochures were tucked in among the produce bins.

I picked up a brochure, and that got the women's attention. Both looked like they were under thirty, one with a dark brown complexion and a quiet smile, and the other with lighter skin and a gigantic smile.

I pointed to the sign. "I've heard of you."

The woman with the big smile smiled even bigger.

"I think you're connected with a homeless shelter?"

"Connected, yes. There's a men's and women's shelter for emergencies that Homefull will direct people to if they need it. But we're about something different. We set up people in low-cost housing. There are work programs. It's about long-term stability."

I looked at the brochure. "I think I knew that. I know someone who used to work there, a long time ago."

Both of the women looked surprised. The one with the big smile cocked her head. "What's her name?"

"It was a long time ago. I think it was called something else then. The Other Place?"

"I might've heard of that. Yeah, it think it changed its name."

"My friend hasn't been there for a long time."

"I wasn't here when it had the other name."

"So you probably wouldn't know her. It looks like things have changed a lot. So there's no homeless shelter anymore?"

The woman looked at her companion, then back to me. "There are the Gateway Shelters. The men's is out on Gettysburg."

"That's a long way. There's also a women's shelter? That's closer? On Apple Street?"

The two women shared another look. The woman with the big smile continued. "I think you'd want the men's."

Oh. "No, I don't need a place to stay. I'm…interested. There's an organization in Yellow Springs that I'm familiar with that helps people get housing. Home Inc."

"You live in Yellow Springs?"

"I do."

"I love it there."

"Me too."

"Does the one out there have a work program?"

"I don't think Home Inc. has that. They're growing. Homefull has been around a lot longer."

She beamed. "This place has been great for me. Got me off the streets, got me a job. I love working in the gardens."

"It sounds like a great program."

"It is. We have mobile food markets. And we double EBT credit so people who need it have a chance to eat healthy."

"That sounds good. You're a terrific spokesperson for them."

Her smile was mesmerizing.

"I'd like to help out," I said. "But if I buy greens and peas and straw-berries, I won't be taking those away from someone else who needs them, will I?"

"No. We have *lots*."

"OK, then one of each of those."

The other woman began packing the food into a paper sack for me, and I handed over some bills. "And maybe you could help me out a little? I'm looking for someone. Her family wants to get in contact with her." I held up my phone with a photo of Henna Winstrop showing. "This is from a long time ago. She's twenty years older now. But maybe you've seen someone who looks like her? Somewhere recently? Here or some-where else?"

Both women leaned in and squinted. It was the natural thing to do. Then the woman with the big smile leaned back. "I don't know…"

The other woman kept squinting at the photo. "There's a lot of new people. Lot of them want to be in the gardens."

"Uh-huh." I kept the photo up, encouraging. "Her mother would really like to find her."

"There might be one…"

The women shared something silently. I waited. Listening. Not pressing. They had to decide what they would do. Trust me or not.

"You say it's her mother looking for her?"

"It is."

"Maybe you might try the gardens. Somebody out there maybe has seen her. I don't know. Kinda looks like somebody that's been around."

I'd seen in the Homefull literature that the gardens were across the river a little north of downtown. "Thanks." I put the phone back in my pocket and reached for the bag of salad fixings and other things. "I really appreciate this."

My gratitude was genuine. I hoped that these women, in this safe place, didn't feel like they'd given away too much. That they somehow knew if I could find this woman they had perhaps pointed me to, I really would offer to help her. If I could ever find Henna Winstrop. She was beginning to feel like a ghost. I felt a step closer to finding her and at the same time like I'd gotten nowhere.

I took my produce and bread out to the truck and backed out of my spot in front of the bay doors and tipped my cap against the sun coming at my eyes. The gardens were a short drive from there. Maybe my luck would change.

I waited at the light in front of the market while a couple strolled with locked hands across the walk. A woman trailed behind them and entered the crosswalk late. She wore a bright pink baseball cap, like they'd give out at the ballpark on Mother's Day as a promotion to support breast cancer research. The cap was dazzling in the sunlight, and I marked its bobbing path across the street.

Then as if she knew I'd been watching her, the woman in the pink cap turned when she reached the curb and glanced back at the truck.

I blinked. An image flashed in my head of Willow Winstrop sitting in my truck in the dark, dripping wet from the rain. But that's not who this woman looked like. She was an older version of that image. It was a vision of Henna, Willow's mother.

19

SHE WALKED UP THE RAMP to the market and went inside. I checked the time. They should be closing. This could be interesting.

A car pulled up behind me. The light had gone green and I was sitting in the turn lane, blocking traffic. I made a slow left turn and drifted into a lot across the street.

I checked the mirrors and saw the woman appear again coming back down the ramp. She swung left and started down Webster Street.

I took a moment to settle on an approach story in my head, then I got out of the truck and went after her.

She had already turned down Ford Street and made some progress. I hesitated. Ford Street was a narrow road that bisected some tucked-away parking lots and the back of an industrial building, then ran up close to a long, brick, gated apartment building.

It was closed-in and quiet and there were no cars or other walking traffic. After that, where I'd likely catch up with the woman, Ford Street became an alley, one car wide and made of old brick pavers that sloped up to the backs of more long, low industrial buildings. There it was even more closed-in and isolated. Not the kind of place I wanted to make contact. Too confined.

I ran back to the truck and wheeled onto Second Street, pushed to make it through the green lights, and cut down onto Canal Street, a leftover reminder of the old Miami and Erie Canal that once floated through the heart of the city.

I paused where Canal Street crossed the end of the Ford Street alley and pulled the binoculars from under the seat. The pink hat was a block and a half away, moving toward me.

From where I was, Canal Street dead-ended in a zag into the back of the White Lotus, a restaurant so small it had no tables, only a single row of stools at a counter tucked in front of a grill and a tiny kitchen. The place had once been a burger joint, a quickie lunch and carryout for downtown workers. I heard they had good Thai food now.

I made the turn onto Third Street and immediately back to Patterson and nosed in at a meter by the library. My view down the alley was obscured, but I stepped out of the truck and into the shade under the trees in Cooper Park in front of the library where I caught sight of the pink hat and waited as it came closer.

She climbed the steps up to Patterson Boulevard and crossed to the library. I put myself in plain sight of her and approached on the paved walk from the opposite direction. When we had nearly closed on one another, I pulled the baseball cap from my head, stopped, and turned as she passed. "Ma'am?"

She looked startled, but she stopped. "Me?"

"Your mother asked me to deliver a message to you."

"My mother?"

"Yes, ma'am. Elizabeth Winstrop? She's been trying to find you."

Her face darkened. "What do you know about my mother?"

"I know this seems unusual. Let me explain—"

She took a step back. I stepped back too, doubling the distance she had opened between us.

"Take your time. I just want you to know that your mother is looking for you, and she knows about your daughter, Willow."

"Willow?"

"You are Henna Winstrop?"

Her face twisted like she had stepped into a Munch painting.

"You look a lot like your daughter." It was true, even with her tortured face. The dark hair and thin features, the curve of her chin. It was like seeing time lapse.

"You know my daughter?"

"I've met her. Briefly. I have a lot to tell you if you want. It's up to you."

The muscles in her features relaxed a tick. "Why are you…talking for my mother? Why are you looking for me? Do you work for her?"

I put my hands in my pockets, trying to show that I wasn't aggressive, and I wasn't going to be aggressive. "Your mother hired me. She wants to know that you're all right. You and Willow."

"How does she know about my daughter?"

I shrugged.

"You've been following me? Have you been following Willow? Where is she? You bastard!"

"I don't know. I'm trying—"

"You bastard!"

I was getting tired of that word really fast. I took my hands out of my pockets and brought my phone with them. "I'm going to call someone you know. Kathy Halstead. Look, here's her number." I held the screen up, but we were too far apart for her to read it. I dialed, and Kathy's phone rang.

"How do you know Kathy?"

"A young man who knows your daughter pointed me to her." Kathy's phone rang again. "With bright red hair?" I pointed to my head. Another ring. "It's kind of a long—" Another ring, interrupted by a sorry-I-missed-you message.

When the short greeting had played, I told Kathy who it was and to call me as soon as she could.

Henna was eyeing me like I had snakes in my hair. I hoped she didn't turn to stone.

My phone buzzed.

"You just called?"

"Kathy. There's someone here I want you to talk to." I held my phone out toward Henna. "Take it."

She shook her head.

"It's Kathy Halstead. I'm giving you my phone." I flattened my palm so the phone rested lightly on top.

Henna's eyes went to the phone but she didn't come closer.

I bent my knees and crouched to the sidewalk. "I'll leave it here. You can take my phone. I'll walk over there." I pointed to the entrance to the library. "Take as long as you need."

Then I backed away, and Henna kept her eyes on me but stepped over and picked up the phone from the concrete walkway.

I gave them a lot of time to talk. Henna watched me and occasionally looked up like Kathy had said something about me that got her attention. Or maybe she was still trying to decide if I was a gorgon and had snakes in my hair.

Finally Henna came over to me and handed my phone back. "OK."

I raised my eyebrows. OK what?

She didn't pick up on it. Henna reached up and took the pink baseball cap off of her head. Her hair fell in dark, curling cascades from where she'd had it tucked up under the cap. It made her look even more like her daughter. Then Henna's face dropped. "I have to find her."

"You don't know where your daughter is?"

She shook her head.

"How long?"

There was water in her eyes. "I don't know. Several days."

"Since you left Kathy's?"

The first trickle eased from Henna's eye. "Yes."

"Why did you wait so long? Why not call the police? Call someone for help?"

"You don't understand."

I didn't. I waited.

"I told her where I was going to be. I called. I texted. With Kathy's phone. Willow has mine. I told her where to go. Where to find me."

Some gears clicked into place. Willow in the truck with the phone she wouldn't use. "She may not have gotten those," I said. "I think your phone could be out of time. Kathy told me that sometimes…"

An eyelid fluttered. Henna didn't reach up to stop it.

"Kathy tried to call you. There was no service."

"I didn't know." Another trickle rolled out of her eye, and Henna shook her head as if that would wipe the track away. It didn't. "It's not her first time. Willow has run off before."

"I understand that. But it's been too long. We need to get some help."

The water came out in deeper rivulets now. "You don't understand. People like me don't call the police. They'll take her away."

A tightness in my chest made it hard to find my words. I made another call and waited while it rang. Marzi's number went to message. I asked her to call me if she could. Henna slumped against the library entrance and watched me. I added a text to Marzi.

Call if you can. It's important.

Then Henna and I looked at each other like strangers who both wanted the last bag of peanuts in the vending machine but neither of us had any money. A longing.

My phone rang. Marzi.

"I'm sorry to call you again at work."

"It's OK."

"I wouldn't ask if it wasn't important."

"I just stepped out of a meeting. It's all right."

"I found her."

One second. "Which one?"

"Henna."

"The mother?"

"Yes."

"What about the teen?"

A breath. "We don't know where she is. Almost a week now."

A quiet sound. A phone shifting to the other ear, or cloth on cloth. A soft sound. Then, "Have you called the police?"

"No."

"You should."

"I know. Henna knows."

A slow intake of air. "What can I do?"

"Talk to her?"

"Yes."

I gave the phone to Henna and walked away to open some room for them. And some room for me. If it was Cali missing I would call the police. I would call everyone for help. I would beg the governor to mobilize the state militia to hunt for her. But they could never take Cali from me.

I could provide a home for my daughter. Food and shelter and stability. Henna had a harder battle to fight. I couldn't imagine the demons that must be whispering recriminations in her head.

They didn't talk as long as I expected. Henna motioned me over and handed back the phone. The call was ended. Henna's mouth was a tight, thin line. "We have to tell the police."

"I know."

"But that lady can help me do it. She'll explain it to them. She said she would help me…"

"She will." I felt like laying a hand on Henna's arm to offer reassurance, but I resisted. "What did you arrange with Marzi?"

She looked briefly confused. "Her name is Marzi?"

"It is. What did you arrange with her?"

"She said you'll set it up. You can take me to her."

"Did she say where?"

Henna shook her head. "She said you'd do it."

"OK." Wheels turned in my head. "Will you go to your mother's?"

Henna rocked back. "My mother doesn't want to see me."

"She does."

She crossed her arms and leaned away.

I stepped up to close the distance between us. "We can go to my place. Or we can pick up Marzi and go somewhere. Or maybe Marzi will let us go to her place. Or we can stand out here on the street and figure it out. But we have to find some place to do this. Now."

"Not my mother's."

I rubbed my eye sockets. "You know your father has passed?"

Her chin lifted. "I know."

"And now your mother…she wants to find you."

"That witch is alone now. She only wants me because she doesn't have daddy anymore."

Something was fitting into place in my head. A decision. A push. "Twenty years is a long time."

Nothing.

"I think sometimes things can change. People can change."

"She told me never to come back. She'd never speak to me again."

"Uh-huh." I swiped the phone and placed a call. It went straight through on the first ring. "Elizabeth?"

Henna's eyes caught fire. "You bastard!"

"There's someone here I want you to talk to."

Henna's eyes screamed bastard again, but her heart must have said something else. She gave way and reached a hand out for the phone.

I heard Elizabeth's voice shouting from the phone. "You found them? Oh my god, you found them?"

No, Elizabeth. I only found one.

Henna's face crinkled and warped. "Momma?"

I turned away again. This was way more drama than I was used to. I'd rather be doing something straightforward and simple. Sprinting in the heat up a steep, winding hill. Carrying the chassis of '78 Buick Skylark in the afternoon sun. Chasing down the bad guys. But some days aren't that simple. Some days, there's drama.

This conversation took longer. I stayed far enough away that I couldn't hear any of it. It would work or it wouldn't. We'd see.

Then Henna pressed something on the phone and walked to where I was lingering in the shade of a tree. She held out the phone. "This is yours. Let's go."

I pointed in the direction of the truck. "You'll ride with me?"

She started across the park where I'd pointed. I guess that was answer enough. We walked to the truck and got in and cranked the windows down. I put the key in but didn't turn it. Henna was sitting where Willow had been when I picked her up in the rain. I still couldn't explain that. How Willow had been in my truck. Coincidences didn't work for me. This story still had more threads to pull.

I hung an arm over the steering wheel. The heat from the wheel sank into my skin. "Where are we going?" I asked.

"Mother's."

I looked ahead at the line of buildings and road in front of us. "We're going to have to make some decisions when we get there. You have to find Willow."

"You have to call that lady to help me."

It only took a minute. Marzi was in. I gave her Elizabeth's address and she said she was on her way.

I dropped the phone into the cup holder. My head formed the words *this is going to be hard*, but I didn't let my mouth say them. Henna's face was stone. The medusa couldn't have done any better work.

I turned the key and we set out for a reunion that was a long time in the making.

20

I THOUGHT IT COULD WORK. Twenty years was a long time to cool off. A long time for the memories of how you thought you'd been wronged to fade. A long time to forget, if not forgive.

And the need to come together to find Willow should be a bonding experience for Henna and Elizabeth. I'd seen that kind of thing in the movies. If you believed Hollywood, and if everyone here was telling the truth, it could work.

My mind was chugging, but Henna was quiet as we crossed over the Mad River and took the ramp up onto Route 4. I let the silence sit between us, figuring she was thinking about seeing her mother.

When I took the exit to wind around the Air Force base, Henna looked over at the spillway for Huffman Dam. "Well, that hasn't changed much." It was the first she'd spoken since we started the drive.

I reached over and turned the radio down. Water churned through the three gates at the base of the spillway. I didn't tell her that dams generally don't change much. That's what the Huffman spillway always looked like. But this was a matter of perspective. It was twenty years between visits for Henna, and a regular event for me.

I tried to keep the conversation going. "Have you been back to Yellow Springs since you…"

She let it hang.

"Since you left?"

"You mean since I ran away?"

"I guess that's what I mean."

"No."

The view of the dam receded in the side window, and Henna got quiet again. I left the radio playing low and kept driving.

We cleared the couple of miles through Fairborn and I made the turn onto Fairfield Pike. When the view opened up on the far side of the I-675 underpass, Henna straightened up. "This looks different."

It was. "Houses went in a couple of years ago. Used to be fields here."

She pointed out the window at the gas station. "That used to be a little grocery store."

"I remember. Long time ago. Then it was a flower shop for a long time."

"My dad used to take me there when I was little. We'd get sandwiches at the deli."

I remembered that too. We passed the station and watched a car pull up to one of the gas pumps. The driver got out and inserted a credit card into the slot on the pump.

"That's progress for you," I said. "I figure there'll be a traffic light here before long."

We cleared the new development and climbed the hill outside of town and passed into the open rural landscape. Nothing much had changed here in Henna's twenty-year absence. That was why I liked this drive.

Henna waved a finger in a moment of recognition. "The old Armstrong building is gone."

Right. Back in town. The granary tower that had been a staple of the city view was still there, but where the building had been was now just an empty grassy patch. "Burned down some years ago."

"I knew something looked different."

I ventured further conversation. "My dad used to take me there to get field corn and dog food when I was a kid."

Henna kept her gaze on the fields passing by out the window. After a long moment she said, "Field corn?"

I grinned. We were having a conversation. "For his grandma. My great-grandmother. She fed the squirrels."

We were quiet for a couple of miles. OK. No more conversation. But I still thought this could work. Henna and her mother could have their reunion and then we could get to finding Willow. You talked, you realized the past was the past, and you moved on. That's what these two needed to do.

Corn and soy fields drifted by. Some cows and a few pigs. Old farm houses. Twin Towers horse park. It was all still the same as when Henna had lived here.

She was slumped in her seat. I tried to reanimate her. "You should see Dayton-Yellow Springs Road. All built up there by the highway now. Lots of traffic."

She looked at me. "That was country road. Used to be you wouldn't see more than a couple of cars the whole drive."

"Not anymore."

"Has Yellow Springs changed much?"

I laughed. "No. Change is one thing that comes slow to Yellow Springs."

Henna gave me a sheepish look.

"There's a Subway. KFC is gone. IGA is a Dollar General."

Her focus sharpened.

I grinned. "All very tasteful. It's mostly the same. Some of the businesses have changed. Some of them have moved around. Current Cuisine and Ha Ha Pizza and the coffee shops and little stores are still there."

She didn't respond.

"There's a hotel downtown now."

"Hotel?"

"On the corner where the old Barr house used to be." Henna looked like she was thinking. I gave her a nudge. "Next to the funky place with the brick arches and the gardens out back."

The light bulb switched on. "You're kidding."

"Nope."

"When did that happen?"

"Few years ago."

We snaked into the sharp turns that led into the last stretch of road before the village. A zig around one soy field, then a zag around the little development in the middle of the fields and cows.

"Big hotel? Like a Days Inn?"

I laughed. "No. But not a tiny thing. Built to look like the old Mills house that was where the school is now. Big front porch that stretches down the sidewalk on Xenia Avenue."

Henna shook her head. "I used to walk past there every day when it was just a great big yard with giant old trees. I can't believe there's a hotel."

"We're getting used to it. Nothing new is popular at first." I pointed to the right. "Marijuana-growing plant over there as you come into town."

She looked at me like I was joking. I gave it to her straight. "Medicinal herb. People are calling it mellow yellow. Fits right in."

"That I believe."

It at least fit the myth. Marijuana use had changed a lot since the town had earned its reputation in the sixties.

I took the turn onto High Street that would lead us across the village to Henna's childhood home. "The people haven't changed much."

We rolled past the assortment of houses, each one almost entirely different from the next.

Henna watched the village go by out her window. "You probably mean that in a good way."

I did. "The people are what make this village the way it is. Everybody still likes doing their own thing."

"And debating about everything, and talking everything to death."

I shrugged. "You remember."

A tiny piece of a grin lifted at the edges of her mouth. "It was always funky."

"No place quite like it." I felt more confident. Henna was relaxed. This could work. We would be at her mother's house in a minute and the two of them could begin to reconnect. Then we could get down to finding Willow.

But then I looked over at Henna and my mood darkened. Instead of Henna I imagined her daughter sitting there in the cab beside me, dripping wet in the dark. And then she'd run off into the dark and the rain.

And I still had no way to explain the coincidence that I had picked her up. And I hadn't brought Willow back to her mother, and to her grandmother. We weren't done here yet.

The second crack in my confidence came when I saw the lawyer's car parked at the curb in front of the Winstrop house.

I wheeled in behind the Infiniti. The compact car in front of that looked familiar. The driver's door opened and Marzi stepped out. My confidence clicked back up a level.

Henna was staring at her mother's house, the hedge at the curb, the stone path walkway, the brick terraced garden under the oriel windows. "Well, this looks the same."

Marzi leaned against the fender of her car. I pointed through the windshield. "That's Marzi."

Henna looked out the glass. Without a word, she unbuckled her seatbelt and got out and walked to Marzi.

I waited in the truck. It was a calculated move. I didn't want to be an unnecessary male body standing between two women who didn't need me.

Henna and Marzi talked for a couple of minutes and then exchanged a brief hug. The conversation continued and Henna raised a hand to wipe one eye. I hoped they were moving toward what Marzi could do to help take Henna through some of the options, how to talk to the police and Child Services when they were likely to get involved.

Then the front door of the Winstrop house opened and Elizabeth appeared on the landing. She placed one hand on the railing and leaned out expectantly.

Henna and Marzi both turned toward Elizabeth. I stepped out of the truck.

Henna took a step forward. Elizabeth came down off the landing. Marzi and I stayed where we were, and mother and daughter approached each other slowly down the walkway, moving toward a rendezvous in the center of the path.

It all looked overly dramatic, like a slow-motion scene from the movies. But I couldn't tell what the women would do when they reached each other. They might hug. They might stare, or shout, or slap. Or something worse.

They did none of those things. Elizabeth stopped before the two reached each other and moved to one side. Henna stepped past her mother, and the two walked one after the other to the front door where Henna pirouetted to reverse the maneuver, moving to one side while Elizabeth passed her to hold the door open. Then they went in.

Marzi came up next to me. "Should we go with them?"

"Yeah." I slipped my hand behind her and we did our own waltz up the walkway.

Samuel Thomas was at the door when we reached it, and he invited us in with a motion that hinted of *Thank you sir, may I have your top hat and coat?* Why did everyone seem so stiff?

The reservations didn't last long. The voices inside were already stepping up in pitch when Marzi and I reached the parlor.

"How could you lose your daughter?"

Marzi and I stopped in the entry arch. Samuel Thomas stayed behind us.

"What kind of mother does that?"

"You! You're that kind of mother. You didn't know where I was for twenty years."

"That was different. You weren't a child."

"I was seventeen. Not a legal adult."

"But your daughter is…"

"How old? You don't know. She's fourteen! You didn't even know I had a daughter."

Elizabeth let slip an unladylike snort. "That's beside the point."

"It's not."

They were in the center of the room, standing by the hearth and amid the easy chairs. The cocktail cart was nowhere in sight. It probably would have been useful.

I moved aside to make room for Marzi to step through. She looked at me like I was absurd and stayed where she was. Samuel Thomas stayed similarly parked behind me.

The buzz lapsed for a beat and in that moment Elizabeth took note of the three of us at the threshold of the room. She didn't try to play hostess. She simply said, "You'd better come in. We have some things to discuss."

Introductions were brief. I announced Marzi to Samuel Thomas and to Elizabeth.

Elizabeth straightened her back. "You're the one with agency experience?"

Marzi tipped her head once. "Yes, ma'am."

"Please call me Elizabeth."

"OK. Elizabeth. I've just talked with Henna some about what might happen in situations like this."

"I assume that you mean when we call the police, which we must do." She turned a stabbing glare to Henna. "To protect my granddaughter."

Huh. And her daughter's daughter. Already Elizabeth was trying to take Henna out of the equation and make this about herself.

Marzi ticked off a miniscule nod. "That's one option."

"I beg your pardon. We have to—"

"They'll take her away!" Henna's cry cut through the room.

Elizabeth offered cold comfort. "My dear, she is already away. We must bring her back. And *they*, whomever you may be referring to, will not take her away from us once we find her."

Henna's face dropped.

I put a hand on Marzi's shoulder. She turned and mouthed *What?*

I shrugged and put my hands up. *What do you think?*

Marzi didn't look pleased, but she stepped in to speak to Henna and Elizabeth Winstrop. "It's tricky," she said. "There's more than one way this might go. But we have to find that girl. And soon." She motioned to Samuel Thomas. "The lawyer may be helpful."

My mouth moved before I was smart enough to stop it. "That's not what Shakespeare said."

Everyone turned to me.

"Now is not the best time," Marzi whispered.

"Sorry. Go on."

Glances passed through the group and settled on Samuel Thomas. He swept a hand out from his hip. "Why don't we all sit down? I can ask a few questions, and maybe we can decide what is best to do next."

No one disagreed, and we moved to take chairs. As we all sat, Elizabeth slipped away from the group. It seemed odd that she might go for the tea pot now, but I realized my false assumption when I saw her lift her phone to her ear.

Marzi and Samuel Thomas were saying something, but I was focused on Elizabeth and didn't make out their words. Elizabeth's face hardened, then fell. She raised her free hand and motioned frantically in a wide, sweeping arc. "Stop!"

She poked the phone and got the speaker on. Then she staggered to the center of the room and fell down on her knees.

The speaker came to life and a panicked voice shouted "Mother!" Henna shrieked.

The voice from the phone shouted, "Mom? Mom?"

"I'm here, baby."

"They won't let me go. They said—"

The voice cut off and there was a muffled grunt and some unintelligible syllables.

Another voice came on, distorted, like someone was talking through a hand held tight against his mouth. "Two million dollars. You have two days, until Saturday. If you call the police or fail to deliver the money, Willow Winstrop will disappear and you will never see her again. If you deliver the money as we will tell you to, we will release her. Keep this phone charged and the line clear. You will receive more instructions later."

The call ended. Elizabeth slumped.

I scooped up the phone and checked the call log. It was a local number. The old land line prefix. I called back.

The number rang several times while everyone seemed frozen as if in a wax museum. Then the call went live and a thin, quiet voice answered. "Hello?" It sounded female and elderly.

"Did you just call this number?" I asked.

There was a moment of silence. "Who is this?"

"I just got a call from you."

A throat cleared. "What?"

"You just called me."

If confusion could have a sound, that's what came through the connection. "I think you have me confused with someone else."

The voice sounded familiar. "Mrs. Tolland?"

"Yes?"

I knew her from town. Her family had been here for generations. We sometimes talked in Tom's Market over the produce. She was picky about her tomatoes.

"Who is this?"

"It's Jackson Flint. Listen, there's been a mistake. Someone used your number to make a spoof call to me."

"A what?"

"A spoof call. It's…" I had too much adrenaline to try to explain it.

"I didn't know I could do that."

"You didn't. Mrs. Tolland, I have to go. I'm sorry about the confusion. I'll see you around town, OK?"

"OK."

I hung up. My hand shook and I took a deep breath to steady it. I wanted to go get somebody. The bastard who made the call. I wanted a fight.

They were all looking at me. "It was a…"

Samuel Thomas reached his hand for the phone and I gave it to him. "We heard."

Elizabeth slouched to a chair and fell into it with a prolonged groan. No one else spoke or moved until Henna released a throttled choke and said, "Oh. My. Holy. Fucking. Shit."

Normally I wouldn't care for a lazy expletive like that, but in this case she'd nailed it. What made me feel worse was that I'd failed them. The threat against Willow had been real. Someone was looking for her. Flame told me. He knew, and he told me, and I lost Willow and they'd gotten to her.

The string of suspects was still long, and I hadn't even uncovered all of the players. I knew almost nothing about the mysterious men who had showed up at the warehouse, or Kathy Halstead's live-in friend Roy. And I knew little about several of the others in the story. It was possible that I hadn't uncovered the kidnapper, or nappers, at all.

I had failed Elizabeth. And Henna. And myself.

Another wave of adrenaline clouded my thinking. I tasted metal, and I felt ready to kill somebody. But there was nobody there to go after.

I went to the kitchen and took a couple of deep breaths and worked to release my clenched fists. Then I felt Marzi's hand on my shoulder. She spoke quietly. "You think it's real?"

I breathed one more time and felt a centering and focus returning. "We have to believe it is."

Marzi's lip quivered. "What do we do?"

I turned us back toward the parlor. "We get Willow back. No matter what."

The other room was buzzing again. I worked to track the conversation.

"The obvious course is to call the police and issue an amber alert. Get everyone in there." The lawyer.

"Just find her. Find her!" Henna.

"I just can't believe—" Elizabeth.

"Unnh." Henna. Really loud. She held Elizabeth's phone limply, as if it was a snake that might try to turn around and bite her.

"What?" Elizabeth took the phone. Her eyes scanned and she swiped. Then her shoulders sagged.

I stepped into the middle of the melee and slipped the phone away from Elizabeth. Henna had looked up what happened to the girl who the amber alert was named for.

I closed the phone's browser. "That was a different situation. Amber wasn't ransomed. It was an abduction only."

"But the police will have resources that—" Lawyer again.

Henna let out another groan, and the confusion of voices started up again. There was too much at once to follow. I motioned to Marzi and went outside to the front landing.

Marzi followed and caught me at the porch railing and said, "What are you doing?"

"Giving them some time."

Her eyes crinkled. "For what? They need help deciding what to do."

"I can't help them yet."

"Why not?"

I looked in through the window. They were still talking past each other with animated gestures. Streaks of garbled language leaked out to us. "They haven't decided yet."

Marzi gave me a long look and went back inside. If I had been a smoker, this would have been the time to tap out a stick and light up. Instead I stretched my back and took in a deep breath and held it. I wanted my head to clear, but something came in and filled my thoughts completely.

Cali. I knew what I would do if it was her. I was certain what I would do. It wouldn't be pretty.

A few minutes later Marzi came back out. "They want you in there. To run them through the whole thing again. The whole story. To see if that helps."

I did, and the others' additions to the story spilled out and overlapped as I went through it. In the end we were all talking through it. Henna had no idea about much of what had been going on. Her story matched Kathy Halstead's. She and Willow left Kathy's house because of the boyfriend Roy. Willow ran off. Henna called and texted her daughter to meet her at Homefull. When Henna got to Homefull and was redirected from there to the women's shelter, Henna called and texted Willow again with the update. And again.

Willow never responded to any of Henna's calls or texts, and Henna had been drifting back and forth between the Homefull offices, the women's shelter, the Second Street Market, RiverScape Park, the library, and every place else she could think of, looking for Willow.

Henna didn't know anything about anyone who was looking for Willow, or for her. She didn't know that her father had tried to find her before he died of a heart attack, or that Robert Winstrop had hired a private detective. Or that Elizabeth had been trying to find her and had hired me.

The surprise for everyone was when I told them that Willow had been in my truck.

Samuel Thomas ventured a guess. "Maybe that was a coincidence. How many people would be driving down that road at that time?"

I shook my head. "Maybe a lot of people. It's a long way. It would take a long time to walk it." I breathed. "And I don't like coincidences."

"But it was dark," Samuel Thomas said. "And it was raining. How many people would see her? And stop?"

Marzi answered. "Jackson would."

Samuel Thomas motioned as if he was resting his case.

I wasn't convinced. "So where did Willow go? I saw her the next day in Dayton. How did she get there? And where did whoever has taken her find her?"

Nobody knew.

The emotions in the room were bouncing off the walls, but the conversation had squeezed to a trickle.

I tried to offer options. "I can press other leads. I can go back and look for Flame. That might turn up something to follow."

Henna looked at me. "But you couldn't do that and help with the ransom too."

"The police would have to manage the ransom. Or all of you. If I go looking for a trail that might lead to Willow, somebody has to follow up on the ransom."

Another moment in the wax museum passed.

I leaned in to Henna. "What do you want to do?"

She twisted and twitched, but no words came out.

Elizabeth stepped in. "It's not her decision to make."

I raised a finger. Just one gentle finger. Elizabeth stayed behind it. I said, "But Henna is her mother."

Henna cleared her throat loudly. "What usually happens? If the police are called?"

"It could go well."

"But if the kidnappers find out? They said they'd make Willow disappear. What does that mean?"

I shook my head. "We can't know."

"But you could get her back. You could do it. You could take them the money and make sure they give my daughter back."

"I would handle it differently than the police. I'd do whatever we have to to make sure Willow is safe."

Henna dug her palms into her forehead and pulled them down over the sockets of her eyes.

"Look, I know this is a hard decision—"

"I want you. No police." She looked at her mother, eyes pleading to agree.

Elizabeth gave one jerky nod of her chin, then looked to Samuel Thomas. Samuel Thomas held up both hands and stepped away.

Marzi watched everything but said nothing.

I spoke to the whole room. "Are you sure?"

Elizabeth answered for everyone. "Yes. No police. Jackson, bring Willow back to us."

21

THERE WERE LOTS OF THINGS I should have been doing. Call Brick. See if we could bring J'Leah in. Set up a base, probably by stuffing everyone into my little office looking down on the main street through the village. Find out if Elizabeth could even raise the kind of money that might look like two million dollars. Secure the Winstrop house. Make sure Elizabeth and Henna would be safe.

Work a plan with Brick to get Willow back at the exchange and then get these sons-of-bitches, assuming there was more than one of them. Better, find an angle to get to them before the exchange. Call in some tech help, try to trace the call. That might be J'Leah. Go back and look for Flame, try to find Kristine from the warehouse, see if either of them had seen anything that could point me in the direction of who had taken Willow. Shake down the squatters sleeping in the warehouse. Somebody should have seen something that I could try to follow.

I could have ticked off more items on the list, but there was only one thing I really wanted in that moment.

I texted Cali. *Òu êtes-vous?*

It was something she would recognize from her mother. Kat and I used to call to each other when we were separated—around the house, in the grocery, across a crowded room. Whenever we wanted to reconnect. *Where are you?* Cali had picked it up when she was still very young, and it had become something we used for just the three of us. *Òu êtes-vous?* I need you. I want you.

Neither Cali or I had used it since Kat had died.

The reply came almost right away.

Everything OK?

Òu êtes-vous?

Downtown with Jenny and Asia.

Can I come get you?

She didn't ask why. *BMU*

I tried out a couple of things. Big muddy underdogs. Bermuda made unreal. Bring my ukulele. Nothing fit.

??

Beam me up.

Before I could try to puzzle it out, another reply came.

Space ship at VA.

And another.

Village Artisans. Painting on the side. I'll be there.

I hadn't figured all that out, but if that's where Cali was going to be I couldn't miss her.

I tapped my phone. *OMW.*

Then I got Marzi to go along. She readily agreed. I wasn't going to leave her alone at the Winstrops, and she wasn't going to let me. We went out and climbed into the truck.

Village Artisans was a co-op of local artists that had kept a shop in Yellow Springs for more than thirty-five years. That was pretty good run for a co-op.

I turned onto Dayton Street and the shop came into view. A series of paintings lined the outside wall, and Cali was standing directly in front of one with a spaceship hovering beside a full moon and throwing a tractor beam down through the trees onto a campsite below. It gave the illusion that Cali was under the tractor beam, waiting to be beamed up.

I slid into a spot at the curb and Cali came up to the open truck window and found Marzi sitting there. Cali offered to sit in the middle, but Marzi waved her off and scooted over. When we were all squeezed in I leaned around Marzi to look at Cali. "Où est la vache?"

She cocked her head.

"There's a tractor beam, there ought to be a cow around."

She nodded once. "Oui, tractor. La vache est partie."

"Tractor beam got him."

"Art," Cali said. "It's what you want to see in it."

And then I really wanted to hug her, but Marzi was between us and it was a tight squeeze and I couldn't reach over.

Cali looked at Marzi, then at me. "Dad, what's going on?"

"I needed to know you were all right."

She gave a puzzled look. In the light of the late summer evening she looked older that I thought she could be, that Cali had grown faster than Kat would have believed if she was still with us. I wanted to commiserate with Kat. It's what parents were supposed to do. Our daughter growing up, but not grown up. Still a little time.

I put the truck in gear and eased away from the curb. "Let me tell you a story. Marzi is going to help out."

For a moment I thought the two might shake hands, they looked so stiff. But then they communicated in some unspoken way that only women can understand, and I felt the atmosphere in the truck cab soften.

I pushed in the clutch pedal and when I drew the shifter down Marzi tilted her legs toward Cali so the stick would not come between them. My hand grazed Marzi's hip as the stick came down into gear, and I felt another unspoken memo pass between the women.

We rolled through town and I started telling Cali about the Winstrops. Henna running away. Finding Willow, the warehouse, the park. That Robert Winstrop had died of a heart attack. Cali perked up when I told her about Kristine and our lunch at the restaurant in the sky. I got to finding Henna and the ransom call. Marzi filled in a few details.

Cali's face contorted. "Is that real?"

"We have to believe it." I shifted down for a turn and the floorboards hummed. I wanted again to be next to Cali, but Marzi was still between us. I tried to give a reassuring look. "We'll get her back."

Then we were at the Winstrops and I realized I didn't have a plan for Cali. I just wanted to know where she was. See her. Connect. *Òu êtes-vous? Je suis ici, avec vous.*

We went in to figure out what should come next.

Elizabeth doted on Cali. I thought Cali would hate it, but there was something about the attention that Marzi and Elizabeth were giving her that seemed to give Cali a glow.

Henna hovered in the background, and I tried not to notice if she saw the way that Cali soaked up the attention. Henna could have used some of the sympathy her mother had to dole out, but there had not been a thaw yet between the two of them.

Then the doting faded into the reality of the situation and a tension came back into the room as we looked at each other with the shared urgency of Willow's abduction.

Cali agreed to let Marzi take her to our home. I reluctantly watched them go.

Then I went over to where Henna was sitting in a wingback chair. "I'm calling in some help." I texted Brick. *Grasshopper.* It was a code we didn't use often, and we didn't take it lightly.

Elizabeth moved to my elbow and looked at my phone screen. "Grasshopper?"

It was a kung fu reference. I didn't try to explain it. "Brick can be trusted."

My phone buzzed.

20?

"I'm giving him your address."

Elizabeth gave tacit consent.

Supplies?

Later. Just get here. We'll want J'Leah.

Then I put my attention on both Elizabeth and Henna. "And I'm going to call in someone else, if we can get her."

Neither of them disagreed. Elizabeth twisted her hands. "What can I do?"

"Put on a pot of coffee."

I could tell she didn't like it, being asked to play hostess, but she went out to the kitchen and I heard water running. I would have made the coffee myself if she'd objected.

Samuel Thomas came over with Elizabeth's phone in his hand. A series of texts were coming in. The phone bleeped as another arrived, then another.

"Instructions," he said.

The number was Mrs. Tolland's again. I didn't suggest calling back to make sure it wasn't her.

Samuel Thomas held the phone out and we crowded around to scan through the texts. He scrolled down the screen. "They want us to use Monero."

"The cryptocurrency thing?"

He nodded and scrolled some more.

"Why that one? Why not bitcoin? Or a wire to an account in some foreign country?"

"It's fungible. Can be converted to other currencies. And hard to trace. Not just hard—they claim it's untraceable."

"Is it?"

He shrugged. "With the right people, the right resources, you could maybe do it. Maybe the feds, working with phone company records."

"That hard?"

"And they're probably using burner phones. We know they're spoofing the numbers. They can set up a Monero account, receive the money there, move it to another account, run it through another cryptocurrency, switch up accounts again. With the open source blockchain coding, they'd be hard to find. Maybe impossible."

I let my eyes drift over Samuel Thomas. "How do you know so much about all of this?"

"My firm had a client. He was using the dark web to move some money around, hide it from his wife's divorce attorney. We had to cooperate with some state authorities, and the client wasn't very happy about it. Things got messy."

Huh. The lawyer had more game than I'd given him credit for. I turned to Elizabeth. "Can you get that much money? Two million? In a couple of days?"

"I don't know. Not cash."

Samuel Thomas stepped in. "This won't be cash. But you'll need the whole two million."

Elizabeth rubbed her temples. "There are substantial assets, but how liquid…"

"I can help with that," Samuel Thomas said.

"Can we do it?"

Samuel Thomas had the look of someone adding numbers in his head, which he was probably doing. "I believe so." He was calm and collected. Not like I would expect from a lawyer who knew that he must act as an officer of the legal system, yet had agreed not to report a child abduction to the police.

My confidence in him was growing. But I hoped we were doing the right thing.

A doorbell ringer buzzed, and Elizabeth moved quickly to answer it. I stepped in behind her.

Brick was an imposing figure in any light, but standing in the glow of the porch lamp in a black t-shirt that stretched tight against his pecs and biceps, he might have given G.I. Joe pause. His hardened muscles and smooth bronze chin jutted out like he'd been chiseled from a block of brown stone. A large handgun tucked into a holster at his left side completed the look.

Brick's t-shirt announced *Your workout is my warmup*.

None of that bothered Elizabeth. She stepped up and opened the door. "We've been expecting you."

I came around Elizabeth and pulled Brick inside. "I said we'd get supplies later."

He touched the butt of his weapon. "Didn't know that meant arms too. You wrote grasshopper."

"There'll be time for that. Let me catch you up."

Henna's eyes were fixated on Brick and the holster and gun at his side. I pointed to Brick's gun. "Maybe you could put that away for now."

He grinned. "Then you probably don't want to see what all else I got out in the jeep." He turned and let himself out the door and came back a minute later without the holster and the handgun. I knew he had something else tucked away somewhere. And he knew I knew it, but the others in the room didn't know it, and they seemed more relaxed.

I made introductions. Brick shook hands with everyone, including Elizabeth and Henna. His hand looked enormous as it circled Henna's.

That done, Brick turned me. "J'Leah is in. She's on her way."

"Tell her she doesn't need to arrive in full battle gear." Then I explained for the others who J'Leah was and that this would be the team to secure Willow's release.

They accepted all of that without debate, and Elizabeth went to get the coffee. She called from the other room. "Henna, will you come in here and help me?"

Henna moved swiftly to help her mother. I took that as a good sign. Then I wondered for a moment at asking the women to play traditional roles and bring coffee for the men who were going to solve the problems. But if that's what it took to get mother and daughter to share a moment together, I could live with it.

We drank coffee and caught Brick up. We agreed that he and J'Leah and I would set up a base in my office. The space would be tight, but that would move us away from the Winstrop house where we didn't want to be seen if the abductors might be checking the place for police or other activity.

We agreed that Elizabeth and Henna would get hotel rooms out of town, about twenty minutes away in Fairborn where they wouldn't be seen. Samuel Thomas would work with Elizabeth to get the ransom funds together. Henna had no distinct role except support, which she appeared to need more of herself than she would have to offer.

J'Leah would be tech. Brick said she knew some people. Could maybe call in some favors, maybe have a chance of trying to trace the number where the texts were coming from. I doubted that, but I wasn't going to stop anybody from trying.

Then J'Leah arrived. She wasn't in battle gear. She'd arrived in tight-fitting dark gray pants and a black shirt that together with her dark brown complexion made her seem like she could disappear into a shadow. I'd seen her do just that.

We spent time telling the story again, catching J'Leah up. We all put each other's numbers into our phones. Then the group split. Brick and J'Leah and I went to my office above the street in the middle of the village, and the others went to get hotel rooms.

Henna had some things still in my truck, and I went out with her to get them. She looked frazzled and stressed like someone had just snuck up from behind and scared her, and she was expecting it to happen again. I guess that's probably the way she felt.

I picked up her bag from the truck seat. "We'll get Willow back."

Henna sniffed and slung the bag over her shoulder. "You have to," she whispered, and slumped away back to the house.

We went to my office. It was after eleven when we got things arranged and rearranged in the little space. J'Leah had brought some equipment and had already tapped into my wifi and boosted the signal. Brick was studying the texted instructions that Samuel Thomas had forwarded to everyone from Elizabeth's phone. I stood in the hallway to give them some room in the tiny office.

Then what felt like only a minute later Brick was tapping me on the shoulder. "Wake up, precious."

I blinked. "I wasn't asleep." I was sitting on the floor outside my office, leaned against the wall.

Brick tilted his head to the side and let out a loud sound like a snore. J'Leah's voice floated out from the office. "Sounded just like that."

I stood up. "OK. What's next?"

"Sleep."

"I was just doing that."

"Not very well. You won't last long in the hallway."

"I don't think we're done for the night yet."

"Not us. You."

"I can't—"

Brick poked my shoulder. "We need anything, we'll get you. You need to sleep. We're going to need you bright-eyed and ready to go."

"Bushy-tailed."

"What?"

"The expression is bushy-tailed. Bright-eyed and bushy-tailed."

Brick shook his head. "Go home."

I did. It was late, but a light was on in the kitchen and I could see a flickering glow from the TV through the living room blinds. Marzi's car was on the street.

When I got inside they were both on the couch, in the dark, watching the TV screen. Marzi and Cali, watching that show about the girl who lived only with her mother in a small town not so unlike Yellow Springs. The show we'd watched together a few nights ago.

They both looked up at me and Cali picked up the remote and paused the video.

"There's no news," I said. "We're going to bed."

Cali's eyes roamed over Marzi, then to me.

I went over and sat down next to Cali. "There's something I should tell you."

Marzi looked over. Her eyes signaled yes.

I put away my dad face and just said it. "Marzi and I would like to start dating."

Cali looked confused, and my heart took a little dive. Then her eyes twinkled and she looked from me to Marzi and back. "That's silly. We all know you already have."

I grinned like a possum in the dark and sat back on the couch with the two of them. Cali started the video, and I watched about a minute of the show with them before I was snoring again.

22

THE NEXT TWENTY-ONE HOURS passed quickly. Marzi was up early and moved her morning commitments so she wouldn't have to go in to work until after lunch. Fridays for her were usually slow in the afternoon and she hoped to be at work only an hour or two. After that she would come back to check in on Cali again.

For breakfast I made salad from the greens and peas and strawberries I'd gotten at the market when I was looking for Henna. I toasted slices of the rosemary baguette in an iron skillet, then cooked soy sausage and eggs.

We lingered over breakfast, though I was anxious to check in with the others and coordinate my day with them. We lingered a little longer when I cut up the pain de raisin and Marzi and I sipped more coffee while the three of us ate it.

Marzi had spent the night in my bed. I slept deeply. I assume she was comfortable enough and did the same. I'd have to find out.

When Marzi woke me last night to get up from the couch and go to bed, Cali had already been in her room. Then both Marzi and I woke before Cali got up. I didn't know what Cali knew or had assumed about the sleeping arrangements. I'd have to find that out too.

My home life was falling out of sync because of work and the situation with the Winstrops. I'd have to remedy that soon. But right now there was work to do.

Marzi took the breakfast dishes to the sink and ran some water.

I came over to the sink. "I can do that later."

"I don't mind."

I laid a hand on her arm. "I really have to go."

"I know." She quieted the flow of water to a trickle and we both looked over at Cali, who was still at the kitchen table and looking at something on her phone.

Cali's head came up. "I'll be OK."

"I'd rather not leave you alone," I said.

"I'm old enough. I've always been old enough."

Now Marzi turned off the dish water.

My jaw worked slowly, then fell into place. "You mean since we lost your mother? You've been old enough to take care of yourself since then?"

"I've been doing it all along."

Cali was right. I'd left her mostly to fend for herself after Kat died. Cali made meals, washed the laundry, got herself up for school and got on the bus and got herself home. Kept up with her homework. Kept up with her friends.

She had learned to do all of those things for herself while we were both grieving, and she'd done it fantastically. And she knew it. And would be better off for it.

Cali turned her phone over and set it on the table. She came to the sink and picked up a dish towel and gently bumped me out of the way. "I'll dry. You go."

I wanted to kiss her on the cheek, but she looked too grown up for that. Instead I finished the last of my coffee, took my cup to the sink, and said goodbye.

A few minutes later, I was navigating the upstairs hallway to my tiny office. J'Leah was inside sleeping on the floor. My bumping and creaking to get to the door hadn't woken her. Nor did my key in the lock. When I stumbled into my desk that had been moved to give her some room to stretch out behind it, that did it. J'Leah had taken the blanket that was usually draped over the back of the filing cabinet and tucked herself into that. She had her backpack as a pillow. The window was open and the air inside the office was cool.

J'Leah's head came up. "What time is it?"

"Morning. You slept on the floor?"

"Yeah."

"I'm sorry about that. You could have gone home."

"I wanted to be here in case something happened."

"You could have come out to the house to sleep. Just a few minutes away."

"This is OK." She stood up and stretched. "You civilians are soft."

"You get used to it. Where's Brick?"

"Went home after you left last night. Said he was going to run some tacticals." She said it with a question on her face.

"That probably means he was sleeping. You want some coffee?" I gestured to the pot on my desk. The remnants looked questionable. I could dump the pot in the bathroom down the hall. The sink was too shallow to get the carafe under, but I could slosh some water in or take one of the water bottles with me, then come back and make coffee with more water from one of the bottles. That was probably why I didn't make coffee here very often.

J'Leah looked at the pot. "How old is that?"

"No idea."

"Then maybe later. You want an update?"

"Yeah."

"Well, there isn't much of an update. Status quo. We haven't had any luck tracing the number. I have a friend who's trying to pull some strings, but people are sensitive about phone records. I've set up a text tree so we can use that to communicate quickly. And Elizabeth hasn't gotten any new calls or texts, as far as I know. She hasn't called with anything."

"I'll check with her. First let me see if I can find Brick." I tapped out a text. *What are you doing?*

Toting Betty around the yard. Thinking. Focusing.

OK.

My phone rang. Brick. "You need me right now?"

"You decide. I'm going to Dayton. Looking for anything that could point me to who took Willow. I have to see the Winstrops first. I'll do that on the way."

He grunted hard. "When?"

"The sooner the better."

Another grunt. Lifting a piece of the Buick. "You at the office?"

"Yeah."

"Let me find a shirt." He ended the call.

J'Leah was looking out the window. I gazed over her shoulder. She spoke without turning from the view. "I wonder where they have her?"

I hadn't been letting myself think that.

"I wonder if Willow is OK. If she's comfortable?"

"I don't know."

"If they're treating her OK. She's just a girl…"

I gave her a moment. "You all right?"

"I will be."

I stepped back and let J'Leah have the window to herself, and I busied myself stuffing things into my bag. Water bottles, baseball cap, binoculars. Phone charger. Granola bars and little bags of peanuts from the filing cabinet drawer.

I took the thermos down from the shelf. "You ready for breakfast? Coffee?" I opened the top of the thermos and sniffed. It smelled OK.

"I'm always ready."

I had the feeling she meant for anything, not just breakfast. "Or do you want to go home. Get cleaned up?"

"I'm going to stay here. I want to be ready. I want to find the girl." She bent to pick up the blanket from the floor.

"There's a restroom down the hall and one at the train station." I pulled the top desk drawer open a few inches and reached in for an extra house key that I dropped onto the desk. "In case you want to use the house." I gave her the address. "My daughter might be there, and maybe Marzi. Call before you go, if you go. You have the number."

J'Leah looked at the key but didn't pick it up.

"Eggs and toast and potatoes OK? How do you like your coffee and eggs?"

"Black, and doesn't matter."

"All right." And I went down to get her some breakfast. Eggs any way. The Jackson Flint breakfast special. I was liking J'Leah more and more.

It took a little while to get the take-out order and fill the thermos and get coffees to go. People liked to take their time at the Emporium.

And everywhere in town. When I got back to the office Brick was there, leaning against the desk. J'Leah was in the desk chair, tapping on her laptop's keyboard.

Brick eyed the paper containers in my hands. "She's working on the trace. And how blockchain works. Monero is hard to break."

"So I've heard."

Brick uncrossed his arms. His t-shirt shouted *Let's get physical.*

I set J'Leah's breakfast on the desk and pushed it toward her. I set another container beside Brick and opened it. Scones and a rhubarb muffin.

Brick picked up a scone. "Don't judge me. I worked out this morning."

"I wouldn't think of it."

I dropped some bills onto the desk and pushed them toward J'Leah. "If you need anything. Food, snacks, water, a book. Anything bigger— equipment, tech stuff, call me and I'll get you a credit card number."

She opened the breakfast container but left the bills where they lay. "You don't have to do that."

"Don't worry about it. I can put it on expenses."

She started in on the potatoes and went back to her laptop screen. Brick picked up a coffee I'd brought for him, and we squeezed out of the office.

It was a bit of tight quarters in the cab of the truck. Brick tried to stretch his legs out, and he put his feet up against the windshield to get full extension. That looked awkward, and he drew his legs back and settled them under the dash. "Tiny office, little truck cab."

I jerked a thumb over my shoulder. "Lots of room in the back. And I like my truck."

"That you do."

"You think you'd be more comfortable in the jeep?"

Brick grunted. "I'd have more fun in the Shelby."

"Sure, but then we'd be stuck sitting in your barn."

He leaned back against the headrest. "Guess this'll have to do for now."

When we reached the hotel where Elizabeth and Henna were staying, we found them in adjoining rooms.

Elizabeth let me check her phone that there had been no new calls or texts from the kidnappers.

I handed her phone back. "Keep that charged and with you. How are you doing with raising the money?"

"Working on it. That's a lot to put together in a short time. It will take some creativity."

"I assume that means Samuel Thomas. Where is he?"

"He'll be over later."

It occurred to me then that he'd been working a lot of hours for Elizabeth. Like me. "Do you know if Samuel Thomas has a family?"

Elizabeth looked surprised. "I've never thought to ask."

I made a mental note to do that the next time I saw him.

Brick was standing by the door and hadn't said a word. Henna was seated at a small table in the room and also hadn't spoken. Elizabeth followed my gaze to Henna. "She took some over-the-counter sleep medication last night. She's still groggy."

"I'll let the two of you work out the logistics of getting her up and going. J'Leah is coordinating communication between everyone. You'll be hearing from her. And Brick and I are going to look for anything, or anyone, we can find in any of the places where we've seen Willow or think she might have been. If you get a call or a message, or if anything happens that you think is important, let everyone know right away."

"Of course."

"And keep your heads down."

Elizabeth looked at Henna. "There's a breakfast downstairs that goes until eleven. I should be able to get Henna going by then."

"That should be safe."

"And she'll need a few things. We'll stick to the stores by the mall."

I must have made a face. Elizabeth's eyes registered a question.

"That's fine," I said. "I'm just not a fan of the mall. Or shopping."

"That's not a surprise."

I looked back at Henna. "Is she all right?"

Henna didn't answer for herself. Elizabeth said, "No. Neither of us is all right. And we won't be until you bring her daughter back."

I noticed the change in rhetoric. Henna's daughter. On that note of solidarity, Brick and I left.

He didn't try to stretch out in the truck again. Instead, Brick took out his firearm and examined it. Checked the safety and the cartridge, lifted the gun from the harness and replaced it.

"That the weapon you used in the Marines?"

"The very one."

It was a Glock 19. We'd had this conversation before, and we would have it again. Brick liked his gun close if he thought he might need it, and he often seemed to think he might need it. Some things you carry with you long after they've been drilled into you.

He put his weapon away and reached under the passenger seat for my lock box. He knew the combination, and he took out the M&P40. "I see you're carrying."

"Not quite," I said.

"What good can this do for you if it's in the lock box?"

"Does what I need it to."

"What's that?"

"Generally, not much. Comfort."

"Makes you feel safe."

"Gives me a better chance that I'll come home to Cali. And a statistically better chance if it's not with me unless I need it."

Brick was quiet for a moment as he handled my gun. "OK. That's a good answer." Then he placed my gun back into the lock box. And he removed his weapon and placed it in the box beside the M&P40 and closed them both up.

"You're going to leave it behind?"

He flexed his biceps. "Can't lock up these guns."

I couldn't tell if lightening the mood and the talk of guns was making me feel better or not. I had a feeling way down in my stomach that they wouldn't stay locked up for long.

I navigated into the city and we parked on Monument Avenue by the river. Then we went everywhere and looked for anything, anyone, that could give us something to work with. The park, the baseball field, all of the restaurants and bars nearby. The library, inside and out. The warehouse, which had some different faces but mostly with the same look about them. The restaurant at the top of the hotel. The convention center, the homeless shelters and the Second Street Market.

We didn't see Flame, or Kristine, or anyone who could tell us anything about a teen who looked like Willow. We got a lot of blank stares. Some requests for money. One woman who wanted to take Brick up on what his shirt said and get physical with him. He took it as a business request and politely shut her down.

The guy in the park was there, singing "Change, change, change. Does anybody have any change?" Brick liked him and gave him what he had in his pocket.

We snacked on the peanuts and granola bars I'd brought, we drank coffee from my thermos, we walked a zig-zagging path across downtown, and all we got was hot and tired.

We checked in with J'Leah. We checked in with Elizabeth and Henna. We heard that Samuel Thomas was making progress getting the funds together. But we didn't hear anything from the kidnappers.

In the middle of the afternoon when I called J'Leah again she said it was hot in my office.

"Sure," I said. "Go out and stretch your legs. You'll probably like the village."

Brick and I were on Fifth Street in the Oregon District, drinking iced coffees. We were over-caffeinated, but that wasn't unusual. He looked at me over his sweaty cup. "You thinking what I'm thinking?"

"We should have heard from them by now."

"You think it's a hoax?"

"I think we have to believe it's real. If we can find Willow, we can breathe easy. Make all of this go away."

"Who would fake something like that?"

I wiped sweat from my forehead. "Good question."

Then we packed it in and headed back to Yellow Springs. When we walked down Xenia Avenue toward my office, there were barricades folded up at the street corners, no-parking signs taped to the light posts, and a series of lines painted onto the surface of the street. The village was getting ready for Street Fair the next day. Our twice-a-year extravaganza. In all that was going on, I'd forgotten.

"That complicates things," I said.

Brick frowned. "Won't be able to get near here, on foot or in a car."

"Not with twenty thousand people in the street."

Then we cut back to Kieth's Alley and the entrance to my office. Some young people were taking selfies at the murals painted on the backs of the buildings. They paused in their picture-taking and waited for us to go by. Some people had enough celebrity to photo bomb in Yellow Springs, but I wasn't one of them.

J'Leah was there in the office to meet us, but she was looking out the window and didn't turn when we came in. By way of greeting, she said, "I love Yellow Springs."

"There's a lot of that going around. Any news?"

Now she turned. "Nothing. It doesn't feel right."

Brick squeezed himself into one of the folding chairs. "We've been thinking that too."

"Should we check in with Elizabeth again?"

I shrugged. "Hasn't been that long. But it might make us feel better."

"I don't understand," J'Leah said. "Where are they? Where is Willow?"

We stewed on that for a while, without many words. I called Elizabeth. There had been no new contact, but Samuel Thomas and Elizabeth had gotten the funds together and were waiting for instructions.

I called Cali. She was at home. Marzi had come over with take-out spaghetti dinners for the two of them. They were watching that show with the single mom who was raising her daughter.

Finally, Brick stood up and looked out the window into the dark night. "Sitting ain't helping. Let's go for a run."

"A run? We must've walked fifteen miles today."

"Yup."

"We're not dressed for it."

He looked me over. Dickies work pants and shirt, already sweat-stained. "Won't matter much. We've got the shoes."

We did, both of us in running shoes.

J'Leah slipped away from the window. "I'm in."

I shook my head at them. But I was bending to tighten the laces of my shoes. "We'll need water bottles."

Brick grabbed one from the desk. "Pre-hydrate. Travel lighter." He downed the whole bottle.

J'Leah and I both took on water too, then we went out into the night to run.

We cruised down to the bike path and turned up toward the Glen Helen nature preserve. Brick pressed the pace a little, and J'Leah stayed right beside him. I hung behind, right off their shoulders.

The trees from the nature preserve threw the bike path into even heavier darkness than the night brought. Ahead of us a pair of eyes shone as a deer grazing at the edge of the tree line froze and watched us pass.

Brick turned at the far edge of the Antioch College campus and we went cross-country over the fields and past the gardens by the solar array and the old amphitheater. The college grounds were quiet, but I knew the ghosts of Antioch past were all around us. Last fall Cali and I had stumbled across on old movie called *The Antioch Adventure*. It was filmed on campus in the sixties when small colleges and the liberal arts were still in their heyday. The echoes of that vibe still lingered in the buildings and grounds as we ran through.

Then we cleared the campus and Brick picked up the pace again as we turned back toward town. Something buzzed in my ear. I thought there was a gnat, but the buzzing was intermittent. Brick and J'Leah slowed. It was our phones. All of them. It was something J'Leah had set up.

We stopped and drew in ragged breaths as we looked at our screens. Elizabeth had forwarded some texts. Several of them. With very precise instructions about how to set up the Monero account. And a photo of Willow. She looked unhurt, sitting in a chair with a black blindfold pulled around her head. It didn't look good.

The exchange would happen at Street Fair. We were to set up the Monero account on a phone and leave it at a place to be named tomorrow. If we did, Willow would be released into the crowd.

Brick looked up from his phone. "Oh, lord. They're going to do it in the middle of Street Fair?"

23

ALL OF US WERE KEYED UP. We wanted to do something *now*. The image of Willow sitting on the chair with the big black blindfold on her face was haunting. J'Leah was ready to kick someone's ass right now. The girl was a child, dammit. J'Leah had seen the effects of what adults can do to children when she'd been deployed, and she'd had enough of it for one lifetime.

Brick and I let her stomp around the office to burn off some energy, and when she'd settled some we sent her to a big box store that was open twenty-four hours a day to buy burner phones and other tech supplies for the Monero account and to set up communication between us that would be hard to trace.

It was late, but Brick and I went back to the hotel in Fairborn for a session working out some details with Elizabeth and Henna. Henna was alert and pacing and twisting her hands and picking at imaginary threads in her shirt and biting her nails. Elizabeth watched the show of nerves until she went to her daughter and placed her into one of the hotel chairs. Then she stood behind Henna and gently rubbed her shoulders. It was a major thaw for the two of them, and Brick and I hung back for a few minutes to let them take it in.

Then we walked Elizabeth and Henna through some scenarios for the next day. Elizabeth checked her watch and reminded us that it was already the next day. That didn't help anyone's nerves.

Brick and I would be on the ground in the Street Fair crowd with the phone, waiting for instructions for the drop and to secure Willow. J'Leah would be in my upstairs office looking out over Xenia Avenue and keeping the communication lines open. Our primary objective was to get Willow back safe. We would be armed and ready to do what was necessary, but the thought of carrying a weapon in the crowded fair made me more than uneasy. We had to look for any opportunity to press an advantage. A chance to keep the weapons away from the crowds.

Elizabeth took a long look at Brick and he knew she was sizing him up. He pointed a finger to her and then held his hand to his heart.

Samuel Thomas arrived and we called J'Leah to put the two of them together working on the Monero transaction. J'Leah was just coming out of the big box store when she answered her phone. "By god, they have more things for sale in that place than some of the villages where I was deployed. The whole village. I mean everything."

"OK. Did you get the phones?"

"I did."

"Samuel Thomas is here. You two need to work on the account and the transfer. Set up the passwords and everything."

"Send him to your office."

I turned to Samuel Thomas. "She wants you to meet her at my office in—"

"I heard. I'll go."

I went back to the phone. "He says he'll meet you there."

"I heard."

I held the phone up in the air. "Anything else?"

Nobody spoke up.

"Call one of us if something happens or if you make progress." I ended the call. "Samuel Thomas, do you mind if I ask you something?"

He looked surprised. "I don't."

"Do you have a family?"

His face softened. "I do. Julie and I have a three-year-old."

"What's her name?"

"Emmy."

I waited for him to show me photos. He didn't. "You have a picture?"

He showed me the background image on his phone. Elizabeth leaned over my shoulder and looked in. It was an image of a woman with long, light-brown hair carrying a girl on her shoulders. The girl's hair was thick and wavy and the color of her mother's. Both of their mouths were open as if they were laughing. "My favorite," Samuel Thomas said.

"I can see why. Have you been married long?"

"Seven years."

Brick and Henna both had come closer to look at the photo. Samuel Thomas seemed concerned. "Is this important?"

"You've been taking a lot of time away from them to work on this."

He looked at the image of his wife and daughter. "I have."

"I hope we can get you back to them soon."

Samuel Thomas turned his phone over. "Me too. Is that all you wanted to know?"

I leveled my eyes on his. "It's enough. Let's go get this done."

Samuel Thomas left right away to meet J'Leah at my office. Brick and I were ready to go, but it took some time to convince Elizabeth and Henna that the best place for them was to stay at the hotel. They wanted to do something. They couldn't just sit there thinking about what might be happening to Willow right now.

Brick finally convinced them. "You have to be strong," he said. "And when we get Willow back you'll have to be strong again, even stronger. It's going to be hard. She's going to need you. That's when you get to do something."

It was a nice little speech. When we left and Brick had squeezed himself into the truck he looked straight ahead out into the darkness. "Where's Cali?"

"Home. Marzi's with her. Marzi's taking some time off work."

"That's good."

I took us up the highway, and when we swung off the exit and the darkness of the back roads had swallowed us up, Brick said, "Supplies now?"

"Yes, supplies now."

"My place."

"Yes." You wanted to suit up for battle, Brick's was the place to do it.

I knew the drill. This wasn't my first rodeo. We were in and out with what we needed in less than ten minutes.

When we got back to my office Samuel Thomas was alert and working on his laptop. Four burner phones and an array of wireless earbuds were sitting on the desk, plugged into a multi-pronged charger. J'Leah was at the open window, looking out over Yellow Springs in the dark.

I left the office door open to keep some air moving and give us some room in the tight space. "How's it going?"

Samuel Thomas looked up from his screen. "I think we're ready. J'Leah is very sharp."

J'Leah turned from the window. "You bet your ass she is. And don't you forget it."

"And a little punchy," Samuel Thomas said. "I think she could use some sleep."

"All of us," I said.

J'Leah stuck out her jaw. "Ask me if I'm ready to go?"

We didn't. Brick waved me aside and came around the desk to J'Leah. He put a hand very gently on her shoulder. "I know you're ready. But we're gonna need you tomorrow. You got to be sharp when this thing breaks open."

"I'll be sharp."

"I know you will. But you done your job for now. You'll be sharper if you get some rest."

J'Leah stiffened and shook her head.

Brick looked J'Leah in the eye. "Stand down, soldier."

J'Leah let her shoulders slump. Brick had done the convincing again. And that surprised me again.

I pulled my key ring from my pocket, twisted one off, and laid it on the desk. "You can take her to the house. Let her sleep in the extra room. I'll text and let them know you're coming."

Brick shook his head. "Let them sleep. I can take her to my place."

"Might be better if everyone were closer?"

He picked up my house key. "I'll put her in the sun room."

I nodded, but I was going to text Marzi as soon as they left. We were edgy enough without a surprise in the middle of the night.

Then I sent Samuel Thomas home to his family and his bed, and when Brick got back to the office we agreed to sleep in shifts, on the blanket J'Leah had used the night before. Brick would sleep first.

Somewhere around three-thirty when I was supposed to wake Brick to take the watch, sleep for everyone made more sense to me, and I tip-toed out into the hallway and curled up on the floor outside my office. It was awkward and stuffy and I didn't have a pillow or blanket, but sleep came quickly. And when I opened my eyes again, so had morning.

24

SUNRISE CAME SLOWLY to the village, canting up through the window in the hallway where I'd been sleeping. The door to my office was still open, and through it I saw Brick sitting cross-legged on top of the desk facing me, his hands palms-up on his knees. He opened an eye. "Rise and shine, precious."

I got up and stretched. "How long have you been talking to the void?"

"Not talking. Listening." His other eye opened.

"What's it saying?"

"Same as always. Like a magic eight ball. The answers are already there, you just have to shake 'em out."

I picked up a paper coffee cup from the top of the filing cabinet and shook it. Empty. I picked up another and shook it. Maybe a few drams of sludge in the bottom.

Brick unfolded his legs and scooted to the edge of the desk. "You don't want to drink those."

I shook the last cup. It had something in the bottom, but the cup was soft and mushy. "You're probably right."

I came around the desk and raised the window and the screen and leaned out. The street was already filling with tents and vehicles and people unloading crates and boxes and tables. In another hour, all of downtown would be packed with booths, filling with all manner of clothes, arts, food, incense, candles, and funky wares. The sidewalks would bloom with buskers and performers, from the very young to the very old, sprinkled with a modest dose of aging hippies. By nine o'clock the stages would open with musicians and dancers, and the festival would begin to fill. The side streets would be clogged with parked cars and people walking in from every direction.

I breathed deep. The morning air was cool and comfortable. The forecast called for a clear day, light clouds, low humidity. High around seventy. A perfect day for Street Fair. It would be packed.

Brick stood up and arched his back like a cat, held that for a long time, then pulled his arms back and stretched them. "You feel sharp?"

I turned from the window. "Maybe could use a few minutes sitting on the desk if you're done."

"I am."

"That or some coffee."

"I think you'd do better with the coffee."

I pulled the window screen back down but left the pane open. "You're probably right."

We walked down into the milieu to get coffee. Brick was partial to Dino's Cappuccinos, and we dodged the bustle on the street to get there. The coffee was hot and fresh.

Early morning was the best time for locals to get around at Street Fair. There was a lot of activity with set-up, but the big crowds wouldn't arrive until later when the festival started.

When we came out of Dino's with our coffees, the double row of canopies along the center line of the street was rapidly filling in. Vehicles moved through slowly at the sides, wheels squeezed between the curb and the piles of wares and supplies and people moving about.

There was a back-up in front of us. A vehicle stopped to unload was holding up a row of drivers behind it.

One of the local volunteers who had been helping to set up the festival for years saw me and pointed. "You got a minute?"

"Always." I knew what he wanted. I set my coffee cup on a window ledge, and Brick did the same. Then the three of us stepped into the street and each took a leg of the canopy a young couple was struggling to raise. We boosted the legs and secured them, then moved to the open hatch of their car and hauled out the crates and boxes inside and piled them under the canopy.

Then the volunteer motioned the young guy into the car and hurried him off. The line of stopped vehicles started moving slowly through again.

The guy tipped his baseball cap at the drivers as they went by, then turned to me and Brick. "I'd buy you a cup of coffee, but it looks like you're already set."

"We are."

The cars cleared out. The man looked up and down the street.

I looked too. "It looks like you've got this under control."

"Always."

We shook hands, and Brick and I retrieved our coffees and went back up to my office. Once we were off the street and above the crowd, the mood changed. It wasn't funky and laid-back Yellow Springs anymore. It was the somber business of getting Willow back safely, and what we might have to do to make that happen. The fun of Street Fair seemed miles away from our level above.

Brick did some push-ups in the hallway, checked the backpacks and supplies, then went back out into the hallway and did some more push-ups. I watched the village out the window, thinking about angles and escape routes and how hard it would be to move quickly through the crowds. I didn't like it. The exchange would be a public safety nightmare that would distract us from getting to Willow and whoever had her. We needed to create an advantage. We needed to know who we were dealing with.

Just when I started wondering why J'Leah hadn't shown up, her slim, shadowed figured appeared in the jumble of people below, moving toward my window.

A moment later we listened to her shuffle down the hallway, then she came into the office and set her coffee cup on the desk and announced, "I love this place."

Neither Brick nor I said anything.

J'Leah picked up on the looks on our faces. "Sorry. I've never seen Street Fair before."

"You haven't seen it yet. Things could get messy."

The change in her attitude was immediate. Like turning a light switch. "Right. Give me an update. Have you heard from the Winstrops?"

We agreed to check in right then. I made the call.

Henna answered. Her voice was clear and sharp. If you can sound bright-eyed over the phone, Henna did. "We're ready," she said. "We're coming out there."

"Wait a minute. We decided that's probably not in the best interests—"

"Jackson." It wasn't a question.

"Yeah?"

"If it was your daughter, what would you do?"

"I'd try to do what…" I couldn't finish it. We both knew it wouldn't be the truth if I did.

"And Samuel Thomas is coming with us."

"There's no room."

"We might need him. He could help if there's anything with the money or something."

"J'Leah can do that."

I heard Henna take a sharp breath. It was loud enough through the phone that Brick looked over. Henna said, "Samuel Thomas has worked for my father for a long time. And now mom trusts him. And so do I. And I think you do too. He could be useful."

"I know, but—"

"And he wants to be there. He deserves to be. When you asked him about his family last night, that meant something to him. He told us. He said he wants to see Willow come back to us."

"Look, I don't think it's wise for any of you to come out here. It won't help us get Willow back. We've got things covered." I was trying to cover my fear. What if we didn't get Willow back? What if something went wrong? What if Willow was hurt, or worse? Would I want the others to be there and see that?

"Jackson?"

"Yeah."

"What would you do?"

I told her the truth. Nothing would keep me away. And nothing should keep them away either. "Come in the back. Find a place to park on Corry Street. Walk through Beatty Hughes Park and the alley. Wear hats if you have them. Sunglasses." I told her where to find the entrance that would take them up to my office. "It's going to be tight. The office is very small."

"OK."

"And you'll have to let J'Leah work. Stay quiet. Stay off the street."

"OK."

I sighed and tried to let my regrets settle. "Get out here. It's starting up."

J'Leah volunteered to go down to Current Cuisine for breakfast sandwiches and fresh fruit. Extra water bottles. Whatever else she thought we'd need. It might be a long day.

Then we locked the filing cabinet and pushed that out into the hall. Moved the desk against the wall next to the window. Pushed the folding chairs against the walls and made just enough room for everyone to get in if they didn't mind their knees touching.

Brick lurked in the hallway. "Anybody else wants to come, we'll have to knock a wall out."

I moved out into the hallway with him.

Brick crossed his arms and looked into the tightly arranged seating in the office. "Where is Cali gonna be?"

He was thinking the same thing I was. Keep her safe. Away from Street Fair. I'd tried. "With Marzi. They want to come down later to watch the belly dancing."

Brick's eyes moved up to mine. "You think that's a good idea?"

"No. But there'll be twenty thousand people here. Chances are they won't get into the middle of anything we'll have to do."

He uncrossed his arms, then re-crossed them. I knew what that gesture meant.

"I don't like it either, but I haven't had much luck convincing them to stay clear."

"Or 'Lizabeth and her daughter."

"Or the lawyer."

Brick grunted. "They've got to do what they have to do. And so do we."

"Pure poetry. I couldn't have said it better."

The others arrived a short time later. Then Brick and I suited up and went down into the village. It had gotten busy. Street Fair was starting up.

It was more grueling than I expected. Brick carried the phone with the Monero account transfer information and passwords. I roamed.

Brick waited. He carried Elizabeth's phone, waiting for instructions. As we'd been told to do.

We didn't expect the abductors to recognize us or know who would make the drop, but we still didn't want the two of us to be seen together. We wanted to create any opportunity we could, and keeping us separated seemed to our advantage.

We had been instructed to have the transfer phone in a paper lunch bag. No police. Nobody else with the drop person. Nobody make any other moves. Just have someone there with the phone, waiting. Sitting in the middle of Street Fair on Xenia Avenue. We weren't told for how long.

J'Leah watched what she could from the office window, scanning the crowds with the big field glasses. She was still hoping to catch a break on tracing the phone number the kidnappers had spoofed from, or even to determine if they were calling from one phone or several, but I felt like that hope had already slipped away.

Brick and I each wore wireless earbuds connected to a burner phone J'Leah had set up for us. We could make hands-free calls, and J'Leah could set up a three-way call almost instantly. She had Elizabeth's phone set up to forward texts automatically. As soon as something came in from anywhere, we'd all get it right away.

I roamed. J'Leah scanned the crowds and kept us in communication. Brick occasionally moved between spots near the center of town where J'Leah would have a view of him out my office window.

I moved from one end of Street Fair to the other and back, trying to stay out of the thickest of the crowds so I wouldn't get bogged down. Down Kieth's Alley, behind Tom's Market, through the schoolyard, down Corry and Dayton Streets, circling the beer garden. Through the neighborhoods and up and down the lines of cars parked in front of the houses, looking for Willow, looking for anything suspicious.

I pressed, moving fast. Whenever I stopped I felt like I was in the wrong place, and I ran off looking somewhere else.

I passed Brick several times. He was always in the shade, sitting, standing, leaning. A pair of sunglasses was tilted back on his head, and his eyes scanned the crown. He wore a loose-fitting long-sleeved shirt over his tee and had a slim backpack tucked onto his shoulders. We never spoke or met eyes when I passed.

I wore light-weight trousers with side pockets and an oversized long-sleeve shirt. It was hot, but it wasn't the heat that was unbearable. It was the waiting.

J'Leah had encouraged me to stay fairly close to Brick, but I passed through Street Fair again and again, moving past the food trucks with the aromas of waffle fries and sausages and wontons wraps. Past the tie-dyed clothes and patchouli incense. Among the buskers and the artists selling their pottery, paintings, and all manner of whimsy. Past the homemade soaps, the lavender farm booth that smelled like a good bath, glancing over the free books in the crazy decorated pick-up truck at the corner.

Nerves can't stay on high alert indefinitely. Eventually my passes through the festival slowed, and my nerves settled, as they do, until a sense of longing to have Willow safe and be done with this moved into its place.

The longing was as grueling as the nerves had been. I was hot and tired and hungry. Elizabeth and Henna had already twice persuaded J'Leah to break in and ask me and Brick for updates. They were probably wondering as much as I was whether this whole thing was right. If the waiting was designed to wear us down, or if there was something more deeply wrong here. If we really would get Willow back today.

By early afternoon I found myself at the John Bryan Community Center and the bandstand, examining the area for its possibilities. It was porous, with lots of tree cover and secluded entry from several directions. A good place to set up the drop. I could wait here a while.

I was wrong. My earbud blooped. A text message had been forwarded. *Walnut and Limestone. Now.*

Dammit. The other end of Street Fair. Through all of those people and booths and food trucks choking off the routes.

I started moving. My ear buzzed and I touched the bud and connected to J'Leah.

"Brick is moving. Travelling south on Xenia toward the destination."

I ran. Darted around the strings of people milling in front of the beer garden, and dodged over to Dayton Street to avoid the heavier throngs of people on Xenia Avenue. I zig-zagging up to Walnut, skirted the barricades and almost took out a nice family licking ice cream at the Corner Cone.

My earbud blooped again. Another text was forwarded.

Put the bag with the phone in the temporary trash barrel. Do not look around. Walk away.

J'Leah buzzed again. "You got that?"

"Got it."

"What's your twenty?"

"Behind the King's Yard, heading south. Where is Brick?" We had agreed that Brick would stay silent to make it seem like he was acting alone. Unless he had reason to do otherwise. Like maybe now.

"My line of sight is gone," J'Leah said. "But he should be arriving at the destination."

"I'm not going to make it."

"Try."

Another message came through. *Move away quickly. Don't look back.*

I cut behind the food trucks and juked through the schoolyard. I tapped my earbud. "Brick?"

I swooped around couples picnicking their lunches on the lawn. "J'Leah, can you get him?"

I heard her voice calling Brick as I ran, but he didn't answer.

I cleared the food trucks, and the intersection of Walnut and Limestone came into view. Brick wasn't there. Everything looked calm and normal. People sat under the food tent eating and listening to a musician play guitar and sing on the stage. Others waited in line for food at the trucks. People walked into or out of the festival from the side streets. The shuttle bus that ferried people from the parking at the edge of town groaned away down Limestone Street.

The trash barrel was there at the intersection. Nobody was nearby or appeared to be approaching it. I closed to within a dozen yards. "Brick? J'Leah?"

"Jackson." It was J'Leah.

"Where is he?"

"Hang on."

"Do you have a line of sight?"

"Negative."

"Has there been a pick-up? Is the phone still in the barrel?"

"No line of sight. Brick has not reported."

"I have visual. No activity. There hasn't been much time. They would've had to take the phone from the barrel while Brick was still right there."

"Hang on."

I didn't like it. Where was Brick? And why wasn't he communicating? Scenarios ran through my head. The golf cart that came around to change the big garbage bags in the cardboard waste containers would arrive and take the bag with the phone. I would follow, by any means available. On foot, a borrowed bicycle. Commandeer a car if I had to.

Or I would wait and nothing would happen. The drop phone was already gone. I was watching a barrel with nothing but garbage. They were getting away. Willow was sitting in a dark room someplace with a bag over her head, calling out to no one who was there to come get her.

I shook the guesswork from my head. That wasn't helping. "Should I check the barrel?"

J'Leah came on. "Advise you find cover and wait. Keep the barrel in visual."

"I want to be close enough to pursue."

"Advise you blend in."

I moved closer to a group of people who appeared to be together, standing and eating from paper boats while they listened to the music.

A few minutes passed. They felt like hours.

J'Leah's voice came into my ear again. "I'm coming down to provide another angle. Give me a minute to—"

"Hold on." Brick's voice.

"Where are—"

There was a loud thump, like a mattress landing squarely after it had been dropped from a high place.

"Brick?"

Another thump, less violent, and some voices in the background. Then a high-pitched yelp, followed by what sounded like wood splitting, and a much louder shriek.

Brick's voice: "Tell it."

A grunt and a whimper. A man's voice. "Let me go. Lemme go! You broke my arm!"

"Tell it."

Another shriek. "Gray CRV. Gray!"

"Where?"

"Walnut Street! Walnut Street!"

"Where?"

"Near downtown." Another groan, weaker, as if the fight had left whoever Brick had a hold on. "Close to town."

"You ain't tellin' the truth and—"

There was a soft thud and a groan, then Brick's voice. "You get that?"

"Got it." I was already moving.

"Have to be quick. Somebody in that car is expecting this guy to check in right about now."

I sprinted. J'Leah came into my ear, but the sound was broken, buzzing.

I ran. Swerved. Avoided. Breathed.

Willow. I had to get to Willow.

"Jackson?"

"Uhn."

"Twenty?"

"In pursuit."

"What backup do you need?"

Gasp. "Hang on where you are."

The man with the broken arm wasn't lying. The gray CRV was there, parked outside of the festival on a stretch of road that got a fair amount of traffic and people walking into and out of Street Fair. I wondered how long it had been there. How they got a spot so close this late in the day.

I slowed and saw the answer. The car was parked across a driveway. They probably didn't expect this to take long. In and out before someone had time to complain about being blocked in.

J'Leah came into my ear. "Twenty?"

"I'm there. I see it. Approaching."

The vehicle was facing away from me. The back of a man's head was framed in the driver's seat. I veered behind a high privet for cover.

Then some luck. A junked lawn mower waited at the curb for one of the scrappers who trawled the village.

More luck. The mower's spark plug had been pulled and was sitting on top of the cutting deck.

I turned my back to the CRV, stepped out from behind the privet and scooped up the plug, and hustled down to the next house where I stooped to pick up a granite stone from a mulch bed. I dropped the plug on the sidewalk, held one hand in front of my eyes to shield them from debris, and brought the granite down on the plug. The porcelain casing cracked off, and another blow fractured the biggest pieces of porcelain again.

I gathered the shards and closed a palm around them. Then I tugged my cap down, crossed the street, and came back at the CRV behind the row of cars at the far curb.

When I neared the CRV I slipped back into the street and took an oblique angle as if to make a long, lazy diagonal crossing. The CRV was directly to my right when I reached the center of the street. I cut my eyes over and saw a face I recognized looking back at me.

William Bennett. The Columbus investigator Richard Winstrop had hired to find Henna.

His face froze when I pivoted to the window and hurled the porcelain shards with as much force as I could muster, stepping into the motion like releasing a good two-seam fastball.

The tiny points of the shards found space between the high-tension lines in the safety glass, and the window exploded into Bennett's lap. I had my arm through the shredded glass and on the door release before he could recover. When I dragged Bennett from his seat I saw a bedsheet draped from the back of the headrests and stretched to cover the cargo area in the rear.

Bennett surprised me. I squared for a fight, but instead he clawed his way back into the vehicle. I went in after him, groping to secure his arms and pat him for a weapon. He was wiry but not strong enough. I muscled him down onto the center console and squashed myself over him with a knee in his back.

Then the bedsheet moved and Willow's head came up from behind the seat. A black blindfold was secured over her eyes and she was gagged. Our heads nearly touched, and she jerked violently and tried to scream through the gag.

I pressed my knee harder into Bennett and reached for the blindfold. Willow thrashed, but I hooked the blindfold and swept it away. "I'm here to help."

Her eyes were wild. Bennett struggled beneath me. We were crammed in like a kids' game of sardines. I reached behind Willow and untied the gag.

She screamed and held up her hands, twisted together and bound with a zip tie. Her wrists were red and cut and ugly.

Bennett struggled. My knee slipped across his back. I reached down and put my left arm around his windpipe. He choked and settled.

Willow tried to yank her hands apart and cried when the ties cut her again.

"Wait. I have to get him out of here."

But she yanked wildly at the ties again, and tears rolled down her eyes. "Get them off!"

I slammed Bennett down and reached my other hand into my pocket, struggled in the small space to get my pocket knife out, then fumbled it and dropped it down the back of the seats. Willow dove after the knife.

I knew I should have immobilized Bennett first. But he hadn't put up much of a fight, and Willow was descending into hysterics.

I moved just enough to give him room. Bennett put an elbow up and it hooked hard into the soft flesh under my chin. I twisted away and Bennett scrabbled and we spilled together out of the passenger door onto the sidewalk.

Some people had stopped a few houses down and were watching us. They had cell phones out and a woman was shouting into hers and pointing at us. It wouldn't be long before someone stepped in or the police arrived.

Bennett came up from his knees slow and clumsy and I knew I had him, but then something was wrong and I saw the glint of metal in his hand. Everything slowed down and my eyes registered the shape of the gun barrel and then the charge exploded toward my chest.

I knew I was falling and couldn't orient, and then a searing pain ripped through my torso.

I blinked and saw Willow running away.

I blinked again and saw Bennett turn after Willow.

I blinked and I was looking straight up at the sky. I breathed and the pain in my ribs inflated like a balloon.

Brick had been right about taking precautions. I'd been a fool to fight him on it.

I let as much air out of my lungs as I could release, closed my eyes, and watched the sky wink away.

Then I curled my knees and rolled onto my side. My hands went under my shirt and grasped at the straps that held the body armor in place. I stripped off my shirt and the armor plates and sat up with a hand pressed against my ribs where the impact had been. I'd thank Brick later. And I'd worry about broken ribs later. Right now I had to get up and move.

I reached to my ear but the bud was gone. I grabbed my shirt, rose to my feet, flipped my phone out of my pocket, and started after Bennett and Willow. They were nowhere in sight, but I could move, and I did.

My phone came alive. "Jackson?"

"Still here."

"What happened?"

"Willow is here. Escaped from Bennett. He's after her. I think they ran into Street Fair."

"Copy." There was a very brief pause. "You can tell me later. What is their entry point?"

"North end. I didn't see them enter. Look out the window." The pain in my ribs was real, but the drive to pursue was greater. I picked up some speed. "Where is Brick?"

"Off site."

"What?"

"He's a few minutes away. Jackson?"

"Yeah?"

"There's a ripple."

I was crossing Dayton Street. Trying to run with the phone to my ear and every step driving a thumping ache into my ribs.

"Someone pushing through the crowd. Heading south. At the Trail Tavern."

I reached the back of the King's Yard.

"Another, pursuing. The one in front is a girl. He's chasing her."

I ran through the back of Tom's parking lot, pushed through the people and the canopies and the strollers and the sun-soaked festival-goers and emerged onto Xenia Avenue. J'Leah was leaning out of the office window waving wildly. I looked up at her and she pointed south.

I turned right and crashed around a young girl playing a flute on the steps beside the market. Side-stepped two boys pulling a rusted red wagon, selling water from a cooler. Pushed between a hairy-chested man in biker gear and his tie-dyed bosomy girlfriend. Some space opened at the intersection of Short Street and I moved into it, but I didn't see Bennett or Willow.

The crowd got thick and I kept pushing, past the dirty looks. Someone eating berries and ice cream at the Presbyterian church strawberry fest shouted "Dude, chill."

Ahead I saw the movement of Bennett pushing through the crowd.

I stumbled up the curb, swung wildly to avoid a lamp post, and then I had a clear line at Bennett. He dodged past the belly dancers twirling on the grass in front of the food tent. The pain in my ribs and J'Leah in my ear faded away. There was nothing except catching Bennett and getting to Willow. I lurched and made a grab and caught him.

Bennett came down beneath me like a giant, squealing bug, arms windmilling in surprise as he tumbled. This time I kept track of his hands. When he flipped onto his back and raised both arms over his face, I cut a hard right between them that drove his head back into the ground. He grunted and lay still and I patted him for his gun and secured it.

He didn't try to get up. I wanted him to. It was too easy at the end. I had more fight left in me.

Two young guys in tight t-shirts ran up and tried to pull me off of Bennett.

"Hey, man, back off. Let the guy up."

I resisted, but they yanked and I popped up and threw a right-left-right and the guy nearest me bent and went down.

His friend stepped back, squared, and raised his fists. I wanted to take him. I wanted to hit somebody hard, again and again. But Bennett was down, and he wasn't getting up. So that left this guy. But I didn't do it. I turned my palms to the man, gestured for him to hold, and jerked my wallet from my pocket. I held out my PI license. The man leaned in to look.

That's when the local finest took me down.

They cuffed me, took Bennett's weapon off me, patted me down, and took my weapon. I watched them bend to check on Bennett, who was still on the ground. And I scanned the crowd intensely.

A woman wearing a Yellow Springs Tree Committee shirt emerged from a booth. She had on a soft safari hat that blocked the sun and made her appear as if she was looking out from a place of deep wisdom. She pointed to the circle of belly dancers. They had broken and were watching the unwinding of the melee with the rest of the crowd. "I think the girl you're looking for is over there with the Egyptian Breeze dancers."

Standing among the women in their long skirts and baubles and bangles and jingle garb was a teen girl with flowing black hair and a wild look in her eyes. Willow Winstrop.

I looked to the woman from the tree committee, but she had melted back into the shadows of her booth.

The police were asking me lots of questions. They had Bennett up, and I told them to look in my wallet. I saw Marzi emerge from the crowd and move toward Willow. Willow cringed and backed away when Marzi came to her, but Marzi said something and the girl's shoulders dropped and she collapsed into Marzi's embrace.

Then Cali came through the maze of people and joined Marzi, and the three of them walked away.

Then I started talking. I knew it would take a long time to explain. The police led me and Bennett away. Street Fair closed in behind us and swallowed up the space where we'd been. The sound of the belly dance music started up again, and the trill of the dancers' shouting and the jangle of their rhythmic steps rose up behind us.

25

IT TOOK A LONG TIME to unwind everything. They took me to the emergency room for x-rays of my ribs. The doc decided they weren't broken, but she and the techs shook their heads when I explained what had happened.

A polite but very firm officer stayed with me the whole time and when I declined the wrap for my ribs he gave me a free ride in the back of his car to the county building in Xenia. I don't know where they took Bennett. I didn't see him again.

The guy I hit after he pulled me off of Bennett didn't press charges. They told him enough of the story that he let it go. Guy got punched for trying to be a good Samaritan. That'll teach him. I'd try to remember to send him a card at Christmas.

They made me tell the story several times. I knew they were comparing it to what Elizabeth and Henna and Samuel Thomas were telling them. We had rehearsed this. We would explain who J'Leah was if her name came up. But it didn't. Brick would remain anonymous unless things got dire.

They had the phone I'd used, which was a burner J'Leah had set up. It had logs and texts to the burner phones Brick and J'Leah had used. But those phones had disappeared and so had the people who had used them.

My burner also had records to Elizabeth's phone, which Brick had returned to my office and the authorities now had. That also had call logs and texts to the missing phones.

They also had the Monero phone, but J'Leah had made sure that wasn't linked to anyone other than Bennett and his partner. None of this made anyone questioning me very happy.

They knew about Brick, but not who he was or how to find him. He'd left an indelible impression on the other riders on the shuttle bus. Bennett's partner had reached into the trash barrel to pick up the paper bag with the Monero phone, then jumped onto the shuttle bus as it was pulling away. The riders had seen Brick run after the bus, waving his arms and shouting, but the driver had driven away.

Brick sprinted down a side street. When the shuttle bus was stopped in traffic near the lot where it would drop off the riders, Brick had re-appeared, running up to the bus and convincing the driver to open the doors by nearly pulling them apart. Brick had gone directly to the man who picked up the paper bag from the trash barrel and sat beside him. A minute later when the bus arrived at its stop the man had tried to run when they were getting off, but Brick had taken him down in the parking lot and broken his arm. He made the man tell him something that the riders generally agreed had included a gray car.

Nobody had intervened with Brick, though more than one of the riders called the dispatcher to report the incident. Brick had sprinted away and disappeared before the police cars arrived.

They told me that Elizabeth and Henna and Samuel Thomas had reported that a man I brought in to work with me matched the description of the man the shuttle riders had given. But neither the Winstrops nor their lawyer knew Brick's real name or how to contact him. That was all true.

That left me, and the interview kept coming back to this: "Who are your partners?"

"They wish to remain anonymous."

"If they haven't done anything wrong they don't have anything to be concerned about."

"You don't need them. You have Bennett, and you have the others to testify."

"Are you aware, Mr. Flint, that you can be charged with a crime for refusing to cooperate with an investigation?"

I was.

They threatened to suspend my PI license.

I told them I had a good lawyer.

They told me it was my civic duty to report the others who had been involved.

I told them I'd done my civic duty. Willow was safe, and they had the bad guys.

They didn't like my answers, and they left me to spend the night in a jail cell.

In the middle of the night, a deputy woke me and released me on the condition that I stay in the area and be available for further questioning, just like on the TV shows. I'd never known before that that was real. I agreed and Marzi drove out to pick me up and we went home to my house to sleep.

I learned in the morning from Samuel Thomas that the thing that had sprung me was Bennett and his partner had turned on each other. In the wee hours of the morning, they had cracked. The case against them was solid, and the county and state police involved became less interested in pressing me to get to my two missing accomplices.

That, and Elizabeth and Samuel Thomas had been exerting pressure to have me released.

I learned that the CRV was stolen. Willow hadn't seen either of her abductors until I took the blindfold off of her in the car. A third man had been involved in the actual abduction. The man whose arm Brick had broken and another who was now in custody had grabbed Willow in the warehouse while she was sleeping. Flame and his two-by-four and the others hadn't been able to stop them.

Willow couldn't describe Bennett or his partners as anything other than voices. The scene in the car was a blur to her, Bennett nothing more than a head and body tumbling out the door and then a loud gunshot blast as she ran away.

I hadn't used my M&P40 and I had lived to come home to Cali, though Brick's interpretation of how I managed that would probably be stupid luck. He wouldn't have hesitated to put a bullet into Bennett with Willow's fate at stake.

Samuel Thomas and Elizabeth had been briefed on the charges against Bennett and his partners, and they explained that Bennett had set the whole thing up months ago when Robert Winstrop hired him to find Henna. Bennett had found Willow too, and planned to hire someone to abduct her, then go to Robert to help him get his granddaughter back, thereby working both sides of the deal and securing the ransom money. But Robert had died unexpectedly of a heart attack, and Henna and Willow moved out of Columbus and disappeared before Bennett could reconstruct the plan for Elizabeth. That set the rest of the story in motion.

The one thing I didn't like was that picking up Willow in the rain had truly been just a coincidence. Samuel Thomas had gotten it right. I was likely to be in the right place to pass Willow as she made her way to Yellow Springs trying to find her mother, and I was the kind of guy who would notice her and stop to offer a ride. Willow hadn't called anyone to help her and hadn't returned her mother's calls or texts, or Elizabeth's, because the phone she'd taken from her mother was out of credit. When Willow realized she didn't have any idea where to look for her mother in Yellow Springs, she got back to Dayton the same way she'd gotten to the village, with a ride from a stranger.

After a long debrief with Elizabeth and Henna and Samuel Thomas, I got called back to the county building to answer more of the same questions again. They still wanted to know who my accomplices were and they wanted the missing phones, but they had the case in hand and the steam was out of them. I was back home by late afternoon.

Brick resurfaced, and he and I and Marzi and Cali were on the front porch decompressing. I asked Brick about J'Leah. "I haven't heard from her since we wrapped things up yesterday," I said. "All of her things are already out of my office."

"She's keeping her head down. Said she and Kathy Halstead are spending some time together."

"Probably good for both of them."

Brick agreed.

Cali asked a few questions and we realized she hadn't heard a lot of the details. We took some time to fill her in. When we finished the story, she asked, "What's going to happen to them? Willow and her mom and her grandma?"

I shrugged. "That's up to them. They're family. They're together. At least they have a chance now."

"Do you think I'll see her around town?"

"Who, Willow?"

Cali nodded.

"Could be. I don't know what they're planning. Willow is fourteen, so she's about a year younger than you. You'd be about the right age to bump into each other if she and her mother stay here."

"Willow would go to the high school."

"Probably."

"Weird."

"That you'd see her?"

"Yeah. And that all that stuff has happened to her already. It's like she's already had an adult life, but she's not an adult. She's just…"

That kind of said it all, so no one tried to finish the sentence for Cali.

Then the leaves on one of the big hosta plants rustled and a calico flash jumped out and came up onto the porch and rubbed against Cali's leg. Cali bent to pet the cat. "Hello, Mrs. Jenkins."

Marzi cocked her head. "Mrs. Jenkins?"

The cat looked at her as if she recognized her name.

Cali laughed and scratched Mrs. Jenkins' ear. "Yes, Mrs. Jenkins."

Marzi's eyes twinkled. "Odd name."

All of us grinned except Marzi. She looked around at our faces. "What?"

Brick pointed to me and then to himself. "Mrs. Jenkins was our fifth-grade teacher."

Marzi nodded. "The teacher you didn't like, huh?"

Brick shook his head. "No. We liked Mrs. Jenkins. She was a good teacher. She just—" He looked at me to finish.

"She had some whiskers. And fuzzy hair. Made her look a little like a cat."

"Uh-huh. And does sweet little old Mrs. Jenkins know you've named a cat after her?"

Brick's shoulders bobbed up and down as he laughed. "Mrs. Jenkins won't care. She's playing tennis in Florida with a rich old man she married."

Mrs. Jenkins the cat moved from Cali's leg to mine. One step closer to the door and her treats that we kept in the cupboard. Always trying to play an angle.

Marzi stood up and stretched. "Let's all walk in to town."

I raised an eyebrow. "Maybe get something to eat?"

Brick answered. "Always a good idea." He reached a hand out to Cali. She smiled at him and let him help her up.

We walked. It was a quiet evening. Street Fair was over and a calm had come back over the village. As we came near downtown, Cali said, "Where are we going?"

Nobody spoke up, so I said, "Maybe get a drink? A foxpossum?"

Marzi laughed. "That's not a real drink. You made that up."

"It's real if you know what to put in it."

Brick snorted. "Nobody knows what's in it. You change it every time."

"That's what makes it so special."

Cali said, "Really, where are we going?"

I shrugged. "What's going on in town tonight?"

A bicycle approached from behind us. Its rider was not holding the handlebars. Instead he held a guitar that he was playing and singing as he pedaled. It was a pretty good rendition of Johnny Cash.

"I don't know," Brick said, "but there's always *something* interesting going on around here."

Made in the USA
Middletown, DE
26 May 2020